SO-AIH-810

Keeping It Clean

Surviving in primitive Japan was bloody hard work for John Adam, and now the big Englishman wanted to wash his hands of violence for a while. When a nice hot bath was suggested by his host, John willingly agreed.

He was mildly surprised when a beautiful young girl led him to the bathhouse. He was even more taken aback when she first took off his clothes, and then hers.

Right then John Adam decided that not only was cleanliness next to godliness—it could turn out to be pure heaven. . . .

John Adam -Samurai

CHRISTOPHER WOOD

A DELL BOOK

Published by
Dell Publishing Co., Inc.
1 Dag Hammarskjold Plaza
New York, New York 10017

First published in England by Arlington Books
(Publishers) Ltd.
Copyright © 1971 by Christopher Wood

All rights reserved. No part of this book may be
reproduced in any form or by any means without
the prior written permission of the Publisher,
excepting brief quotes used in connection with
reviews written specifically for inclusion in a
magazine or newspaper.
Dell ® TM 681510, Dell Publishing Co., Inc.
Reprinted by arrangement with the author.
Printed in the United States of America
First Dell printing—April 1974

CHAPTER 1

MY TRAVELS BEGAN WHEN THE MAN CAST HIMSELF ON
to the pike I had snatched up. At least, that was my
impression of the incident, though a nervous flinch of
the arm or a jostle from one of the serving wenches
might have helped the blade on its way. I remember
the feel of it, like a knife sinking into pumpkin, and
the blood spreading all over his doublet, and my inside
voice saying 'Adam, you poor hapless fellow, you're
done for this time.' And done for I damn nearly was.
On the spot. All for lifting a fallen purse and defending myself against the drunken sot who laid claim to
it.

But there is little justice or mercy in the world and
I was overpowered and borne away to gaol by a rabble who could barely restrain themselves from tearing
me limb from limb. Two days later, I was condemned
to death without a word being spoken in my defence,
and a date fixed for my execution which would leave
me dancing on air two days before Good Queen Bess
led England into a new century. A sobering thought
and one I will leave you with whilst I impart a few
facts about myself.

My name is John Adam and I believe myself to have
been about twenty years old at that time and a native
of Plymouth, a seafaring town in Devon, a county in

the south-west of England. My mother was an amiable woman and, for the price of a glass of sack, downright benevolent—as my father would have been the first to acknowledge had one ever found a trace of him. I grew up a wild boy and might well have made my appointment with the gallows earlier had I not had the good fortune to be apprehended whilst thieving from a manor house on the moors about the town. My good fortune derived from the fact that the owner of the house was a gentleman whose wife had died in childbirth leaving him with only one child, a prodigiously fair daughter, and not the son he so desperately wanted. Loyal to the memory of his wife the old buffoon still yearned for a male heir and it was in this guise that I suddenly found myself cast. I was taught to read and write, clothed in fine raiment and responded so well that even the servants, who had been hard put to conceal their loathing, began to accord me the respect my birth did not deserve. I might have been there still had not the demon lust invaded my loins and I conceived a mighty passion for my benefactor's daughter. I have no wish to talk of it for the details are still painful to me but suffice to say that I found myself between her sheets and was found in the self-same position a few hours later. One might have thought that my benefactor would have welcomed this union but one would have been wrong. My backside was against the miry road within minutes and the whole of my future lay behind me.

It was this sad state of affairs that led me to return to my old ways and on which I brooded whilst awaiting execution. My gaoler was the meanest cullion I had ever set eyes on. Fat and bald with a small wet mouth surrounded by a scrub of tacky hairs giving it the appearance of a virgin's private parts. Inside the

mouth a graveyard of blackened teeth stunk like rotten
fish and there was a rime of salt around his armpits to
confirm the impression of one's nostrils that he was a
prodigious sweater. This gorbellied hilding delighted
in verbal torture and would recount with glee the
length of time he had seen men dance at the end of a
rope and the post mortal functioning of their bodies.
A favourite jibe was to ask if I had a few pence with
which to purchase small boys to hang upon my legs
and thus shorten my agonies.

I had answers to all his jibes but kept them to myself
for my one aim was to render myself so abject in his
eyes that he would have no fear of me. To this end I
barely raised my voice and moped in a corner of the
cell letting my head drop lower on my chest with each
day that passed. On the eve of my execution I sank
down on my knees against the wall and waited for the
wretch to bring the platter of maggot-shit that served
as my evening meal. I listened to his footsteps approaching and knew that if my ruse did not succeed,
the next of their kind I heard would be coming to
lead me to the gallows.

"Faith! I think I find you praying. Your sort will
find no favour in that quarter. It's Hades for you my
pretty rogue." His voice was coming through the grill
and I held my breath until I heard the bolts rasp
back.

"Come on. Sit up. I bring your victuals. I want to
see some life in you tomorrow."

He found this monstrously amusing and from the
corner of my eye I could see his shadow heaving up
and down with laughter.

"Have you no spirit in adversity? A man half dead
would see the jest in that. Come, turn your head towards me. I would like once more to look into your

fair brown eyes before the rope pops them out like snail's horns."

The lump swung towards me and I tensed my muscles ready to spring. He had never ventured so close before.

"I take your silence badly boy. I think it earns a cuffing. But first take your food. It would be a crime to waste it."

He hurled the platter at my head and as he did so came so close that I was able to lash out with both arms and scythe his legs away from under him. My hands were manacled but there was enough chain between them to wield like a scourge and rising from one knee I struck him with all my force across his beastly face. He stumbled back with the blood streaming from his cheek. He was beginning to shout but I silenced him with another blow which slewed his mouth across his face. As he staggered forward I pinioned him by the shoulders and used his momentum to half run with him across the cell, projecting him with such force into the window bars that his head wedged between them like a marrow. In this position he began to set up a pathetic yammer until I stepped back and aimed a kick between his legs that jerked him forward as if he had been triggered off by a charge of powder. His head burst through the bars and the gross hulk collapsed putting such pressure on his neck that it snapped with the cleanest, sweetest sound that could ever have been grateful to escape from his body.

I snatched the keys from about his waist and unlocked my wrists. My fellow prisoners were now beginning to raise an outcry and their plaints redoubled when they saw me free. Much as I would have welcomed their presence as a diversion there was no time to release them so I hurled the keys into the nearest cell and took off into the night.

Now my mind was in a turmoil and I had no other resolve than to put as great a distance between myself and Plymouth as possible. In this aim I was to succeed beyond my wildest dreams.

I sped into the town and being not rich in friends made my way to one of my acquaintances, who was a bum boatman. This good fellow willingly informed me of the vessels that were in port and I repaid him with a jar of ale and—when we retired to water a Spaniard's ear behind the tavern—a tap on the nowl that left me the temporary possession of his boat whilst he recovered his senses.

Here again cruel misfortune was my enemy for in the darkness and with a high swell running I lost all sense of direction and unwittingly blundered aboard a merchantman bound for trade in the East Indies instead of the vessel of my choice.

'Tis simply said but that ill-fated act was akin to sentencing myself to prison for three years. I have no wish to impart a geography lesson but our search for trade took us round the continent of Africa, into the Red Sea and to Surat in Northern India, before we crept down to the trading post established at Bantam in Java, one of the East Indian islands. The experience was one that might have done for a less dastardly novice than myself. The crew were the most villainous bunch of cut-throats that ever attempted to bugger an albatross, but resisting their advances was the least of my problems. Filthy quarters, ropes-end discipline, stomach-turning food—the meat was so bad as to poison the maggots and to tap a piece of bread was to lose half its weight in weevils—sickness, drowning, brawls, a brush with Dutch privateers, a minor mutiny—after which the three ringleaders were hung from the bow-

sprit until their rotting bodies dropped into the water
—plus the natural hazards of drought, monsoon and
tempest—made it unremarkable that our number was
diminished by a third before we reached Bantam.

Our trading activities had not been profitable and
the Mace—no doubt named after one of the spices we
sought—was still weighed down with quantities of
lead, iron, tin, quick silver, hides and broadcloth. It
therefore came as no surprise when I learned that we
were to press on to the Moluccas, or Spice Islands,
and if our efforts were unsuccessful, attempt to set up
a trading post in a country called Japon which stood
on the very edge of the world and was where the sun
rose.

Needless to say, the Moluccas yielded up not a single clove and we settled to a north-easterly course
which five months later saw us hove-to off a small island with a greater land mass looming behind it. I
was standing in the stern with one Twist, who was
something towards being a friend, his malice being so
securely wrapped in stupidity as to be almost indistinguishable. A light rain was falling on to a flat sea
and Twist was spitting contemplatively into the water,
taking pleasure in his contribution to the pattern of
rain drops.

"I ask myself why we have hove-to here," I said.

"To take on water," said Twist, continuing with his
spitting.

"That is why I ask myself," says I, "because I knew
that if I asked you I would invite the full weight of
your stupidity. We are but a half day's sail from our
destination. What need have we of water?"

"I do not know," said Twist, and gobbed again.

I was prepared to leave the matter there but my ship-
mate, temporarily running short of saliva, was disposed
to bequeath more words.

"Or perhaps it is the muskets?" said he.

"The muskets?"

"Those we took on at Bantam. It is said that they were for trade with the Japons."

This was indeed true. Fully five hundred muskets had been taken on in Java under the captain's personal supervision and they had been guarded night and day ever since.

"A fine place to do trade," I said huffily, not anxious to concede that this loon could be sharper than I.

"I have heard that the Japons prohibit the bringing of arms into their country," says he. "If that be so then it is likely that some secrecy surrounds our presence here. We are probably waiting for another vessel."

I did not answer but looked out towards the island. Half a league away a black conical cliff rose sheer from the water and was joined by a belt of undulating, densely wooded greenery to a sand bank that faded away below the surface of the sea. It was like the painting of a bird with upturned beak, composed of black head, green body and yellow tail. Behind the island lay another stretch of water and beyond that a vista of distant mountains sheathed in clouds. This, I surmised, was the mainland of Japon.

As I looked at the black cliff a vessel appeared before it like an actor stepping on to a darkened stage.

"Zounds," I said, "I think you may be right. What is it?"

"A junk. A black junk."

"And being rowed towards us. Do you see the oars?"

"And the hull, like a tortoise's shell."

It was in fact more like a Noah's Ark with banks of oars on each side disappearing into the hull so that no men could be seen. The deck was raised and appeared to be composed of sheets of metal interleaving like scales. All in all it seemed a formidable vessel but

I could see no sign of gun ports that might threaten us. Rather it seemed to be built to offer the maximum of defence.

"They move it well," Twist said admiringly.

"I would like a sight of one of them," I said, " 'tis strange that they have no man on deck."

"See one and you have seen them all. Like little yellow dervishes they are. Features all pressed into their faces as if they'd been turned out of baking tins. Yellow-hued, slit-eyed—"

"How many have you seen?"

"We picked up two after a brush with a pirate junk off the Malay peninsula. When we pulled them out of the water they felt such shame at being taken that they begged to be thrown overboard again."

"And did you?"

"No. We hung them."

The junk was nearly abreast of us now. The oars picking up in perfect unison, the struck sail plucking at the wind like a snarled pennant. Most of our crew were crowded against the rail and I could see men opening the hatches below which the muskets were stowed. Perhaps Twist was right. The junk hove-to with a flourish, two oars length away from us, and glancing towards our bridge I saw the captain address the mate who stepped forward with his hands cupped around his mouth.

"Now you'll see 'em," said Twist.

But I didn't. Not then. As I gazed down, a row of hatches popped open like eyes and I found myself staring into the mouth of a cannon pointing directly at me. Almost instantaneously the piece was fired and I ducked away to catch a glimpse of Twist as a cannon ball tore his head from his shoulders and a fount of blood gushed from his neck and then fell back like a spring in summer. I did not need to bend my eyes from this unwholesome sight because the treacherous broadside lifted the ship like a boot under a table. I was hurled back against the rail and before the vessel could right itself a severed spar and its incumbent sheets crashed down upon my head and whipped me overboard as smoothly as a rabbit into a poacher's bag.

Down I went, fighting against the death-hug of the sail but feeling that I was already dead. I have no other recollection of the incident than the panic that overtook me and the increasing difficulty of moving my limbs. At last, a desperate, unavailing thrust sprang the padlocks on my mouth and nostrils, inviting the ocean to overrun my senses. To my surprise I breathed in air. My limbs were still suspended in water but I could breath. The thought came to me that by some miracle I had struggled into an air pocket and thus found temporary deliverance.

But with my face pressed against the opaque window of the sail I could see that I was not alone. Dark shapes swirled about me. Sharks. The seas hereabouts abounded with them.

No doubt they were plumbing their meagre resources of courage to find enough spark to attack. Sharks are prodigious cowards unless they smell blood. On the voyage to Japon the second mate had received six inches of steel in his lower belly and had been slipped over the side because there was no better place for him. His body had hardly touched the water before it was wittled down to a bloody core.

The recollection of this incident did little to abate the terror that still gripped me. If I stayed where I was I would soon exhaust my meagre supply of air, whilst to strike out for the surface would be to render myself totally vulnerable. It was probably only the strange-

ness of the stricken mass before them that prevented
the sharks from attacking immediately. As if to refute
the thought, there was a flash of white and my shroud
received a fearful buffet as if a shark coming in to attack had veered away at the last second and lashed
out with its tail. The blow knocked me sideways and
I could do no more than snatch a lungful of air before
my head was submerged again. Now there was nothing
for it. I must try to make the surface. Forcing my body
down I felt the grip of the sail slacken and with a few
frenzied wriggles was free and clawing my way upwards.

I came up battling, putting as much kick into my
strokes as I could muster to deter attack. With every
second I expected to be lighter by the weight of a leg
and with my head above the surface my limbs seemed
to be dangling below like bait. I had feared that I
might find myself alone in the shark-infested sea but
the smoke-hung stern of the Mace was only a score of
yards away. Around the rudder was a tangle of twisted
sail and spars and I reckoned that this might afford me
some kind of perch. To this end I struck out with a
speed that surprised me and was in no time attempting
to preserve my balance on a flimsy raft of spars tucked
on beneath the overhanging cliff of the stern.

Around me the water was streaked with red like a
painter's palette. Supporting my conjecture, came a
swift vomit of guttural speech from above, a scream,
and a twitching body that plummeted into the water
but six feet away from me. Hardly had I recognised
it as the bosun, his neck half severed, than the sea
thrashed and the corpse was snatched from my sight
as the sharks launched themselves at it.

I clung on desperately and was grateful that the
stern prevented me from being detected from above.

The Japonian tongue was like nothing I heard before with its short sharp flurries of barked speech, made all the more intimidating by the fact that I had no sight of those delivering it—only ample evidence of their disposition. Two more bodies were hurled over the side and sounds of resistance faded away to isolated musket shots. The devilish jabber took on the intonation of self congratulation.

In my position I felt as secure as a goose as Christmas approaches. To climb aboard was to get my throat cut and I would no more have thought of swimming in that water than trying to walk on it. That left staying where I was and although normally a man who prefers to do something rather than nothing, I was easily persuaded to restrain my impetuosity.

I could not see the junk but a concentration of gabble on the starboard beam suggested that the pirates were converging on their vessel. What were they up to? The question was made more difficult by the sounds of oars rattling against the ship's side and the swish of blades. The junk was being rowed away.

Now, perhaps, was a good moment to try and scramble aboard the Mace. The pirates were probably going to fetch a larger vessel before finishing their plundering. Above me a gun port loomed invitingly and I stretched upwards to take a grip on the shred of rigging that might guide me to it.

At that second the rudder gave a slow deliberate movement, my platform was gently nudged aside and I was toppled into the sea. I came up in a state worse than panic to see the Mace moving away and my perch disintegrating. The accursed Japons must have put her under tow. Before me was a piece of rigging trailing in the water. I struck out in desperation and my fingers brushed against it. Then it moved away, sinuous, like

a snake swimming. I forced myself through the water
and this time my hand closed about it. Another heave
and I was in a position to haul myself from the water
and there, speeding inexorably towards me like a nightmare come to life, was the dorsal fin of a shark. My
heart that had been threatening to beat its way out of
my chest now suddenly swelled up with terror so that
it seemed to rob my body of movement. I hung there
like a rabbit fixed by a stoat. It was not until the fin
keeled below the surface as it spun over to take me
that the spell was broken and drawing my legs I kicked
with all my might. One, two, three times I lashed out,
the first blow connecting with the brute's snout and
the others exercising my panic. Still churning the water,
I hauled myself up the rope until my legs were hanging free and I was desperately feeling for a foothold
on the threads of rigging. Every second seemed to give
the shark an eternity of time to take me and I was
gibbering with fear before I finally slotted my foot and
scrambled a few feet to safety. Below me I saw a
flash of white and enough teeth to fill a charnel house.

By now the movement of the ship was causing the
rope to swing back and forth like a pendulum and I
tried to increase its momentum so that I might reach
out for the gun port. In this I was unsuccessful for
the overhang of the poop was too great and I merely
succeeded in further exhausting myself, since the rope
was cutting into my flesh as if it was cheese, and my
hands had less grip than a virgin's thighs. I decided
that I must drag myself up to deck level before my
strength failed altogether.

The rain that had been light was now falling persistently and the sky darkening almost as if a lamp
were being turned down. The conditions made the ascent more difficult and twice I nearly lost my grip be-

fore I was able to raise my head slowly above the stern rail.

In front of me stood a man with his back to me and his hands resting lightly on the wheel. He was small but broad and wearing baggy trousers and a loose jerkin that came down to his knees. His hair was pulled back into a truncated pigtail and there was a long sword tucked into the wide sash around his waist. An arm's length away a musket was propped against one of the hatches. At first glance the appearance of the first Japon I had seen fell short of what I had imagined. It was difficult to conceive how the like of this squitty little runt could have overrun the Mace, even allowing for the surprise engendered by their treacherous attack. But perhaps I was looking at a particularly malformed specimen. I clung below the rail and reviewed my situation. The vessel was undoubtedly being towed to harbour and I knew that my best ploy would be to wait until the merchantman neared land and I could risk swimming ashore undetected. However, in my present condition this was impossible. Soaked to the skin, exhausted and racked by cramp I must find shelter on the deck or risk dropping into the sea. Five paces in front of me lay a crumpled heap of sail. If I could reach that I would be able to gather strength for the next stage of my escape. Noticing that the wheel was still and the helmsman showing no sign of movement I pulled myself up and swung a leg over the rail. Immediately the little yellow hellion turned round.

At first his face registered surprise but in an instant the neat, flat features crumpled into an expression of demonic rage and he uttered a shrill bark, like a dog waking up to an intruder. In one continuous movement his sword materialised in his hand and he was darting towards the rail. Terrified out of my wits I

barely resisted hurling myself into the sea but fought
the impulse and with the rope still in my hands scrambled to my feet and kicked from the rail. As I swung
out, the sword hit into the wood where my body had
been and a chunk like a stick of firewood danced into
the air. Swinging round in a half circle I crashed back
over the rail, and sprawled across the deck four paces
from my adversary.

The little devil came for me like a greyhound for
a leveret, his sword raised above his head with both
hands. I hurled myself sideways to dodge the blow
and made a dash for the musket. Lack of height
seemed in no way to impair his speed and it was only
by vaulting the corner of the hatch that I kept myself
intact. Behind me came a sharp hiss of exasperation
and wasted breath as another blow tasted empty air.
The musket now hung like a prize before me and I
snatched it up and wheeled round in one movement.
My pursuer was once again primed to attack but at
last I had a stroke of luck. The poisonous dwarf in
front of me lost his footing on the bloodstained deck
and, for a moment, wavered. Quick as I'd cover a
dropped ducat with the sole of my foot I gave my natural impulse full rein and layed the musket squarely
against the varlet's head. He took off like a shuttle-
cock and tumbled head over heels into the scuppers
where he lay twitching. It was a blow from which I
derived a great deal of pleasure.

Any pause for self congratulation was denied me as
there came a sharp report at the same instant as a
musket ball buried itself in the mast beside my head
and showered me with splinters. I spun round to see
another Japon scuttling amongst the hatches on the
fore deck. The man was forty paces away and must
have come from the prow. I gripped my musket imag-

ining that the pirate would attempt to reload his own weapon before advancing. I was wrong. With a wild shriek the creature leaped into the air like a game-cock and drove towards the poop deck as if at the head of sixty men, his sword flashing in his hand. I was in two minds and happy in neither. I assumed that the musket was loaded although I was not sure. To press the trigger was a certain way to find out. But if the shot missed? Then it would be a question of taking up the smitten helmsman's weapon and in the rôle of swordsman I felt I might not be the equal of the treacherous termite. Better to rely on the musket at close quarters. Stepping forward to the rail I tried to hold my aim steady on the centre of the man's charging body, hoping with the gesture to persuade him to take cover or even surrender. It was a hope unfulfilled. The sight of the musket induced no slacking in momentum and if anything served only to make him come on even faster. Foolhardy little runt! Despite my growing fear I could not help but admire the courage of the man. I would have no more thought of exposing myself in his position than I would of flying. I tightened my grip on the musket and depressed the barrel. His foot hit the bottom stair and I could see the stubble of his shaven head. Up came his face, teeth bared, lips coated with spittle, shrill screams exploding from his mouth. His sword was held out before him like a lance and I had my eye on it, but quick as a snake's tongue his left hand dropped to his waist and he sent a dagger skimming for my throat. The weapon clipped my shoulder and sent me stumbling backwards. As I fought to keep my balance he was upon me, so close that I could smell him. Still fumbling I pressed the trigger with his sword almost in my guts. The recoil speeded my fall and I sprawled across the deck gritting my teeth against the pain to come.

But nothing happened. I stared upwards and there
was only a thin wisp of smoke hanging in the air, the
petulant flap of a loose sheet, the rain still falling. Uneasy at what I might see I scrambled to the rail.

Below me the Japon lay stretched out upon his back,
his legs slightly apart and his arms extended above his
head. Slowly but persistently a red stain spread
through the linen on his chest and his teeth peeped
out of his dead mouth like those of a slain rat.

Warily I descended the ladder and skirted the body
to pick up the sword that lay behind it. Gingerly I
prodded the body with my foot and then peeled back
the jerkin with the tip of the sword. The musket ball
had entered the chest in the region of the heart. He
must be dead.

I turned round relieved—and was almost struck by
the body of the first pirate leaping from the poop deck.

Instinctively, ducking away, I lashed out backwards
with my sword arm and felt myself make light contact
as if flicking something with a whip. Blood spouted
from the man's neck like wine from a freshly tapped
cask. The chance blow had sliced through the front of
his throat and a torrent of blood struck my chest. The
pirate hung motionless for a moment and then slowly
toppled sideways across the legs of his comrade.

The incident was over so quickly as to almost defy
my comprehension that it had taken place. Even as I
looked down at their leaking corpses I had no confidence they were dead. This worry I removed by
ramming a sword through their bodies until I felt it
bite into the deck. I was in no mood to receive further
shocks.

The eerie darkness that had fallen about the ship
was now akin to dusk and the rain came down more
heavily. I crept towards the prow conscious of every

sound and movement, fabricating a Japon out of every shadow. Above me the sky was the colouring of a ripe plum and sullen gusts of wind nagged the slack sails.

It was at this moment that I became conscious that the vessel was not moving. I pressed forward, fearing that the crew of the junk had heard the shots and were returning to investigate, but the rope made fast to the prow hung down like a spent cock, whilst far ahead the junk was pulling away fast towards the cliff face. At first I could not understand why the pirates had abandoned their prize but even as I looked towards the junk the sky grew a shade nearer total darkness and I knew that some great storm was near, the threat of which must have driven the Japons to shore. Since they did not seem to be faint-hearted fellows their caution made me fear the worst.

High in the masts the wind whistled shrill, whilst at deck level the air was stifling. The sea though calm, twitched like the hide of a beast anticipating a blow. Ahead the island was an outline and behind it the land mass had disappeared into the gloom. It was as if God was preparing to destroy the world.

Picking my way through the debris I tried to think of what precautions I could take against the inevitable storm. But there was nothing. I was as powerless as one of the rats now creeping across the silent holds. Stepping over the wide stream of blood that trickled haphazardly towards the scuppers I skirted the dead Japons and took up a position beside the wheel. At least, here I might be able to steer some sort of course against the storm.

As I layed hands upon the wheel the vessel shuddered as if striking a cross current and a great gust of wind burst into the slack sails sending them beating against the air like a flock of startled pigeons.

Looking round I saw what at first glance appeared
to be a white line marking the boundary of the dark
horizon. But it was a line that moved. Jigged, danced,
broke and joined again. It was a wave, one wave, one
huge wave. Bearing down upon me like the vanguard
of an advancing army. From left to right as far as
the eye could see, it stretched higher than a house.
Curling, curving, girding itself to destroy whatever lay
in its path. At a distance it made no sound but was
presaged by a wind that tore at the masts as if chained
to them against its will and striving to be free. The
gusts threw me against the wheel and the vessel stirred
ominously as if scenting its destruction. I tried to look
away and prepare myself for death but the sight was
too awe-inspiring. What had once been a great ship
now seemed no more than a piece of driftwood waiting
to be swept away in a flood. It was coming closer now
and a deep roar began to thunder in my ears. I braced
myself against the impact. Then it came. Spread ea-
gled against the wheel I felt myself lifted up and moving with the ship as if encased in a coffin being tipped
into a grave. Around me I heard the vessel crying out
in its death agony. Creaking, cracking, splintering,
bursting. The wind and sea vying with each other for
possesion as it fell; careering, twisting, sliding lurching
down the glass face of the great wave.

The impact.

The world turned upside down.

Cold water breaking over my head.

Nothing.

CHAPTER 2

THE FIRST THING I WAS AWARE OF WAS THE WARMTH
all around me. Above and below. And the softness.
And the pain. The pain came when I moved. From my
arm because I was lying on it. But not just because I
was lying on it. There was something else.

I opened my eyes. The sun was too bright so I
closed them. That accounted for the warmth above. I
moved the fingers of my good hand and felt what
seemed to be warm sand. I opened my eyes again and
it was sand. I was lying on a beach. Between two
dunes. I tried to move my wounded arm and the
pain made me wince. When I looked up again there
was a girl standing beside one of the dunes. She wore
a long, brightly-coloured robe with one side crossed
over the other and held at the waist by a wide sash.
She had small delicate features and her hair was long
and black and fastened behind her head by a silver
clasp. She was beautiful. As I watched with growing
interest she undid the sash and removed the robe revealing that she was wearing nothing underneath.
She was very beautiful. I felt an immediate twinge of
desire which, in my condition, rather cheered me. I
could not be in too bad a way to regain my normal appetites so soon. But, as my eyes rummaged her firm
small breasts, an unsavoury thought occurred to me.

Supposing that I was in purgatory, and that the pain
and the incipient heat beneath me were intended as
reminders of what awaited those who were not prepared to eschew the baser earthly appetites? It was
not too much to conceive that a God who had played
so many tricks on me could treat me in this fashion.

I ignored these warnings and watched fascinated as
the girl stepped away from the dune and began to
scoop a shallow trench in the soft sand. This she settled into like a dove into a dust bath and began to
cover her limbs with more sand until she was buried
from the waist down. The significance of this action
was lost upon me. Humming an unmelodic tune she
began to pat herself indulgently and exhibit every sign
of physical well-being. Small beads of perspiration
glistened on her forehead and, while I looked on
amazed, wisps of steam rose from the sand as if from
a cooking pot. Could she be boiling herself alive? Had
I skirted purgatory to reach a hell whose victims conducted their own torture? Could these crafty Japons
become so inured to pain as actually to take pleasure
in it?

It was while I was debating the answers and enjoying the spectacle of the girl ruminatively scratching
her private parts that she turned her head, saw me,
and opened her mouth to scream.

But she did not scream. Shaking free from the sand
she reared up as if I were some monstrous insect. Without taking her eyes off me she cast about for the robe
in such a panic that I felt forced to forget the pain and
try to placate her with some gesture.

When I moved she screamed.

It had not occurred to me till then that she imagined herself in the presence of a corpse, but this was
clearly the case. I tried to soothe her with words but

this only seemed to add to her terror. She pulled the robe about her, half stumbled over a dune and started to run.

I sank back and closed my eyes. By God, I was a luckless rascal. The girl would alert her village—probably the pirate village—and they would come and cut my throat—or worse.

I tried to pull myself up and let out a cry of pain in the process. This was well done because the girl faltered in her stride and turned back as if having second thoughts about me. I emitted a low moan redolent of enormous suffering and sank back piteously. If I could draw her to my side I might be able to render her incapable of alerting anyone to my presence. Two groans and a short sharp squeak later my half-shut eyes disclosed her standing above me, nervous yet compassionate. She had a beautiful face, that girl. Large wide-set eyes and full, bow-bend lips like a woman of Europe. Although her skin had a faint golden hue there was little to identify her with the Japons I had despatched in the Mace. Even as she was within my reach my resolve began to weaken. Gazing down at me she was more like a guardian angel than a minion of the devil and I could sense that I was once again about to become a victim of my own soft-heartedness.

She knelt down before me and spoke in what I took to be Portuguese. Since my only words in that language consisted of a sentence employed when asking a whore the price of her services I felt ill-equipped to reply and shook my head.

She spoke again, this time in what I took for the Japonian tongue, and I replied in English. Now it was her turn to indicate that she could not understand and we faced each other, lost for a means of communication. Eventually she smiled her good intentions and brushing the hair from her eyes began to run her fingers lightly over my arm. When I winced she made a cooing noise as if soothing an obstreperous child but continued calmly with her examinations. At last she sat back on her haunches and mimed the breaking of a twig. I found it easy to agree with her, for my arm was swollen out of all recognition. I gave her thanks, to which she replied with a bow, and struggled to my feet. It was surprising that despite her slender frame the girl was strong and not loath to prop herself under my arm like a crutch.

Looking around, I could see that I was on the narrow bar of sand that had reminded me of the bird's tail when seen from the sea. Some baulks of timber lay scattered across the beach but there were no obvious relics of the Mace. The sea now proceeded towards the shore in a series of orderly wavelets. On the right was a cluster of black rocks topped with greenery beyond which the land appeared to fall away before rising steadily through well-wooded slopes to the high point of the island. What, from the ship, I had taken for a steep cliff could now be seen as a mountain, its dark peak blunted as if beaten down with a hammer. Its stark outline made me think again of the pirates who had presumably perished in its shadow. I wondered if the girl belonged to them. Her ability to speak Portuguese suggested that she came from no ordinary family. Perhaps her father was some renegade privateer using the island as a base for attacks on European merchantmen trading with Japon? I allowed my whimsical imagination full rein whilst waiting for the girl to give some indication of her plans for me. This she did by disengaging herself from me and moving towards the rocks, beckoning that I should follow.

I felt vulnerable in the open and was glad we were

making for the shelter of the trees. The girl led the way through the rocks and up a narrow path that scaled the cliff face. All around shrubs and greenery crowded the steep slope like troops gathering for embarkation. At the summit, tall trees fragmented the sunshine and the air was cooler. As I had surmised the land sloped away gently and it was as if we were standing on the rim of some giant platter. I had expected to be led inland but the girl beckoned me to follow and traced a path along the perimeter of the cliff edge. Every few paces there were outcrops of black rock and it was by one of these that she stopped and looked round carefully as if to make sure that we were not being followed. Satisfied, she took my hand and guided me down a narrow path that dipped over the cliff edge from the course of a dried up waterfall. In situation it was perfectly concealed from above as was the broad grass-covered ledge which widened out twenty feet below. At its back was the opening to a cave and looking round I could see that the surrounding cliffs were peppered with holes like sand martins' nests. Far below, the beach had disappeared and the sea chewed angrily on the rocks. Used as I was to heights, the descent fair froze my sinew, but with the pretty child tripping before me casting encouraging glances over her shoulder I was loath to show fear. Now, standing outside the cave she did not release my hand but drew me forward protectively as if introducing me to my first day at school. Inside, the cave was formed from the same black rock that had broken through the surface of the cliffs, and divided up into a number of passages that led off like fingers from a glove. The air was musty and a faint glow illuminated the entrance to one of the passages. My guide called into the darkness and fumbled in one of the alcoves, whilst I looked

about me anxiously. She found a candle and lit it from
a flame surmounting a glacier of wax that billowed
to the floor like a lace farthingale. There was no answer to her greeting and holding the candle aloft she
led the way down one of the passages, explaining that
she was surprised that her father was not there. I
moved after her cautiously, still suspecting treachery.
The walls were porous and uneven like crudely cut
hunks of black bread. I was about to ask her how she
could exist in such a place when a slight bend in the
passage revealed a pool of light that seemed to be
thrown down from one of the walls. The girl quick-
ened her pace and I followed to see that the light came
from a small room hollowed out of the wall to make
a large alcove. It was not empty. At one end was a
chest covered by a white cloth and bearing a lamp
and a spilled flask of wine. On the wall above it hung
a crucifix and before it lay a strip of coarse rush matting. On the matting knelt a man with head dropped
forward on to the spilt wine so that at first glance it
seemed that blood was gushing from a wound in his
temple. At second glance I realised I was looking at a
man besotted with liquor. He wore a longer version of
the girl's robe, and had a shaven head but was plainly
European. Much puzzled I looked around the room
again before it came to me.

The man must be a priest and the girl's father!
Some devious papist rogue who had podded one of
his flock. I could be a missionary if that was what con-
version entailed. Hence my fair deliverer's pleasing
features. A Portuguese Japon. I looked back to the
man. Why was the deviant drunk? Perhaps out of remorse or frustration at not having sufficient opportunity to indulge his weakness. I could not envisage any
congregation flocking to this place. And how long had

they been here? The girl was more than a child.

I put on my helpful face but she took my arm and began to pull me away.

As if awakening to our presence the man began to extend his hand across the trunk, his fingers snatching at the ruckled cloth. His head turned slowly and I thought he was about to vomit. Instead he uttered a low, drawn-out cry of terror as if he recognised some instrument of torture and sank back on to the floor. The eyes were wide open, the mouth twisted in pain, the lean features glistening with sweat.

I was not sorry to be drawn away from the sight and wondered if it was induced by some strange melancholy, sister to the grape. Certainly the man seemed to have something eating at his mind. The girl led me swiftly down the passage to another chamber where a pile of blankets lay folded neatly in a corner. She indicated that this was to be my chamber and held the candle until I had settled on to the bedding. As she left the room the light drained away and I could see the jagged outline of the entrance thrown up by the glow in the passage. I lay back in the darkness listening to her voice, alternately chiding and soothing, rising above the background of her father's babble. The pain in the arm had settled into a persistent ache and I felt uneasy about leaving it much longer without treatment. I also felt hungry. Very hungry. But above all, tired. A weariness that engulfed me sucked me down as into a quicksand; swept over pain and hunger. Before I could think more I was asleep.

When I woke up I was cold and stiff as a swart's hampton. Immediately I missed the motion of the ship beneath me. The dank, stale air was no stranger to my nostrils but the absence of any movement, the silence of my surroundings made me wonder where I was. It

was almost a relief when the pain nudged me sharply
back to reality. But with increasing panic I found I
could not move my arm. It seemed pinioned by my
side. I fumbled desperately with my free hand and
felt two tightly-bound splints of wood. Thank God for
my sweet deliverer. My first fear had been that the
smitten adjunct had become gangrenous and was
about to drop off. There was now a candle by my
bedside and with an effort I picked it up and scrambled to my feet. The room was empty and so I made
for the passageway, eager to find food, and wondering
what state I would find my host in. I was soon to find
out.

Casting a glance into the alcove I saw the man himself kneeling in the midst of perfect order and mumbling pieties as if he was the most devout prelate in the
world. There was no reminder of the previous night's
carousing. I made to pass on but the rogue unclasped
one of his fervent hands and held it up to stay my
progress while he continued with his incantations. I
had to admire the spirit of the fellow. Whitgift himself
could not have appeared more pious. Eventually he
completed his orisons and rose wearily to his feet. He
was a fine featured man with sensitive, nervous eyes,
the flesh around them wizened like an apple-John. The
likeness to the girl was very strong. He took my good
hand and applied a modicum of pressure suggestive
more of gentility than any lack of desire to make me
welcome. To my amazement he then addressed me in
slow but perfect English.

"I hope that you have been able to sleep," he said,
obviously relishing my surprise. "We live very simply
here, as you will have observed, but I can see that my
facility with your tongue perplexes you. My name is
Perez, Sebastian Perez, late, very late, of Lisbon. I am

a Jesuit priest and hence fortunate enough to have been schooled in a number of languages. I am here trying to bring faith to this barbarous land."

And not above exploring some novel techniques to effect conversions, I thought to myself.

"And mighty glad of it, I am," said I. "My name is John Adam. From Plymouth, England. My ship was overrun by pirates and broken up in a typhoon. I think I must be the only man of our crew to reach shore."

"We have seen no others. It is a miracle that you are alive."

"I thank your—your daughter and yourself—for your part in it," I said, waiting for him to acknowledge the relationship, but he did not.

"Is your arm causing you much pain?" he said.

"A little, but less than I might expect. Again, my thanks."

"Thank Somi. She devoted most time to tending you. We have both become accomplished nurses since our arrival in this land. It is important to build up trust before one can win a convert with these simple people. The mind through the body, you know."

"Indeed," I said, wondering how he could preserve a serious face whilst saying the words. I do believe that priests surpass even women for self-deceiving hypocrisy and that papists beat the lot. Still, they can name their daughters well. Somi suited the pretty child.

The smell of food invaded my nostrils and its competition for my attention must have been obvious. Perez took me by the arm and led me towards the mouth of the cave.

"You must be in need of food. We can talk later. I am afraid that your arm will take some weeks to heal.

It is broken you know." I nodded. At that moment I was more conscious of how hungry I was. If the limb had dropped off I would have started eating it.

Outside the cave Somi was tending some cooking pots resting on a charcoal fire. She greeted me cheerfully and bid me to sit down and prepare to eat. At first sight this presented a difficulty because there were no chairs or tables readily to hand but Perez, sensing my perplexity, was quick to settle on a mat placed before a small varnished table raised no more than two finger widths from the ground. Here he sat back on his haunches in a manner that I found exquisitely uncomfortable when I tried to emulate it. As I struggled to achieve a more bearable position Somi placed before me two red lacquered bowls, the largest of which contained rice and the smaller what appeared to be raw fish soaked in a kind of vinegar. Two round sticks about the size of a quill were also produced which I assumed were intended to stir the food. Having done this and waited unavailingly for a spoon or fork to be produced I poured some of the fish into the rice and began to direct the mixture into my ravenous mouth with my fingers. Glancing round I was perplexed to see that Perez was holding the two sticks between the fingers of one hand and using them with such dexterity as to be able to pick up a few grains of rice at a time. He also made no attempt to mix the contents of the dishes but helped himself to each alternately. The delicacy of the operation made me feel something of an oaf but I was damned if I was going to let a couple of renegade Portuguese see me discountenanced so I continued shovelling away with a will until my platter was empty. I sat back licking my fingers with all the elegance I could muster whilst Somi giggled and Perez shook his head indulgently.

"It was thoughtless of me not to remind Somi to provide you with a spoon. One adapts to new ways so quickly that one forgets the old." He went on to explain that it was the custom of the country to use these hashi or chopsticks when eating all cooked food and to handle it in the European manner was considered most barbarous. I conceded that it might be, but observed that it was better I was given a spoon, or the use of my hands, otherwise I might starve to death before a grain of rice passed my lips. I was also on the point of saying that the serving utensils were so small as to barely supply an adequate meal to a sparrow, but left the thought unsaid. In this respect, my fears were groundless as Somi replenished my rice bowl three times. On the fourth occasion that she came to the table she filled the bowl with what appeared to be hot water coloured green by a powder giving a faint aromatic smell. This I was informed was made from the leaf of a plant called cha or tea and drunk throughout the country as an aid to digestion or to combat the effects of too much wine. I found the bitter taste of the brew not to my liking and this impression was obviously apparent to my host because Somi was sent to fetch a flask containing a pale amber liquid which was served in a small varnished bowl. This I was told was sake, and distilled from rice. The news did little to enthuse me but I found the wine quite palatable and wished again that there was a larger vessel available to enjoy it. Nevertheless, feeling that I must fit myself to the habits of the country, I tried to attack it in small sips rather than empty the cup in one draught. Watching Perez sitting back easily on his heels it seemed strange that this man who had once come to teach the Japons the ways of Europe should now have adopted so many of their own. Perhaps it was that, having tried to win acceptance by fitting in with their mode of life, he had somehow been overtaken by it. It was strange too that in these sparse surroundings a meal should be served with such style. After my flirtation with the pirates I had believed myself come to a land of warrior savages but if my hosts mirrored their ways they must be more refined than I had imagined.

As the weeks passed and my arm mended I found myself more at ease in the company of my hosts. My days were spent in taking sand-baths, as Somi had been doing when I first saw her, or exploring the woods and slopes about the cave. Perez, fortunately, showed no repetition of his behavior of the first night. He never referred to his relationship with Somi or mentioned her mother and said little about his reasons for leaving the mainland beyond that he feared a great persecution of the Christian missionaries was at hand. I noted that although Somi was a dutiful daughter she showed her father more respect than affection.

Perez's congregation was comprised of half a dozen poor fishermen who arrived at nightfall wearing wooden clogs and an all-pervading stench that clung to them like a garment. They were the foulest smelling fellows I have ever recoiled from. Leaving their clogs at the entrance they would make obeissance to me and scuttle through to the inner sanctum to take Mass, or Konsham as they called it. The sound of their voices trying to bend themselves round the papist chants were scarcely more pleasing than a choir of tom cats.

From listening to these men and the time I spent with Somi I began to pick up the rudiments of the Japonian tongue and attempted to employ my few words upon them. I also learned how the name of this country came into being. It was originally Nippon or

'the origin of the sun'. This was pronounced Jih-pun
by the Chinese and corrupted by the Portuguese to
Japon.

With regard to my future, Perez told me that the
port of Nagasaki for which the Mace had been
bound, and where the Portuguese merchants had
their factory, was a day's sail away. It was agreed that
when my arm was completely healed one of the fishermen would transport me there so that I might find a
ship to take me back to Europe.

Perez told me that they dwelled in the cave primar-
ily because the Christian faith was outlawed throughout the land on penalty of death and also because he
feared the pirates who sometimes roamed forth from
their stronghold at the other end of the island and
plundered the local fishing settlements. Their presence
on the island had been an unwelcome surprise when
he and Somi had taken refuge there but so far they
had remained undetected. The structure I had seen
from the sea was in fact the shell of an extinct volcano
which had once spurted lava like puss from a boil and
finally split asunder in one last great eruption, so that
its cone now presented the perfect harbour. It was here
that the pirates had their stronghold with an access
to the ocean through a narrow passageway overhung
by towering cliffs. It occurred to me that the junk must
have been intent on towing the Mace to this channel
when the typhoon struck and that my adversaries
might well have reached sanctuary rather than being dashed against the cliffs as I had originally supposed.

I resolved to take a closer look at this end of the
island but said nothing to Perez about my intention
because the man was as nervous as a novice catamite
and scarcely moved from the caves but to cast an

eye over what Somi was doing. For a man several
scruples less than perfect he was Cerberus himself
when it came to the conduct of his daughter's affairs.
It was always the same in my experience, the greatest
libertines make the most suspicious fathers, and show
me a mother who would part her legs for a dray horse
and you will find her daughter has a chastity belt before a christening mug. Why they deny their progeny
what they find so pleasant themselves I will never conceive.

Somi herself was both a puzzle and a frustration to
me. For the most part she was cheerful enough but
prone to moods of melancholy and introspection in
which her mind seemed to be swelling in a kingdom
of its own. At these times she would walk for hours
amongst the trees, or along the beach, before returning and being her old good-natured self again.

Being the creature I am, I was intrigued less by her
moodiness than by her female charms and in this respect the interest was all on one side. The child reso-
lutely refused to respond to my gambols. It was not
in truth a refusal, more the fact that she seemed to
have no conception that I was a man, with all the de-
licious possibilities that this entailed. I on my part had
a very clear and increasing cognisance of the fact that
she was a woman. The minx would sit cross legged
before me in the sand inviting me to explore her but
with such damned unaffected innocence that I began
to feel like some tuft-buttocked satyr every time I
glanced at her. She would touch me, tease me, pat me
like a friendly beast so that I had to bite my tongue
and turn upon my stomach. It became so I almost welcomed the intervention of the wily Perez who read
me like some book forbidden to his faith and was
assiduous in rationing the time I spent alone with his

daughter. I felt the desire but was incapable of pressing the matter. I have lain with some terrible old malkins in my time and sold their drawers for kerchiefs; I have lark-tongued my way into the bedchambers of the quality; but these were all women who knew the game we were playing. Faced with Somi's wretched all-pervading innocence I was powerless.

And so the matter might have rested until my departure for Nagasaki had not Perez's flock come bundling into the cave one night showing twice their normal degree of animation. Such was their panic that I forgot the smell that usually drove me out as they came in and drew closer whilst they gabbled away to Perez. From the odd word I understood and Perez's asides to Somi, I gathered that there had been an attack on the pirates stronghold and that the island was alive with bands of armed men. I was eager to inspect the situation, being inclined to believe that the words of these simple fishermen were much exaggerated but Perez flew into a rage and utterly forbade me to leave the caves. Furthermore he said that there would be no mass that night and that his congregation should leave singly and return with all speed to their villages. From his utterances it became clear that he imagined that the bloodshed presaged some general slaughter of the Christians on the island and was an extension of the purges being conducted on the mainland. I tried to reason with him and say that it was probably no more than some local feud between rival bands of pirates, but he would hear nothing of it and persisted that this was what he had been fearing since his arrival on the island, until I almost lost patience with him. Somi looked from one to the other of us like a dog torn between two masters and eventually led him away to bed much agitated. I waited until the last of the Japons had stolen away into the night and having loitered by the mouth of the caves and heard nothing except the sea washing against the rocks followed her to see what additional succour I could bestow.

When I came to them it was to find Somi remonstrating with her father. He sat haunched up on a pile of blankets in one of the small caves which served as his bedchamber. He appeared agitated near to sickness and was already slopping sake on to the floor as he tried to fill his cup. With some difficulty I persuaded Somi to leave us and settled down to reason with him but the man seemed unaware that I was there and looked beyond me to the wall as if studying some painting I could not see. His lips were moving but no sound came beyond the almost inaudible transcription of his thoughts. Without taking his eyes from the wall he would spill some sake into the cup and dash it back like a draught of physic. His pupils dilated and he seemed to be going into some kind of trance. All in all it was a most unnerving spectacle and one I felt singularly ill-equipped to deal with.

Suddenly he started forward and seized my wrists, turning his gaze on me like a magnifying glass concentrating the rays of the sun so that I almost flinched from it. He was a little, bird-like man but his grip at that moment bit like pincers.

"The faggots were wet," he said.

"Wet." I repeated weakly.

"It had been raining heavily." I began to speak but he bore over me as if my interruption had launched him like a vessel into a swift and dangerous current.

"Sixty-five of them in the dried up river bed. Some little children, no more than five or six years old, held tight in their mothers arms and crying out 'Jesus receive their souls.' While the kindling spluttered they

called sayonara to the crowd and began to sing the
Magnificat, so that those Christians amongst them
could not forbear to join with them. And as the flames
enveloped them they sang 'Laudate pueri Dominum'
and 'Laudate Dominum omnes gentes', never failing,
right unto the end of their martyrdom. And I skulked
in the crowd and did not dare raise my voice until it
was all over. And then when the smoke cleared and I
saw the blackened husks I could bear my perfidy no
longer and howled the Te Deum Laudamus until the
judges turned their eyes upon me and sent soldiers into the crowd and I fled again. My God, how many
times did Peter deny Christ? Three? I have done it
scores of times whilst small children roast before my
eyes and I hear their bodies burst like chestnuts on a
fire."

"This was the persecution on the mainland?"

"Was and is and will be. Christianity is not a plant
that will ever grow in this soil. Whatever I may say or
try to do that is what I really believe. How strong must
a man's convictions be that he can witness small children being burnt at the stake and believe it is God's
will and that it is right?"

"From what you said the martyrs believed it themselves."

"They believed what I said, I and others like me.
But if we ourselves have doubts, then how much
greater is our sin when we send others to die for our
words."

"Why do you stay here?"

"Because I am a rogue. You know that, I see it in
your eyes. The way you look at me. You are right to
despise me."

"But why do you stay?"

"Because I have the faith like a thorn in the sole of

my foot. I cannot rid myself of it. I cannot comfort myself into a position where I can tear it out. When I first apostatised with Somi's mother I had some standing in the community. I felt I could exist as a man rather than as a priest. I was so alone, so misunderstood. I could see that these people had no real conception of what I was saying. Talking of another God in a country which has hundreds. As a stranger they paid me respect but I made no impression on them. As months grew into years I realised that they were converting me."

"And Somi's mother?" Uncharacteristic delicacy had made me steer clear of the subject until now.

"Do not speak of her I beg you. Her death was God's final judgment on me. He was telling me that I could never escape my obligation to Him; that He had made me in His thrall."

So the mother was dead.

"You say you doubt, yet you still believe."

"Exactly. In my heart I know I have no volition in the matter. I say to myself that I stay here because of the child, because it is the only life she knows, but in reality it is because I cannot flee from my duty, my obligation. There is a voice within me that is not me that talks to these poor fishermen."

"But what will happen to the girl when you have gone? What life is there left for her in this place?"

"I think of that, and I think of that day in the river bed near Nagasaki. I see her face in the flames and I know, I know. Oh my God. We are doomed. Little-children Jesus receive their souls; I have sinned and I am punished through eternity. That child carries my guilt."

All through this speech his voice rose higher and higher until it cracked into an outburst of sobs and he threw himself down on his litter still crying out about the scene he had witnessed and his fears that he would see it happen again. I tried to comfort him but he babbled on, becoming increasingly incoherent until he toppled into an uneasy, snorting sleep.

It was obvious that he was existing on the edge of his sanity and for Somi's sake at least I resolved to try and force the two of them to return with me to Europe. It was a miracle that the girl could be as sane as she was, living with such a father. I returned to my chamber bearing the sake which had fortunately not been spilled and drank a toast to my lack of faith which I was determined to make apparent to any Japon that I met on my way to Nagasaki. How men could burn each other at the stake because of a difference over religious beliefs was something I had never properly understood.

CHAPTER 3

WITH THE HELP OF THE SAKE I SPENT A RESTFUL NIGHT and awoke determined to allay Perez's immediate fears by proving to him that any bloodshed on the island was not caused by an incipient purge of Christians. My arm was now perfectly recovered so there was no worry in that quarter.

Perez slept peacefully as a babe suckled on brandy and I tiptoed past him to meet Somi who was undertaking her ablutions at the mouth of the cave. The minx was stripped to the waist but made no speedy move to cover herself so I was tortured by the stooping pose which swelled her firm young breasts and fanned the fire always glowing hopefully in my loins. She asked me where I was bound and when I told her that I intended to take a look at the pirate stronghold, surprised me by expressing a desire to accompany me. I reminded her of her father's condition but she said that if he was not awake by now he would probably sleep for several more hours and would be safely left. Eventually it was agreed that we would leave a message by his bedside, which she did by using a small paintbrush as we would use a quill, and we set off for the volcano. A low mist hung above the ground and the grass was wet with dew. Somi danced ahead of me and pointed to the sun rising over the edge of a flat sea and bade me listen to the birdsong which was throbbing from the trees as from a minstrel's gallery.

"Is it not beautiful?" she called.

"Passing fair," I grunted feeling somewhat like an old dotard suddenly gifted with offspring.

"Do you not go for walks in your country?"

"Only to get from one place to another and when denied the use of a horse."

"The Japons are great lovers of nature."

"What do you mean by that?"

"They have affection for natural things. Trees, birds, flowers. They will stand for half the night watching the new moon."

"More fools them. But why do you say 'they'? Do you not consider yourself a Japon?"

"I do not know. Sometimes I think I am. It is a thought that disturbs me when you talk of us coming to Europe with you. I have no real feeling for my father—I know it is wrong to say so but it is true—and he is Portuguese. I may be more alone there than I am in this place."

"But you do not belong here. You do not look like a Japon. From what I have seen, your ways are not those of the Japons. All their women shuffle along, hardly raising their eyes from the ground."

"You have seen only peasants. There are others. I remember them in Nagasaki."

She gazed towards the ocean.

"What are your feelings towards your mother?"

"It is difficult to remember her. She died when I was a child. I do remember that my father did not live with us then. He was ashamed of what he had done, but later he felt more guilt at leaving me 'outside the faith' as he called it. He tried to take me back. I know that he made my mother very unhappy."

"How did she die?"

"She was burned at the stake."

She saw my eyes widen. "Oh yes, she learned her faith from my father, but she was stronger than he."

So that was it, Perez had cause for nightmares. I could see why Somi was so distant with him.

"How did you escape?"

"She gave me to him so that he might have some excuse to save his own life. I think, too, that in her heart she believed he wanted her dead and so died as much for him as Christ."

"He is most conscious of his guilt. Last night he bared his soul to me. He is a man in torment."

"I know that. But it does not change how I feel for him. He has made me—and made me what I am—a creature who belongs nowhere, who belongs to nothing. But come, let us talk no more of this. I was happy when we left the cave. Let me continue so."

She skipped away from me as if our last words had not been spoken and began to gather the blossom that abounded nearby. She was a creature of light and shade, there was no doubt about it. Now I could understand her lonely walks. In many ways she was exposed to the same demons as her father but some quirk of nature made her able to vary her mood magically. If either of them had been able to open their hearts to the other their troubles might have been resolved but I sensed that this would never happen.

As we came nearer to the centre of the island the trees thinned out and we entered glades covered in small brightly coloured flowers so delicately patterned that they might have been embroidered on green damask. Somi fell upon her knees and began to add some of their number to the blossoms she had collected, stopping every few minutes to hold up a bloom and ask me if its like was to be found in England. There was a small stream nearby, cascading merrily down the hillside, and glad to see the wench in happy mood again I sat down by it and watched her in the meadow. Away from the oppressive caves I drank up the fresh clean air and began to feel more myself. As I have observed before I am no country boy but I had to concede that there was some pleasure in the spectacle.

The pastoral idyll was quickly shattered. Sweeping my eyes round towards the open ground I saw a man advancing up the slope towards us. Luckily at the moment that he came into view he was turning round and addressing a few words over his shoulder. At the sound Somi froze and the smile fled from her face. The man had now turned his back on me so I covered the ground between Somi and myself in half a dozen strides and pulled her down beneath me. We lay in a slight depression in the earth and, raising my head above the grass line, I could see three more men come into view. They were all Japons and looked like warriors. Two swords in their waist sashes, one short, one long, and shaven headed but for a tuft behind like my adversaries on the Mace. One was well splattered with blood and all were grimy as if they had been in a fight. Most ominous, they were gazing around them intently as if looking for something. I held my breath and felt Somi's heart fluttering beneath me like a bird. They were holding a conference but thirty paces from me as if deciding which direction to take. Suddenly there was a bellow like that from a wounded beast and a fifth Japon hove into view. He was altogether the most remarkable I had seen yet. Smallish, as seemed to be the rule, but no-necked and

thick as two men. In this I do not exaggerate. He
rolled above the ground and his upper arms were as
thick as an Englishman's thighs. In all respects he was
like a truncated oak tree and his face villainous beyond comprehension. His eyelids loomed out of his
head like pursed lips and were visors through which
he peered so piercingly that I buried my face in the
ground beside Somi feeling that I must have been
seen. When I looked again it was to see him strike one
of his subordinates, for he was surely in command,
such a blow that the fellow staggered back half a doz-
en paces and nearly fell. The speech welled up in his
throat and spewed forth in a great spate of rage that
chilled my blood. As he turned towards me again I
could see that half a nostril was missing and there was
a great crease across his face that must have been the
scar from a sword blow. His face was hideous enough
without the sounds that emanated from it. Another
bellow and his minions started forward again. I began
to breath more freely waiting for him to follow—and
then the damned Somi let out a squeak. In my attempt
to remain concealed I must have been crushing her.
None of the others heard it but their leader pricked
up his ears like a stallion and wheeled in our direction.
I swear my heart came into my mouth and I had to
swallow hard to force it down again. Two strides the
brute took and cocked his head on one side. I held
my breath and swore that if the girl made another
sound she would die under my hand before he could
close with us. And then, blessed release, some small
bird began its chirping croak above us. I saw the creature's eyes rise to the trees, probe the source, and turn
slowly away. As my water thickened into blood the
brute took one last look round and marched over the
lee of the hill.

Hardly had he gone than Somi was squirming beneath me.

"You nearly killed me," she accused.

"Right," I said. "Why did you have to make that noise? God knows what they would have done if they had seen us."

"You were crushing me. I had to speak. Anyhow, how many were there?"

"Five in all. Did you not see their leader. Zounds, I have never set—"

"Five! Surely they would hardly be a match for you—what about those stories you have told me. How many pirates was it you slaughtered on your ship?"

I had in truth sketched an outline of my adventures around the Mace and made reference to my brush with the boarding party which accounted for the wench's presumption.

"Enough of your impudence or you'll feel the back of my hand," I said, still shaken by our narrow escape.

"I think you unkind to be malicious. I am sorry if I have upset you. I am certain you are just as brave as you speak. Now, will you release me or do you have other plans?"

She made this last remark with a cat-like flexing of her lower body that I found more than a might intriguing. It is a fact that often after moments of panic I have found my body charged with a desire for love-making. I wondered if this strange creature's instinct might be the same.

"What plans do you think I might have?"

"I cannot look inside your mind, though it is near enough to do so. This is the position in which men and women make babies, is it not?" The effrontery of the minx. She looked up at me through drowsy eyes and showed the tip of her tongue through half parted lips. I took a tress of her hair between my fingers and I felt its soft sheen chafe me like strands of silk.

"Something approaching it. Where did you glean that information—not from your father?

"No, I saw a couple amongst the rocks. At first I thought the man was killing her. I was terrified and started to cry out."

"He must have been grateful for your intervention."

"He did not seem to hear me. The girl shouted at me to go away. She was like a mad thing."

"And did you?"

"Eventually, when I had seen enough. They did not care. After a while I stole away and like a dutiful daughter went and asked my father what they were doing."

"And as a dutiful father, how did he reply?"

"He was much confused, but said eventually that it was what must be done to multiply the species."

"An obligation and a drudgery?"

"He was no enthusiast for it but I had seen enough to know there was an element of pleasure in it. What would you say?"

"I would say you might be right."

"Only might?"

I had moved off her body but was at no pains to stray further than I need. Her robe was splayed open to above her thighs and I could see that there was some kind of cotton loin cloth about her maidenhead. I felt that if our conversation continued on its present lines it was not going to stay there much longer.

"It is not always easy the first time—or pleasant. I would be a liar if I said it was."

Good, honest Adam. I wondered how many men would have spoken so true in my position.

"But it becomes better?"

"Much."

Her mouth was asking to be kissed so I made myself a gentleman for her sake and settled on it like a lusty bee probing for pollen. It was a small mouth but an ardent one and had learned its lessons well amongst the rocks. Whilst thus pleasantly engaged I was not letting my hands grow idle but loosening the sash around her waist so that I could draw it back to reveal her like some tasty sweet meat wrapped in a napkin. Supine, her breasts were undulations but I browsed amongst the nipples cheering them with the friendly pressure of my teeth until she folded her arms about my head and hugged me close to suffocation. In the furthest reaches of my mind was the unpleasant thought that our position was, to put it mildly, vulnerable should my short, thickset friend and his companions return, but I rejected it as being ungallant and not in the best tradition of my countrymen, and set about loosening my fair charge's loin cloth. At first I thought her fingers were my adversaries but I soon found that they were working with a will towards the same purpose, and better equipped to do so.

Instinct is a wonderful thing if given full rein occasionally and no sooner were her own possessions laid bare than she turned upon my own. In this pursuit she was aided by my wearing a kimono, or robe, similar to her own so that there was little to prevent her taking me in hand, so to speak. This she did with exclamations combining both a pleasing element of awe and, at the same time, an equally satisfying modicum of alarm. I, in part, sensitive soul that I am, shared her trepidation and set out to reconnoitre the territory to be invaded. In this design I was hindered by the eel-darting shudders that ran through her body no sooner

had my fingers lit upon her honey pot. Initial explora-
tion confirmed that there was to be no easy access and
so bearing in mind the demands of the situation and
increasing pressures that I was under from it, I reared
up, gobbed upon my weapon, cried 'God for Harry,
England and St. George' and drove into her breach.
She let out such a cry that I could see clear down to
that small thing that waggles at the back of ones
throat and we danced about the ground like fire crack-
ers. Out of respect for bastardy I tried to draw clear
of her body but she would have none of it and clung
to me like a stoat to a chicken's neck until I popped
my seed inside her and lay gasping for breath in the
damp grass. My God, I thought, if this is the passion
of an innocent child what will she do to me when I
have corrupted her?

Unfortunately, with the sating of my lust I found
my ardour cooling to vanishing point. 'Omnia animal
post coitus triste est' as, I believe, one of the more per-
ceptive mediterannean greasers said. It was not that I
liked the girl any the less, rather that I could not see
what I had been so excited about a few seconds before. It seemed slightly ridiculous. However, I had
been forced to cope manfully with this situation in
the past and so fed her cheeks a few pecks and hoped
that my detachment was not too obvious. She for her
part murmured and gurgled, and hopped from one
language to another like a cricket trying to find the
right endearment. It was a pleasing sound and given
this leisure I would soon have granted her a reprise
of what she so clearly desired. However, in my cold
state anxiety was speedily flowing back into the channels recently filled by lust and disengaging myself I
tried to make it clear that we must put some distance
between ourselves and the armed men. To this touch-

ing regard for her safety she slyly replied by asking
why I had not had this particular impulse earlier, so
that I was forced to yank her to her feet and tell her
to put one foot squarely before the other in case I had
an impulse to box her ears. This she seemed almost incapable of doing and reeled along beside me, chattering and giggling like a tipsy tavern wench. I felt
I would never be able to keep pace with her lightning
changes of mood, but I was not averse to trying.

"Was I like the English ladies?" she asked.

"Smaller."

"Is that good or bad?"

"Good."

"Shall we do it again?"

"Yes."

"Now?"

"No."

As far as possible I kept to the line of trees that
skirted the open ground in the middle of the island
and was alert to any sound or movement. I had decided that we might as well press on to the volcano as
the armed men had been travelling in the direction of
the caves which made an immediate return there im-
politic.

Once away from the grassland the ground rose
steeply like a horse's neck rearing sharply from the
soft undulations of its back.

Scorched shells of trees began to loom up amongst
the eager saplings and the ground was ridged, hard
and shiny like black sealing wax. Despite the omni-
present evidence of the eruption small plants and
patches of greenery had managed to force their way
through the crusty lava and clung tenaciously to the
hillside.

I was worried that we might be too easily seen once

the cover of the trees had been left behind and so
moved round within their shelter until the land suddenly dropped away into the sea and the great black
face of the cliff reared up above us. From our position
it was difficult to detect an opening but as we crept
further round I could make out a dark fissure which
might have marked the entrance.

By this time tiredness had dimmed Somi's chatter
and she was loath to go further but I informed her
brusquely that it was in my mind to carry through
my intention and started to scale the side of the volcano, telling her she could stay where she was if she
so wished. I soon heard her grumbling behind me as
I scrambled upwards. The slope was steep and I was
often on my hands and knees not caring to look downwards. I was attempting to strike towards the split
in the rock, thinking that this might afford me some
preview of the pirates' stronghold but I was soon glad
to find any foothold and my progress became slower
and slower. In this situation I was not pleased to find
Somi overtaking me with ease, my words obviously
having stung her proud nature.

As we neared the summit the way grew less steep
and the ground beneath our feet disintegrated into a
soft carpet of ash that clung in drifts like black snow.
It was a strange stuff to walk on and warm to the
touch which perturbed me not a little. I had an un-
healthy feeling that it might suddenly turn white hot
or that a great gob of lava might envelope me like
molten bird shit. It seemed a poor reward for having
scaled six hundred feet.

Ahead of me Somi, who had moved over to the
right, called to me and pointed towards her feet warning me to be careful. I was nearly at her side before
I saw the fissure which was no more than eight spans

wide and running down the volcano like a scar. It
seemed not wide enough to take a sea-going vessel. I
looked down and could make out the sea twinkling in
the gloom like silver fish at the bottom of a barrel.
Gazing down the chasm it seemed that the opening
widened towards its base and was overhung by the
cliff on which I was now lying. It was an eerie place
and not one in which I would like to have navigated
with a high swell running. Looking towards the heart
of the volcano a bar of light fell like a gap between
two curtains and I could clearly see part of a dwelling
squatting at the base of the cliffs. It was a weird sight.
Like half a painting picked out in a darkened room.
We pressed on in silence, following the rim of the
chasm and crunching through the ash which swirled
and leaped when caught by a sudden movement of
the wind, I approached the centre of the volcano with
some trepidation since I had seen nothing like this before and had no idea what might be lurking within its
crater. In this mood of what more ingenuous men
might have called fear I was stopped in my tracks by
something that filtered up before me.

Smoke.

A thin column rising steadily until it disappeared
into the clear blue sky. I looked at Somi who spoke
my thoughts.

"Is it still alive?"

I did not answer but pressed forward until suddenly the ground opened up before me and I stood
on the edge of a great hole, a hundred feet across, that
plunged down like the mouth of Hades. The farthest
wall was illuminated by the rays of the sun but for
the most part it was dark as a crypt. So this was the
core of the volcano. After a while my eyes became
accustomed to the gloom and I probed the depths

for signs of life. Taking as a starting point the dwelling
I had seen illuminated by the sun. I soon discovered
that there were many caves, like mouseholes, sprinkling the lower cliffs, several with structures of wood
built about their entrances. Some of them had roofs
of thatch and even, in a few cases, tiles. There was no
style about them and they huddled against the rock
face as if trying to escape from the water that pressed
in upon them. Living in such stygian gloom would
have made me a very sullen fellow within hours and I
strained my eyes to catch some glimpse of those who
dwelt in them. It was while thus occupied that another
column of smoke drifted up. Directly beneath me the
faint glow of flames, a shower of sparks. Not an eruption but a fire. At this moment my eyes finally came
to terms with the darkness and I could see that the
floor of the volcano was littered with slow burning
fires, the embers of some greater conflagration. The
cliff walls were scorched, and blackened baulks of timber paid witness to the dwellings that had been de-
stroyed. No sign of human life but as I looked there
was something stirring. Two men. Two men wrestling
on the ground. No, unpleasant revelation, it was a
pack of curs tugging at a corpse. Even as I watched
one of them broke away and almost guiltily stole off
to find its own prize. Now as I peered more closely
there were more corpses smeared like shadows about
the water's edge. Perhaps, heir to my imagination, the
smoke drifting upwards seems to bear the sweet sickly
odour of scorched flesh. No other movement down
there than the dogs rooting amongst the bodies of the
slain. It was like an open grave, begging to be filled
with earth.

Somi's face was wrinkled with disgust.

"The men we saw did this?"

I nodded.

"I think they played some part in it. But I wonder how they could have approached this place undiscovered?"

"Perhaps through the caves. I believe that there are many passages through the rock, like those in which we live."

"The junk is gone, taken for a prize I imagine. Have you any idea of who the attackers might be?"

"None. The Japons are a very war-like people and are always fighting each other as you will find."

"At least we can allay your father's fears. This does not seem like a nest of Christians."

I took one last look down into the charnel house and turned away, eager to leave this dreadful place. With my back to the pit my spirits lifted. The rich green of the tree tops, the white-crested ocean fraying against the shore, the comfortable body-rise and fall of the ground below—this was the place for living men. I turned for Somi but she was still upon the ground propped up on her elbows and using her eyes like soft magnets. She picked up a handful of ash and let it drain through her fingers; held my glance and pursed her lips as if trying to blow away a feather. Set against this black volcanic ash she looked like a pearl in a jewel box and very much worth having. It was really not to my credit, I reflected as I settled down beside her, that I could perform in such a fashion in this place.

CHAPTER 4

I STUMBLED DOWN THE SIDE OF THE VOLCANO WITH MY thighs aching, and not just from the steepness of the descent. My God, if that child was a novice in experience she was no stranger to enthusiasm. Her passion was the nearest thing to physical assault I had so far encountered. Yet, afterwards she was so meek and pliant you would not have thought her capable of a peck on the cheek without concocting a blush.

It is this facility in women that so much annoys and intrigues me. One moment they are in your power, heaving and thrashing beneath you, crying out that you are the most sublime lover in Christendom. Then, they lie back like contented cats and crown your efforts with indulgent smiles. I am certain they have no more recollection of their words than a man who bangs his thumb with a hammer and cries out in pain and anger. If this attitude seems unreasonable coming from a man who has already confessed to a certain post coital quiescence, let me admit it as such but say that the undisciplined fluctuation of a woman's whims makes its own significant contribution to my weakness.

But enough of these observations. Let me return to the present. We came out on the cliff very near where we had started our ascent and I deemed it advisable to

make our way homewards keeping close to the sea.
Both because I wanted to take advantage of the cover
of the trees and because I was interested to see if
there were any vessels lying off the coast which might
be connected with the raiders. I began to wonder if
the Square Root, as Somi had called him, and his
friends, were in fact the remnants of the pirate band
that had been defending the heart of the volcano rather
than its transgressors, but on reflection I thought not.
From their demeanour it appeared more likely that
they were the attackers searching for any survivors
with the intention of affording them a speedy passage
to the next world. These reflections made me step warily and I counselled the gabbling Somi to stop her
prattle and keep behind me like my shadow. Of these
there was a profusion as it was, by now, some time
into the afternoon and the sun had moved from above
our heads and was playing hide-and-seek among the
trees before us. The Japons seemed to be well equipped
with trees, cedars in profusion and some most graceful, swaying slightly with their branches extended
above the ground, like the arms of a dancer. There
were banks of moss, rust coloured, dark as velvet,
sweet smelling bushes garlanded with flowers and a
contented buzz of insects.

A feature of the landscape was the number of ra-
vines that cut into the cliff top, some so deep and rock-
filled as to require skirting. It was whilst moving up
the side of one that I suddenly saw a man with his
back to me, standing twenty paces ahead. Somi's hand
joined mine and we sunk to our knees behind the nearest tree. The man's position suggested that he was on
guard—but more than that. There was about him an
air of expectancy as if he was waiting for something
—or someone—and that their appearance was immi-

nent. He was pressed against a tree with a musket held
in such a position that it might speedily be raised to
his shoulder and his whole frame charged with concentration. As we watched, his position changed not
at all and I was grateful that we had not blundered
into him. As it occurred to me that he was lying in wait
for someone so, for a second, I wondered if it might
be us, but on consideration I could find no substance
for the thought. It was unlikely that we had been noticed on the volcano and there seemed to be enough
faction on the island to occupy the inhabitants without recourse to us.

I was intrigued, and shaking off Somi's restraining
hand, made my way stealthily from tree to tree until
I was but half a dozen paces from the man. I could see
that his position commanded a view of a clearing in
which nestled a slight rill broadening out into a pool.
The area about the pool was trampled down and suggested that this was a watering place in common use.
In front a path probed away between the trees and it
was down this that the Japon was peering intently. He
must be lying in wait for someone or be a most circumspect guardian of the pool. To substantiate this
view there came a bird-like warble from somewhere
along the path. This was obviously a signal, for the
Japon stiffened and half raised his musket shrinking
in close to the protection of the tree. The fact that he
was not alone made me still more uneasy and I
watched the path with no little trepidation.

After the passage of a few seconds there was a ripple of movement through the trees and the figure of a
man appeared, ambling down the track. He was a
Japon, that was clear, but rather taller than any of his
countrymen I had seen. He had a rolling gait, almost
a swagger, but at the same time the movement of an

athlete, so that there seemed to be no moment at which his weight was not perfectly poised for action. He looked dangerous and covered the ground as if prepared to dispute every inch of it. He wore a knee length tunic crossed at the waist and held by a broad silk sash. It was wide in the sleeves which finished on his forearms. There was a circular motif emblazoned on each breast with some of their bird-dropping lettering on it, and a couple of gourds jostled at his waist. A short sword was tucked into his sash but his main weapon he held across his shoulders like a yoke. As I watched, he pulled it down and threw it from hand to hand so that it seemed like some bauble close to his heart, which he must always be touching. There was in the movements an intimation of easy mastery. As he drew nearer I could see that the front of his head had been shaven—but not recently. The hair was sparse and wispy and the man's whole appearance unkempt and uncaring. As to his features they seemed more pronounced than his compatriots, almost English, and perhaps for this reason I felt an immediate bond with the fellow.

Engrossed with him, I had almost ceased registering the man in front until I saw the barrel of his musket sidling up the side of the tree. I knew I would be mad to intervene and that it was no affair of mine; but at the same second some ridiculous impulse made me feel that I could not see the stranger cut down without doing something. The man was twenty paces away now and reaching for the gourds at his waist. Below me, the muscles on the Japon's arms began to tighten. Before I really knew what I was doing I had stepped forward swiftly and brought my clenched fist down on the fellow's neck. Whether through this or the buffet his head received against the tree trunk, he

dropped like kiteshit. Bang! A shot rang out and at
first I thought it was the musket exploding on impact
with the ground, but down the track the stranger
leaped to one side as if a bullet had narrowly missed
him. Quicker than sunlight he unsheathed his sword
and holding it before him in both hands turned in a
circle looking for an adversary. He did not have long
a wait. A lance curved through the air which was contemptuously cut in two with a flick of the sword
rather as one swats an insect. Closely behind it came
a Japon charging from the undergrowth with his
sword raised above his head. The stranger did not
change his position but merely leaned forward dropping his sword so that it was now pointing towards
the ground. His attacker came on a pace, a scream
rising from his lips. Still the stranger did not move.
Only when the sword was about to fall did he suddenly firm his wrists and there was a flash of steel. I
swear that I did not see the blow it travelled so fast,
but the man went down with blood cascading from
the area of his armpit and a look of amazement on his
face that seemed to be captured in a dream. Such is
my nature that I was impressed by this more than I
was horrified and watched amazed as my hero spun
like a top seeking new adversaries. A lesser man (a
role in which I could speedily cast myself) would
have taken to his heels but this Japon flexed and
growled like an angry mongoose. Another attacker
reared into view and was collapsed like a struck tent.
A throat-back honk and two more ambushers broke
cover to present themselves with swords unsheathed.
No waiver. Battle was joined as if the combatants were
pulled together by a magnet, and steel fell like sheet
lightning. My champion was invincible. An arm
twitched across the sword, the blood gushing from the

severed flesh. It seemed a separate unit storing its own red brew, spilling it across the earth. Before I had switched my gaze the meat bag shapes of the attackers had collided with the ground. The man sought out trouble and engulfed it. He wheeled again—then a shot. Pulling him away from his legs, spinning him on his face. The musket had been recharged. As soon as I saw him falling I started forward, and then back. I had no weapon and an overpowering conception of my value to myself. The Japon I had smitten was stirring so I kicked his head hard against the tree and snatched up his musket. Before me my man was clawing for the weapon that had been jarred from his grasp and I could see blood spouting from his sword arm. A man moved from the trees, a musket dangling from his hand, and kicked the sword away. Obviously savouring the moment he plucked it up and hissing hate advanced towards his fallen foe. Fallen but not finished. The man whirled in the dust like a stricken stag fighting for its feet. I thrust the musket to my shoulder, and remembering my tuition on the Mace, squinted along the barrel, trying to hold my aim steady on the sniper's chest. He had the sword above his head when I squeezed the trigger. I blinked through the puff of smoke to see my target stagger, falter and fall, a smear spreading across his stomach. If I felt a sense of smugness at a good deed well performed, it was shortlived. The recipient of my solicitude abated not one fraction in his efforts to lay his hands upon his sword and having succeeded scrambled to his feet and came for my position at a pace that suggested he had more on his mind than mere congratulations. It occurred to me, in the second that I had available, that he thought the bullet had been meant for him, and failed only by mis-aim to make its mark.

I dropped the musket and stepped forward, trying to remember the Japonian word for 'friend', but of course, I could not. My gesture, or perhaps it was my features, must have had some effect on the man because he came to a halt before me and considered me from below, brows furled like crimpled linen. He was snorting with effort and menace and his eyes were wild. Eager to reassure him I pointed to the man I had shot and then to my own chest, wrapping the whole pantomime in a winsome smile.

The Japon weighed me up for one second and then letting out an exclamation of exaggerated disgust, drew back his weapon to dispatch me. I heard my own gasp of terror begin to well up in my throat, and then the urgent voice of Somi, crying out something I could not understand. Whatever it was, the man stayed his sword and listened whilst Somi continued to gabble away, explaining, as far as I could make out, the contribution I had made towards the saving of his life. Eventually he began to nod and even smiled when the ambusher, lolling against the tree, was pointed out to him. It was unfortunate that the poor devil began to stir at this moment, because the first and last thing he could have seen was his intended victim's sword blade a split second before it took his head off. This action was completed as casually as a man slices a turnip in two and with as little display of emotion. I watched the severed head bound away amongst the trees, and felt that I was speedily losing count of the slaughter. Human life seemed to carry a very low premium in these parts.

My champion listened for a second with his head cocked on one side like a thrush harking for a worm and then, satisfied that there was no immediate danger, sought, with some difficulty, a dry portion of his latest

victim's tunic and wiped his blade on it. The wound
in his own arm must have been a slight one for though
there was much blood he gave no sign that it pained
him. His weapon cleaned, he drew himself up to his
full height, which was not much inferior to my own,
and bowed his head.

"I give you thanks," he said. "Both of you. The one
for saving my life and the other for restraining me
from slaying my deliverer."

He turned to me.

"Your death would have been regrettable."

I fully agreed with him and said so, whereupon he
smiled again and said that it was best that we left this
place, as there was a likelihood of our skirmish having
been heard and more armed men arriving. I noticed
that he was quick to seize both the muskets, which
were obviously much prized by the Japons as we had
heard. It was as we were leaving the glade that I saw
him examining me quizzically.

"Where is your sword?" he demanded.

"I have none."

"You have no sword? No man of substance or who
respects his own person walks without a sword in this
country. Take up one of these."

I could see that there was sense in what he said, but
expressed a preference for a musket, if I must be
equipped with a weapon. The man shook his head
emphatically.

"No. The muskets have been stolen from my master
and I must return them to him. Arm yourself with a
sword." I noticed that he used the word tanegashima
for musket, and later found out that this was because
the first armed Portuguese to set foot in Japon had
done so on an Island of the same name. Obediently I
cast about and picked up the first that came to hand

but my mentor was not satisfied. With an exasperated snort he snatched the weapon from me and ran his finger along the blade contemptuously. "Not fit to chop firewood."

So saying he struck a blow at one of the corpses, which half severed its leg above the knee. This seemed to confirm his opinion because he hurled the sword into the undergrowth and told me to hand him another. This grisly butchery continued until the glade was littered with limbs as this warrior Japon sought a blade that measured up to his demands. All this was done with neither relish nor distaste, but purely as a labour which must be performed with diligence if it was to be performed at all. I am not noted for being over squeamish but I found the sight repellant and transfered my attention to Somi. She had obviously benefited, if this is the right word, from her Japonian upbringing, for she viewed the episode with a stoicism akin to indifference and was only anxious that we should not stay too long in the place.

"What kind of man is this?" I asked her, for in bearing, valour and prowess with arms, he was obviously no pot boy.

"He is a samurai," she said respectfully.

I had heard the fishermen who came to the caves use this word and further questioning of Somi revealed that such men served a great lord in much the same way as a knight would have done his master, a few hundred years ago, in England. It occurred to me that the concept of chivalry might differ somewhat between continents, but in fairness, I had to admit that King Arthur and his Knights had sometimes been less than 'gentil and parfit' in their actions.

"Which master does he serve?" I asked.

Somi shrugged her shoulders.

"I do not know. But he comes from the mainland. There are many like him, each serving a daimyo."

"A daimyo?"

"That is the name for the ruler of a kingdom."

"And how many kingdoms are there?"

"Many. Upwards of sixty. Always making war on each other. I had hoped that we were safe out here."

At last the samurai seemed to have found a weapon that satisfied him, for he approached me and pushed the long ribbed hilt into my hand. "With this you may be able to bruise the skin of a peach—if you hit it hard enough. Now, tell me, what are you doing here and how comes it that you speak our language—albeit so badly?"

I explained that I had been shipwrecked, without going into details of our mission, and told him that Somi had nursed me back to health. I could see that he was suspicious of me and also weighing up Somi, so I took the initiative and asked him his business on the island and why anybody should want to kill him.

"My name is Kushoni," he said, pausing sententiously as if anticipating a reaction to this information. When none came he continued, obviously a trifle discountenanced.

"My lord is Taisake, Daimyo of Figo and I am here upon his business. We have employed the pirates who dwell in the volcano yonder, to obtain us muskets to defend ourselves against Shimazn of the Satsumas, who squats upon our threshold. But these pirates have betrayed us. They have kept the muskets and, I believe, attempted to sell them to the Satsumas for a higher price than we have already paid.

"And so you have put their stronghold to the sword."

"Not us. I came here with a few men to see what could be done to recover my master's goods and I find the island in turmoil. We have been beaten to the thrust."

"So a creature who is almost as broad as he is tall is not one of your men?"

Kushoni looked up sharply.

"A man who has no nose and a face disfigured by fire? Where have you seen him?"

"A few hours ago. Towards the other end of the island. Do you know him?"

"Too well and if he is here that confirms all my suspicions. The man is Nomura. He is a samurai to Shimazu, if such a carrion-eating, child-torturer can bear so honourable a title. How looked he?"

"As if he had been in a fight. There were four others with him."

"As I thought, they must have tried their own treachery on the pirates and seized the muskets without paying a tael."

"They had no muskets with them, and looked as if they were searching for someone."

"Yes, that is strange. Perhaps it was me. Nomura bears me no love. He has probably completed his business and indulged himself with the time to settle a few old scores."

"How would he know that you are here?"

"I expect that one of his skulking dogs observed me on my travels and reported the news to his master. There are some who can put a face to my name and a name to my face."

The last words were spoken with not a small degree of reproach.

"But this man Nomura has not been here?"

"No, he probably waits elsewhere. That is why we must tread warily."

"Where are your men?"

"Near enough."

For my part, I felt less inclined to believe that Nomura and his men were stalking Kushoni. I had a suspicion that the muskets all the fuss was about had been in the hold of 'The Mace,' and I had seen that vessel broken nearby to where I had miraculously been washed ashore. The muskets were probably rusting at the bottom of the sea. If that was so then it was understandable that Nomura having paid the treacherous pirates in their own coin, should have found nothing and be combing the island for his prize.

I kept this conjecture to myself because I did not want to exhibit my past involvement with the muskets for fear that the ruthless Kushoni might imagine me a party to their disappearance and consider that I was hiding them somewhere. I felt, from my limited experience of this man, that this was an impression it was in my interests to shield him from.

Whilst this conversation was going on, we were moving cautiously through the trees in the direction of the canvas. I was wondering whether it was wise to let Kushoni see our dwelling place when he suddenly stopped and put his hand on my forearm.

"I must leave you here," he said. "Again my thanks. May good luck attend you."

He nodded curtly to Somi and strode back along the path the way he had come. Before disappearing from sight he turned and raised his arm stiffly in a gesture of farewell, which I felt was really made so that he would see whether there was any move to follow him.

"The man seemed to think that we should know him," I said.

"I have heard of him, although I was not going to give him the pleasure of knowing it," said Somi smugly. "He is the champion of the Figos, whose kingdom

lies across the strait. They are sworn enemies of the
Satsumas as he described, but, I believe, having the
worst of the arguments."

She went on to describe how one man, Hideyoshi,
had succeeded, by war and intrigue, in uniting some
of the more powerful kingdoms and that upon his
death—inevitably, it seemed to me, at the hands of
one of his own generals—his heir had found himself
fighting for survival. The rulers of Figo and Satsuma
had thrown in their lot with this heir but he had been
overthrown in battle. As a result of this lack of judgment their estates had been pruned by his successor
Ieyasu, with Taisake, the Daimyo of Figo, suffering
worst. Somi could suggest no reason for this, but it
seemed to me a simple case of divide et impera. Show
more favour to Satsuma and set two potentially dangerous rivals at each other's throats. Ieyasu was obviously no stranger to the rules of perfidious Albion.

We pressed on our way with me determined that it
would be best to lie low until the competing factions
had realised that there were no muskets on the island.
Once the strife had died down I could make my way
to Nagasaki and then to Europe, taking the fair Somi
and her father with me.

We reached the cliff face without mishap and
stepped smartly down to the cave entrance. As usual
there was no sign of Perez and I wondered if he was
still sleeping off his elbow-bending of the night before.
But eventually he came stumbling down the passage,
his face longer than a list of my sins. He looked so
woebegone that I could not resist making mild sport
of him.

"Tell me villain," says I, "where have you hidden the
muskets?"

For the effect my words had I might as well have

asked him to dice his scrotum for chewing tobacco. The man's worth dropped open like a trap baited with his tongue.

"How . . . ? Who . . . ?" he stuttered.

By sheer chance my jape had hit upon the fact that he did know something about the muskets. And Somi? I searched her face but unless she was a consummate actress she appeared genuinely bewildered.

"Where are they?" I pressed. "And where did they come from? Were they part of the cargo on my vessel?"

Perez nodded.

"The fishermen found them on the shore when the ship broke up. I thought that they might fall into evil hands so I persuaded some of my congregation to hide them."

"There are many evil hands searching for them now. Where did you hide them?"

But I never achieved an answer to that question. There was a sudden bellow behind us and even as I spun round the mouth of the cave was filled with armed Japons, crouching ready to strike. In their midst stood Square Root, his body shutting out the sunlight and a look of self-satisfied malevolence etched across his twisted features. Beside him, on a halter, swayed one of Perez's congregation barely recognisable through the mask of blood that covered his face. As Square Root took in the scene he barked out an order and the creature was yanked away to the edge of the cliff. He started to cry out but a flash of steel cut his scream in half and sent him spinning out of our vision. Beside me Somi sucked in her breath and Perez, who had waited for this day so long, let out a whinny of terror. Square Root smiled and I felt sick.

CHAPTER 5

NOMURA'S SMILE WAS HORRIBLE. ONE SIDE OF HIS FACE was incapable of registering emotion and the movement of the other plucked at the scar tissue as at the strings of a broken instrument. Unlike his companions, he did not have a weapon in his hand but stood opening and clenching his fists like hungry jaws. My eyes fled past him to alight with the flies on the sprinkling of blood that soaked up dust at the cliff edge. No solace there. Some orders bubbled from the brute's mouth and three men sprung forward to seize our arms and bind them so tightly that the cord near severed our wrists. Not content with the pain this caused, they struck us to our knees so that we were forced to cover against the cliff to avoid the blows. This spectacle their companions gave every sign of enjoying and even joined in with a few sly kicks. I thought that they would finish us then but Square Root gave another order and most of his band, which comprised about eight men in all, took off into the caves. Perez was moaning but Somi, though obviously terrified, let out no sound. I turned my head and smiled at her, which was a pointless gesture and earned a kick from one of the guards where I could least afford to receive it. Nomura, as I now knew him, had disappeared into the interior and was the first out, bearing the crucifix, before which Perez's flock had made their absolutions. This he hurled down before the priest and ordered him to spit on it.

Perez refused and received such a kick that his body was near lifted from the ground. This prompted Somi to let out a wail and try to stagger to her feet, whereupon she was brutally hurled back against the rock. In the mood of uncontrolled rage that now prevailed, I could see no hope for us and only prayed that our end would be swift. It seemed that Perez's fears must be correct and that we were to perish in some Christian purge. But Square Root did not follow up his assault. Waiting until the last of his men had reappeared, each bearing a portion of the luckless priest's possessions, he set to questioning them. To my alarm, I recognised the word 'Tanegashima.' The Japons shook their heads, and as one, all eyes were turned back to us. Perez was hauled to his feet and two men supported him whilst Nomura spat words into his face. Each time the poor devil's head began to drop it received another swinging cuff and I prayed that he would reveal all. I had no belief that this would save us, but at least our end might be quicker.

But it was not to be. No sounds but exclamations of pain passed Perez's lips, and I felt that with his resolution the man was trying to atone for his weakness many years before. Nomura became steadily more furious and eventually exploded with a blow that tore the priest from the grip of those who held him, like a door from flimsy hinges.

The poor fellow sprawled across the earth with blood pouring from his nose and Square Root turned to Somi and myself. The girl was huddled against the cliff face with her head tucked into her shoulder so as to shut out the spectacle of her father's suffering.

Nomura gazed at her and for a second his lizard tongue popped out of his mouth and scuttled along his lower lip in lustful anticipation. It was a sight to perturb the most experienced whore in Christendom. Then he turned to me. I tried to meet his gaze with a look of haughty contempt, but I made a precious poor job of it and felt my features settle into pease pudding. He seemed to be stripping layers of flesh from me with his eyes and it occurred to me that this was a task he would probably prefer to set his hands to. What he was thinking I could also make a guess at since it was easy to relate my foreign presence with that of the muskets which must have been brought in from outside the country. He took a step towards me and I bit my lip.

"Where are your muskets?"

He used the Japonian tongue and it was one of the first times I had heard his voice sink below a demoniac bawl. Like his features, his accent had a burned quality as if the flames that had scorched his face had singed his vocal chords. I shook my head and answered in English that I could not understand him, adding for good measure that I was only a poor sailor who had been shipwrecked on this coast. My answer he clearly did not understand and cast about amongst his followers to find out if there was any one who could speak English. There was not and so he turned back to me, drawing his sword and pressing the tip of the blade against the underside of my chin.

"You have five seconds to lead me to the muskets," he said "or stay silent and I will open your windpipe."

The muscles in his forearm were knotted like worm casts and I watched them flex as he prepared to make good his threat.

The danger of pretending that I spoke no Japonian

was that I would render myself expendable and it seemed that—'Aaargh!"

Square Root had obviously waited long enough. The blade was removed from my throat and I closed my eyes. Within the same second my blood splattered across the ground. But not from my neck. A sharp pain from my left ear told me that the bastard Japon had neatly spliced one of my lobes. He had a devious sense of humour that was to be sure and any relief I felt at being alive was speedily dissipated in a desire to make the torturer pay for his indignities with his life. But at that moment there seemed little chance of retribution. Square Root moved away and hurled me contemptuously onto my back whilst his creatures jeered and begged to be allowed to test their swords on me. He silenced them with a word and settled on his haunches, letting his eyes drift over us whilst he considered his next ploy. He was like a cat with three mice, wondering which to torment. Finally, his gaze settled on Perez, who was snuffling in the dust and scarcely able to draw breath through his bloody nostrils. A flurry of orders and two men started up to the cliff top, whilst those remaining set to scooping out a hole in the earth before the cave. Thoughts of a grave passed through my mind, but when the hole was about four spans deep and half as many wide they ceased their labours and looked at each other expectantly. Eventually, to my digust and the cheers of his fellows, one of the Japons removed his loin cloth and squatting over the hole used it as a privy. Another followed suit and those not primed to defecate contented themselves with pissing on the effluence. If that was not enough the two men returning from the cliff top with long staves cut from saplings had lit upon our store of night soil. This the others went off to fetch in any utensil not shattered in their ransacking of the caves.

If the accumulation of human excrement seems strange to western readers let me digress to inform you that the Japonian soil is not overrich and that all forms of manure are employed in its cultivation. Somi had informed me that it was not uncommon for a man to be able to sell his stools for a few taels and certainly the disposal of ordure as is our custom would seem uncommonly wasteful by the Japons. Perez's store was for the benefit of his congregation and another example of his attempts to insinuate himself into their good graces.

By one means and another the pit was soon half full of ordure and playing havoc with my nostrils. I could see no purpose in it, other than to insult and humiliate us still further, until the men with the staves began to erect them in a tripod above the hole. At that point new fears began to infiltrate my mind. It did not seem possible that what I was imagining could take place but before my eyes Perez was suddenly seized and dragged towards the pit. Nomura took him by the scruff of his neck as if he was a bag of straw and holding his head above the filth asked him once more to reveal where the muskets were hidden. If I had known, I would have disclosed everything at that moment, but the priest only mumbled words I could not catch and closed his eyes. Nomura snatched up the cross and screaming at him to look at his bauble for the last time hurled it into the pit. He then drew his dagger and stabbed his foot against Perez's head so that I thought he was going to cut his throat. Somi, who had been mumbling with horror at this spectacle, let out a series of shrill screams and writhed and twisted on the ground in an effort to get nearer her father. I must confess that I was struck dumb with terror and nausea and could only watch transfixed as Nomura pressed his blade against Perez's temple and severed one of the veins so that the blood spouted on to the ground. I could see no reason for this except as a prelude to death of a thousand cuts, which I had heard the natives of China practised, but by this time I was so confused as to imagine myself a participant in a nightmare and have no real comprehension of anything that was taking place. Square Root's men then produced a tangle of cord and—most disgusting sight that I have ever witnessed—strung up the poor creature by the heels, so that his head and half of his body dangled in the pit of excrement. I could scarce contain the contents of my stomach whilst Somi let out shriek after shriek, like a mother bird seeing its young trampled underfoot.

Nomura watched the ritual enacted to his satisfaction and then turned back to us, calling out that we could still save the man's life if we revealed the whereabouts of the muskets. Somi was beyond hysteria and begged the brute to have mercy but she might as well have asked a snake to disgorge its prey. I considered pretending that I knew where the weapons were hidden but I knew too that this would only yield us a temporary respite. I suspected also that if Square Root believed me Perez's life would be immediately forfeit as was that of the poor mangled fisherman who had presumably betrayed us under torture. I also knew, and this was my most positive conviction, that I was a craven coward and no more likely to play the hero than to steal away into a hole in the ground— a facility I envied every worm in Christendom at that moment.

"I ask you for the last time," Nomura's voice rasped out. "Then it is the 'ana-tsurushi' for each of you and we will draw lots to see which of you dies first."

'The hanging in the pit.' I remembered that Perez had mentioned this torture and its use to make martyrs apostatise, and I could believe in its effectiveness.

Nothing coherent coming from either of us Nomura ordered our legs bound and bent behind us to be fastened to our wrists. And so we lay, trussed up like chickens, whilst night fell and the Japons settled down to preparing themselves a meal from our rice supply.

And what a night it was. Racked by cold, cramp and the damn insects that crawled over my body, I could not close my eyes. Above all I was afflicted by the moans from the pit. At first I kept thinking that the priest must soon be dead but then I realised that the purpose of slashing his forehead must be to give the blood some vent and prevent him escaping into the blissful release of unconsciousness. Every few hours, just when his silence seemed to have presaged the worst, there would come a low muffled moan as if there was no longer any holding back his agony. Throughout the night the Japons relieved themselves upon the poor creature to add to his torment and twice Square Root ordered him to be dragged free of the pit and questioned further. But on neither occasion would he give in and so was toppled back into the excreta. Even allowing for the continuing exposure to it, the smell on such occasions was stomach turning.

Frankly, I was surprised when morning came and there was still movement from the pit. The sky lightened and a damp, cold mist soaked me to the marrow of my cramped bones. I was in a fair degree of pain but it seemed craven to consider it in relation to Perez's sufferings. Nevertheless, it being my nature I did, and tried to wriggle some life back into my limbs without drawing too much attention to myself.

For the most part the Japons had spent the night in the caves and stirred themselves fitfully to kindle a fire and cook some rice. I was surprised that they could conceive of eating in such a stench but the proximity of the pit seemed to worry them not at all. Last to arise was Square Root, who strode from the cave and extended a hand for food, as if this was the only gesture required to receive sustenance. Taking the bowl of rice that was obediently proferred, he squatted before us and manipulated his chop sticks with the speed of knitting needles. His repast finished he stood up and walked towards the pit where he reached out and plucked Perez like a dead flower before casting him to the ground.

At first I thought it was a corpse lying there. The face was a hideous grey and daubed with excrement, and a column of caked blood stretched from his temple like a worm extending itself. His limbs were leaden.

And then one eye opened. Naked. Vulnerable. Like the knob of a bone revealed through flesh. Then the other, twitching against the flies busily adjusting themselves to the new position of their meal.

Nomura sent for water which was dashed into Perez's face and squatted down beside him. He had a fan in his hands which he waved daintily before his truncated nostrils—and with good reason, though it seemed a ridiculous affectation for such an ogre.

"I hope you passed a restful night and were not disturbed," he sneered. His followers sniggered.

Perez made no answer so he continued in a light bantering tone, wholly unlike his usual bawl.

"If my pleasantries make no impression let me pursue another line to win an answer. I have in mind to produce an entertainment for you. And it will feature someone dear to your heart. Your child, mistress or wife—no I forget. There is a constraint against marriage in your faith, isn't there? Well, your child or mistress then. Whichever you would lay claim to if you were in a talkative mood. But in case she is becoming nervous let me assure you both that she will not have to perform alone. I can promise you the participation of as many actors as stand within ten paces of us. I hope you take my meaning because I am trying to wrap the matter up in as much gentility as possible. And—" his voice began to regain some of its normal stridency— "this is a spectacle you will watch if I have to prop your eyes open with splinters of wood. Now, let me make one last appeal to your good sense. If you want to save the girl tell me where the muskets are hidden."

There was a silence like that within a coffin when the lid slams shut and every eye was on the priest. He made no movement and I wondered if he had heard or understood a word. Square Root closed his fan slowly and tapped it sharply against his knuckle, as if contemplating a transaction. Somi sobbed piteously and the preparations for her humiliation began.

Two of the stakes that had supported Perez were erected, three spans apart and Somi's feet were lashed to them at a height from the ground so that her rump barely touched it. Her arms were then bound to pegs above her head thus rendering her totally vulnerable. I felt a sense of disgust both general and particular. Call me squeamish if you will but I have never enjoyed the spectacle of rape and had frequently endured the jibes of my shipmates for not participating in the sporadic outbursts of ravishing that characterised their trips ashore. In this particular instance, having been the girl's lover, I felt a sense of personal outrage. It offended my honour to see the malformed freak leering down at my property. Perhaps, too, I remember

the surprise with which I considered the existence of
such an emotion—there might even be a trace of affection influencing my feelings. Square Root rapped
out some instructions and his henchmen cheerfully fell
on Perez, hauling him to his feet and holding him in
such a manner that he would have a clear view of the
proceedings. I noticed his head jerk back and eyes start
to blink with alarm as a realisation of what was happening permeated his numbed consciousness. Faced
with her father thrust into view above her, Somi's sob-
bing redoubled in intensity and she turned her head
away and closed her eyes. It was a sight to melt the
coldest heart on earth but Nomura bent and ripped
the garments from her as if they were no more than
damp petals resting on her body. The men responded
to this sight with cheers and guffaws, clearly relishing
the part they were soon to play. I struggled and
shouted in frustrated rage but my bonds only cut
deeper into my wrists and my outcry earned me a few
contemptuous kicks from those who clearly begrudged
every second of the spectacle they were missing.
Nomura did not bestow me a glance but cupped
Perez's jaw in his hand and bade him take good note
of what was about to take place. Saying this he stepped
back and surveyed Somi who was thrashing like a
stranded fish. His hands went to the sash at his waist
and he slowly withdrew his swords and raised them
aloft before placing them carefully in the ground beside him. Next the knot was loosened and the sash removed. He unwrapped his robe, or Kimono as they
call it, and handed it to a henchman. Now he was
naked except for his sandals, bound to the knee with
leather thongs, and his loin cloth. He paused another
few seconds to savour the pleasure to come—and no
doubt to add to the torture he was inflicting on his

victims—and then unravelled his loin cloth. As he half-turned I saw a scar like a furrow running down his chest, so deep that a child could have put his fingers into it. I saw that and the weapon of his rape. Like him no length, but short, thick, brutal. A cannon primed to blast its vile seed into her half exploited innocence. His men crowded round as if at a cock pit, almost letting Perez fall in their excitement. Square Root dropped to his knees and shuffling forward placed his hands under the soft flesh that squirmed before him. Lifting her buttocks from the ground he pressed his body closer to make connection. Then—

"Stop!"

I had not heard Perez speak for so long that I thought the voice belonged to a stranger.

"Stop! Stop! I will tell you everything you want to know. I will show you where the muskets are hidden for God's sake stop."

Nomura looked up and them down at Somi and I thought it most likely that he would continue to fulfil himself. Certainly his men seemed cast down by the unexpected success of their master's plan and those holding Perez shook him angrily as if trying to make him shut his mouth. Nomura looked down once more and then, regretfully, released his grip on Somi and rose to his feet.

"Lead us to them," he hissed "and if you lie her womb will be lined with red hot coals."

His tone said he meant it and in fact was the easiest man in the world to believe whenever he uttered a threat.

Somi was cut free and immediately threw herself into her father's arms from whence she was peeled like a starfish and trussed up again. No concession was made to her nakedness and the Japons crowded around, touching and pinching her in the most odious fashion. Perez had not the strength to lead the way on foot and so was carried by two men with Nomura by his side, whilst Somi and I were in the middle of the column.

At a word from Nomura we started off and pressed round the edge of the island northwards of where I had first come to the caves, and through an area which gave increasing evidence of volcanic matter. Steam spurted from the ground as if it was the lid of some gigantic cooking pot and the terrain became more barren and open. I was waiting all the while for some situation which might afford me the opportunity of escaping but there was no relaxation on the part of the Japons who were always pressing hard on our heels, and as the trees became scarcer so did any expectation of freedom. It was at this time that Perez directed us into a narrow ravine, which was more like a deep trench. The walls closed in on either side so that a man could not spread out his arms and the rain had scored a treacherous furrow in its bottom which had even the surefooted Japons stumbling and cursing. In our trussed up condition Somi and I spent more time on our knees than on our feet with nothing but the kicks of our irate captors to propel us to an upright position. We proceeded in this fashion for upwards of a hundred paces with the undergrowth closing in over our heads so that we seemed to be almost in a tunnel. The appearance of this greenery suggested the presence of water and in the not so far distance I could hear what sounded like a waterfall. Now when I caught a glimpse of sky it had turned a sullen grey, then black so that I was reminded of the typhoon that had brought me to this hellish place. The wind grew chill and in an instant torrential rain fell like silver bullets, so our condition was made even more miserable. The gully became a river and the ground beneath our feet so slippery as to be impassable. Limbs aching, mud-covered, borne down by pain and fatigue, I could have wished to die at that moment but I had no such good fortune, as our captors vented their irritation by lashing out even harder. Ahead I could see that Perez was sprawling in the mud and watched as Square Root screamed to his bearers to snatch him up before he drowned. I could not believe that the man could endure much more of such treatment and still live.

At last the rain began to slacken and I could make out an end to the ravine. One moment I saw Nomura framed in the opening with clear space around him, the next a figure reared up above him on the brink with a boulder in its upstretched arms and dashed it down on the brute's head like a blacksmith smiting an anvil.

Now I swear that the blow would have shattered an ordinary man's skull to egg yolk but that bastard Japon hardly flinched. One step back, and a shake like a dog coming from water, and his sword was in his hand. And well for him that it was.

There was a yelp from our rear and another Japon leaped down into the ravine. All I could see of him was that he had a white band around his forehead and this might have been more than the man behind me for he fell back with a hands breadth of sword having snake tongued out of his kidneys. I was in my customary position sprawled across the mud and felt in no mood to change it radically though I did crawl to Somi's side and cover her glistening body with my own. As we cowered there another of Nomura's band slumped across our legs, carved from neck to nipple by the new arrival and those in front scrambled over each other in an effort to get out of the ravine. There was no sign of Square Root and Perez and soon no sight of anybody. Our deliverer drove the rabble out of the ravine like a charge behind grapeshot and we were left alone. A trace of wisdom would have made me retrace my steps to safety but, fool that I am, I struggled forward to see what was happening.

At the mouth of the ravine the ground opened up to present a vista of open rock spread at the bottom of a long waterfall that skirted rather than flowed over it. Men battered and slashed at each other as if on a stage and the whole area of their conflict was patterned with small pools that hissed and bubbled like boiling cauldrons. This sight I took in at a glance before trying to single out the protagonists. Nomura was at once recognisable, bearing Perez on his shoulder whilst defending himself desperately against two men. I recognised at once that he was using the priest as a shield and even as I watched he ducked his body into a blow so that it fell squarely across Perez's shoulders. At the same moment he stepped back into one of the pools. Despite the lashing rain and the sounds of carnage, his scream burned into my ears like molten pitch. Perez, always close to death, died with that movement. As Square Root leaped for the nearest rock his prize fell from his shoulders and plunged into the boiling water. Immediately a man dropped down in a vain attempt at rescue but even as his arm reached out there came a realisation that the gesture was useless. Whether dead before or after, Perez nodded and bobbed like a pudding in a pot. Nomura fought on, but in desperation, looking round to gauge the fortunes of his followers. One was pinned down beneath a pike and as I watched swept into a pool where he kicked

his life away until his puppet legs lackeyed to the
frothing water. Another, gauging that all was lost,
took to his heels, running along the rim of the waterfall. Six paces and suddenly he was running without a
head. The body buckled, staggered, fell; the head
bouncing behind. I gazed, amazed, scarce able to reg-
ister what I had seen. At that instant another of our
tormentors threw down his weapon and followed the
passage of the first. This time I watched his flight with
more care and saw that as he ran beside the waterfall
there was a sudden flash of light which turned into a
sword arm. Someone was standing behind the screen
of water to strike down an enemy that passed. The
latest victim fared no better than the first, his headless
corpse ending up abreast of the fellow, as if racing it
into the next world.

Like a tinder fire that springs up, then as quickly
subsides, the action before my eyes had shrunk to individual clashes. Nomura still held out against his two
opponents whilst on the far side of the river bed another couple appeared, one of whom I recognised, with
a relief that almost surprised me, as Kushoni. His opponent fought with all the desperate agility of a cor-
nered rat and his terror was well founded. Kushoni
parried his wild blows as if they were being made
with a pig's bladder and then suddenly flexed his wrists
in a movement that sent his sword into the man's
chest below the armpit and near sheared off the whole
of his shoulder. That left Nomura to be dealt with
and I thrilled to see the bastard mastered. My cer-
tainty was heightened when in running one of his
adversaries through he lost his grip on his sword and
stood weaponless and ready for despatch. His remaining opponent raised his sword in two hands but with
remarkable agility in so compact a man Nomura leapt

in below the blow and struck his own with a straight forearm that stove in the man's ribs, like the sides of a rotten barrel. The noise rang out like a musket shot and that coupled with the brute's ability to shake off a boulder on the head made me fear that he must possess superhuman strength. My hopes now rested on Kushoni who was bounding across the bloodied arena but Square Root snatched up a pike and took off on the path his luckless predecessors had followed. I watched enthralled to see him share their fate but this bloated butcher must have had eyes in the back of his head, for while skirting the screen of water he cunningly hung his pike so that the man lurking there suddenly toppled out holding his stomach together like Polonius from behind the arras in Shakespeare's play.

This hazard disposed of, he turned and hurled the pike at Kushoni with such venom and accuracy that my champion was forced to throw himself to one side to avoid being clove in two by it. By the time he was on his feet Square Root had scaled the far bank and disappeared.

Now the scene resembled the last act of tragedy. The ground looked as if it was bleeding. Corpses, some still stirring, littered the terrain and above all stood Kushoni, breathing deep and exploring a slight wound as he wiped his sword blade on a convenient corpse. The cauldrons bubbled, peeling flesh from bone, and the steam slunk away, beaten down by the persistent rain.

Once again I experienced the repetition of a feeling that I was living through a nightmare. Taking care in no way to suggest a threatening pose, I stepped from the ravine and called out to Kushoni.

CHAPTER 6

UPON SIGHT OF ME KUSHONI DROPPED INTO HIS CATLIKE crouch and his eyes flashed fire. Their blaze was soon extinguished when he recognised who I was.

"Ei, ei," he called, "you are always jumping on me like a damn squirrel. Have compassion on an old man's nerves."

"Your nerves seem strong enough," says I, "in better condition than ours I would warrant."

"Yes, I am surprised that you were spared. I thought they might well cut your throats when we attacked."

"Your consideration is touching, if a trifle belated."

"Had you been my own child, it would have made no difference. My obligation to my master overrides all. Now let me cut your bonds, unless you relish that position."

This he did, nearly severing one of my wrists in the process. "Ah, forgive me. Put near any flesh my sword conceives an appetite. Now where is your companion?"

In the turmoil I had forgotten Somi and retraced my steps to the ravine to find her slumped in the mud a few feet from its opening. I wondered if she knew that her father was dead. She appeared half way to that condition herself. Kushoni glanced at her and turned away, almost primly.

"She needs clothing," he said gruffly and proceeded

to rob the nearest Nippon of his robe as if stripping muslin from a leg of pork. I loosed her wrists and pushed her arms into the robe, drawing her of necessity to her feet. The movement brought her to her senses and catching sight of Kushoni over my shoulder she uttered the words I had hoped her condition would deny her.

"Is my father still alive?"

My silence must have told her all because she started to sink back, burying her fingers like talons in the wall of the ravine.

"Tell me, tell me the truth. He is dead, dead, I know it."

Her voice was rising into a shriek.

"He was a brave man . . ." I began, with faltering voice because I am abject in this kind of situation and incapable of supplying any succour that relies upon words alone. Kushoni was equal to the moment.

"The priest is dead," he said brusquely, "but the boiling water must have killed him instantly. He could have known no pain." It occurred to me that even one as clumsy as myself might have imparted the news with more grace. Somi must have agreed with me for she surrendered herself to body-rending sobs so that I could hardly support her. Still, for all Kushoni's clumsiness, the news could not have come as a surprise to her and was probably better exposed than cloaked in my mumbles.

"Had we not better be away from here," I asked quickly, "before Nomura returns with more men?"

Kushoni shook his head.

"Most of his fellows have returned to the mainland. I saw three Junks put out as we came here. He will look a long time before he finds support. I still have time to find those muskets."

He looked at me searchingly.

"It may be difficult for you to believe," says I, "but I have no knowledge of their hiding place and did not even know of their existence when we last met."

"That may be true and even if you lie I am not likely to fare better than Nomura in extracting the truth. I am a poor torturer."

"And I am glad to hear it. Also you lack assistance at this moment." This was indeed so because, as I have already pointed out, Kushoni was the only man left standing. The brave fellow who had leaped into the ravine lay in a pool of his own blood that aped the rock pools, steaming about it for sheer size. The only man still moving was one of Square Root's followers and his release was short-lived because Kushoni slit his throat casually as he might have snipped himself a nosegay. The place, never a favourite with me, was now becoming more than my tortured senses could stand and I cast about desperately for some route that we could take away from it. Out in the open I could see a small temple nestling picturesquely on the side of the hill and suggested that we catch our breath there till the rain ceased. Kushoni was loath to delay his search for the muskets but I made much play of the wilting Somi and eventually succeeded in leading him up the hill.

When we approached the temple it was to find it a ruin but the roof still held and we stole gratefully inside. Somi had ceased her weeping but cast herself down, red-eyed and disconsolate in a dry corner and I, not having the expressions to comfort her, sat by the doorway with Kushoni looking down upon the rain-swept countryside.

"Was it chance that you lit upon us in the ravine?" I asked him. Kushoni shook his head.

"No, we came upon you at the caves—"

"What! And watched us tortured?"

"No, no. A fisherman told us what passed and when we crept up it was to find you on the point of setting off."

"And so you followed that you might be led to the muskets?"

"Exactly."

"But what prompted you to attack?"

Kushoni gestured at the sky.

"This accursed rain."

"What do you mean?"

"Our muskets. Do you not remember the two I seized? With those we could have scotched Nomura and thrown such a scare into the others that they would have hurled themselves on to our swords. I had packed a charge for that mound of gristle that would have blown his black heart through his backbone. But then the damned rain came and our powder was soaked. I had to attack where the ground favoured us, or risk being stranded in the open when the priest exposed the muskets. Remember, we were four against nine."

"And now all your companions are dead."

Kushoni looked not a wit cast down by the reproach in my voice.

"But what better way to die than in the service of their master."

I could think of several and looked at him hard lest he was playing with irony. But his face did not change.

"You express an opinion which would not meet with universal acceptance in my country," I said. "As a rule men there prefer to live their lives rather than give them."

"Not so here. Our lives—or the life of any man fit to be called one—are ruled by honour. There is no

point in living if you purchase the right at the price of
your own self-respect. Courage, loyalty, service. These
are the things that matter. I saw you wince when I
cut the throat of one of those dogs but he was dross.
Grovelling for mercy, he forfeited the right to our respect."

"You cannot believe that only the strong should
survive?"

"Only they have the right to make their voices
heard. Your peasant or fisherman has his position fixed
by birth and circumstance. He is there merely to provide for those with greater aptitudes."

"Would you believe that if you were born a fisherman?"

Kushoni looked perplexed.

"The question is meaningless for I was born a
Samurai."

"Yes, but that was mere chance was it not?"

"I think you must be trying to make me angry. I
have told you that I am a Samurai."

There was no point in labouring this matter. The
man obviously had no idea what I was getting at. Better to change the subject.

"So, with Perez, die your hopes of finding the muskets?"

"Was that the name of the priest? Dwindled not
died. I believe that they must be hidden somewhere
near here. How did that Jesuit dog get hold of them?
I have always suspected the motives of his brother-
hood."

I explained to Kushoni that the Mace had probably
been carrying his master's muskets and what had sub-
sequently befallen them. He sucked his lips and his
brow furled like a caterpillar's back.

"Ei, ei. They do not seem over smitten with good

fortune. I hope better luck greets us if we light upon them."

"What do you plan to do?"

"When the rain stops we will search until nightfall. If we have found nothing I have a Junk hidden not too far away and we can return to Figo. Unless you would prefer to stay here?"

I assured him that I would not and that I could answer for Somi in this respect. A trip to the mainland would tie in very well with my plans for reaching Nagasaki and I could see nothing to bind Somi to her father's death place. I only wished we could get under way immediately as I had grave uneasiness that Nomura might be lurking nearby or engaged in rallying fresh recruits to hunt us down. This thought I passed on to Kushoni but he merely gave one of his less eloquent grunts and indicated that we would proceed as he had outlined.

Rebuffed, I turned to Somi who I could see had been listening to our conversation.

"Why do you so glibly say that I will come with you?" said she.

"Do you wish to stay here?"

"I might as well die here as on the mainland."

"Why do you talk of death. I know that—"

"You know nothing. My mother and my father are dead. Can you not understand that God has laid his curse upon us. Our flesh is weak. As my mother gave herself to my father and perished so I gave myself to you and secured my father's death. God will strike us down."

"Your grief deranges you," said I, "there may be some sad irony in your father's death but it has no root in what you and I have done."

She shook her head. "You lie or you deceive your-

self. In my heart I know that I will perish like them.
I have their blood and I have sinned."

Her voice rose to a shriek and I looked to Kushoni
who was regarding us as if we were putting on a play
for his amusement. I felt sorry for the wench as I had
come to believe that her difficulties arose from the conflict between her passionate nature and the constraints
of her papist upbringing but I was in no humour to
discuss the matter. Luckily, it was not necessary for
no sooner had I turned my back on both of them than
there came a piercing scream and I spun round to see
Kushoni dancing in the air as if he had stepped on a
scorpion. He was jabbing at the floor with his sword
and a cloud of dust and fragments rose from the rotting boards. As I approached him he dropped on his
knees and tore up one of the timbers. Below, nestling
as innocently as eggs in down, were row upon row of
muskets.

Kushoni sank back upon his heels.

"By the sword of Hideyoshi, there is luck for you. I
see this little flicker of light at my feet and it turns out
to be Dame Fortune winking at me."

"Or perhaps ill-fortune, bearing in mind your earlier remark."

"Never mind that now. How many will the girl be
able to carry?"

"My God! Have you no compassion? Would you
turn her into a beast of burden, so soon after her father's death?"

In truth this remark was as much a plea for myself
as I could see the way things were going.

"If these arms can be brought to Figo she will be
doing much to avenge her father's death. Three of
my men died so that she could live—"

"You mean so that you might seize Perez and
through him the muskets."

"No matter, the end was the same. Do you think that you would still be living if I had left you with Nomura?"

"No, but—" and then I gave up. I was speedily learning that there was little point in arguing with Kushoni. We tore up the rest of the floorboards and uncovered about three hundred muskets. This was but a half of the Mace's cargo and I imagined that the rest of them must be rusting on the ocean bed. Kushoni was overjoyed and chuckling to himself as if he was uncovering nuggets of gold. No sooner were they lain out than he began plaiting creepers and testing to see how many could be carried by one man. I must say that for a person of superior rank he was well able to turn his hand to anything and this I put down to his military training and the general hardiness of his race.

It was obvious that we could not transport all the muskets in one move and so it was decided that we would wait for nightfall before making our way to the seashore. I suggested that we try to light a fire as Somi particularly was now shivering pathetically, but with the discovery of the arms Kushoni had become wary as a cat with kittens and would allow nothing that might betray our position. All he could offer for our comfort was some cold rice and strips of leather which might once have been meat. With this mixture sitting like lead dumplings in our bellies, Somi and I fell into an exhausted trance which in our condition was an adequate substitute for sleep.

We awoke, shivering, to Kushoni's prods as the last grey dregs of light were wrung out of the sky. Like beasts of burden we were festooned with muskets and began to totter down the incline towards the waterfall. I had hoped we would avoid this grisly place but Kushoni made us retrace our steps across the apron of rock where the springs bubbled like pots on a hob and the ghastly corpses merged with the shadows so as to set my teeth on edge. Even in the gathering darkness I could see some fragment of cloth stirring in a pool and imagined the flesh of Perez boiled clean from its bones. I feared what the sight might do to Somi but the girl moved as if in a trance, gliding across the rock like one of the spirits that must now haunt the place.

To my relief we skirted the ravine and pushed on through wooded slopes with the ground falling away beneath us. It was now quite dark and had started to rain. My God, if there was ever a more miserable fellow than myself at that moment, I have difficulty in conceiving of him. I was as cold as a mermaid's quim.

We clattered on stumbling and cursing, or rather me stumbling and cursing and Kushoni hissing at me to be silent. Then suddenly we were out in the open and I could feel the wind and hear the sea. Kushoni told me to rest still and I, needing no second bidding, was almost asleep before my body had reached the ground. The next thing I recall was the presence of two men gabbling to Kushoni, and myself stumbling on along the beach. Then the shock of water round my ankles. Everything now came as a surprise, my reactions were seconds behind each event: a boat rocking before me, the muskets over the side, Somi being half-lifted after them, myself eager to follow near swooning at this sea-borne cradle. But no. Kushoni and one of the guardians of the boat dragged me back the way we had come—or it might have been any other way for all I knew, though our destination remained inescapably the same. This time the shadows at the waterfall had some substance. They turned and drew away from us, watched from a respectful distance. All except one that continued to worry a corpse so that the arm twitched and shuddered as if it still retained some life. Disquieting spectacle. Perhaps it was the dogs from the volcano or perhaps the island abounded with their kind thriving on the rich pickings to be found. I indulged an urge to kick one but it merely withdrew its snout long enough to show me its teeth and resumed its rummaging. Feeling as I did, I refrained from carrying the dispute further.

Back at the temple I begged to rest but Kushoni, probably wisely, would have none of it. More muskets were heaped upon me and without even pausing to relieve myself I was started down the slope again. In fairness to Kushoni and his companion, they did not make a beast of burden out of me to spare themselves. Both of them were so laden they looked like sticks of bananas. I had hoped that this trip might see the end of the muskets but there were still some left and this thought stayed with me past the wild dogs—who were now grazing like sheep and following their leader's example in ignoring us—and all the treacherous, rain-sodden way to the boat. Sure enough, I had no sooner cast one of my legs after the last musket than I was pulled back and told that my mighty labours were not at an end. I attempted to indicate that I was in the last extremities of exhaustion, which presented no difficulty, but had to be content with a flask of sake thrust between my lips and a kick up the backside for comfort.

The journey back to the temple I have no recollection of, but it was upon our return when my spirits, if I can use so inflated a term for them, were a trifle in the ascendant, that something happened. Kushoni suddenly clapped his hand on my shoulder and hissed that we all should be silent. I listened and sure enough in the distance I could hear the sound of men's voices calling to each other. Very faint at first but getting louder at a speed that suggested they were being borne on something besides the wind. Sure enough there came the alarmed whinney of a horse and high above us a light flickered through the trees. We were on a steep and heavily wooded slope from which the roots broke clear and afforded some hand hold. Now we clung on in silence as the skyline above filled with torches and we could hear the shrill cries of the horse-men as they urged their mounts down the slope. Fear honed my dulled wits but Kushoni's companion was the first to move. Shedding his load like a snake its skin, he hauled himself amongst some giant roots that reared beside us and squeezed between them into the cavity formed by their separation from the bank.

Whether he intended to take his muskets with him I do not know but Kushoni bundled them through after him and hauled himself up still accoutred. No mean feat considering the weight he was carrying. I was now left in the open with the sound of falling stones and the horses crashing through the undergrowth get-ting closer every second. I took a step towards the tree, slipped and fell. Try as I could my limbs seemed to have no power left in them. I tried to struggle to my knees but I had no more strength than a sickly kit-ten.

"Quick, quick," hissed Kushoni.

I felt one of the roots before my nose and started to pull myself to my knees. Ten paces away a light was dancing behind the trees and a small avalanche of shale glanced off my ankle. The horse stumbled and the rider cursed. My hand went up and brushed against Kushoni's, lunging down desperately. His finger closed over my wrist and he hauled me upwards with such force that my arm almost parted company with its

socket. Zounds, but that man was strong. I shot
through the opening like a woodpecker into its hole
and all three of us collapsed on each other with a clatter that made me feel discovery was inevitable. Light
streamed through the screen roots and I waited for the
exultant screams. In all this time I am certain that it
had never occurred to any of us that the horsemen
might not be searching for us. If it had, the man's guttural rasp outside our hiding place was sufficient to
confirm our fears. Nomura in a rage was not a sound
easily forgotten. Luckily at this moment his anger
was concentrated on his terrified mount and to that
beast we probably owed our lives. Snorting and wheeling, it nearly pitched its rider amongst us before
slithering down the slope, leaving us clinging to an
uneasy silence. Seconds turned into minutes and we
could hear our breathing—as I realised then, one of
the sweetest sounds a man can listen to. The last echo
died away down the hillside and we were alone.

"We stay here," said Kushoni and I think at that moment I was asleep.

When I awoke, or rather, as was my habit in those
times, was shaken awake, an early morning greyness
hung in the sky and the rain had stopped. We struggled out from the roots and continued our descent toward the shore. Christ, if my vocabulary could encompass the words to describe the aches and pains
that prevaded my body. Every muscle, or its erstwhile
repository, groaned with the burden of my limbs. The
heavens may have been leaden but my body was
heavier.

When we broke from the trees it was into a vast
void, a nothingness, composed of mist that eddied and
swirled like smoke, opened up long enough to present
a view of the sea then swept over our heads, so that a

man might be cut off from his fellow five paces away. The constant movement of the mist, its breaking and closing, made it difficult to preserve a sense of direction and I was soon at odds with my companions as to where the ocean lay, let alone our vessel.

"This way, this way."

"No, over here, follow me."

"You are both wrong, you imbeciles, that way takes us back to the trees. The boat lies yonder."

"*Lay* yonder. What if it put to sea when the horsemen came?"

"Then it will return with the mist."

"If he can see where to go."

"At least Nomura and his band will share our difficulty."

At that moment there came a distant yet unmistakable drumming, gaining in intensity every second. Someone was galloping towards us. Fast. Our eyes probed the swirling clouds, not knowing where to turn and suddenly the mist thinned out so that one could see above it. Before us lay the ocean and, wonder of wonders, the lop-sided sail of a vessel that could only be ours. There was no time for self-congratulation or relief because the head and shoulders of the horseman reared above the mist a few paces in front of us. He was wearing some kind of shoulder armour and a head piece that curved around his ears and nose and made him look more devilish than he might actually have been. In his hand he held a lance. He might have seen us had his attention not been gripped by the boat. Reining in his mount so that it pawed the sky, he let out a triumphant shout and veered toward the ocean.

"If the boat goes we are lost," said Kushoni, and started after him. The rider had spurred his mount a few feet into the waves and beyond him I could see a flurry of activity aboard our vessel as the helmsman struggled to bring it round. The rider shouted again and pressed forward to make contact. The sail shuddered then filled with a movement that I knew presaged the vessel's smooth withdrawal—and our deaths.

"Hold hard!" I shouted in English.

My words had no effect on the passage of the boat but the Japon wheeled round and threw up his lance. But not fast enough. Kushoni was directly behind him and despite his load still swift enough to send his sword flashing across the man's belly The Japon crashed from the horse, his foot still caught in the stirrup, and was dragged past me, a trail of red in the white spume. More shouts came from behind. We pressed forward with the water over our waists. Kushoni was first to the boat and disgorged his muskets over the side before turning back to protect us. I saw him close with another horseman who came thrashing out of the mist in a sheet of spray. I clung to the side of the vessel and felt spent. But small lithe fingers closed on mine and I saw Somi's sweet face mounting encouragement. She and the helmsman hauled me aboard and I sprawled gasping in the bottom of the boat like one of the millions of fish that had preceded me. Somehow I wriggled free from the muskets and peered over the side just in time to see another horseman pitch into the ocean and Kushoni turn towards us. The vessel was shuddering again and our companion aboard. The helmsman sprang to the crude rudder and the boat quivered unexpectedly. Kushoni strained towards us as if held back by ropes around his waist. Five paces, four, three, two, one, so near, reach out, now, now! A lance thumped into the gunwale missing him by inches and then the mist closed over everything like a curtain. We were gliding smoothly out to sea. All aboard and safe.

I said nothing but found a crude shelter in the middle of the boat and fell into it. I seem to recall that Somi offered me the succour of her arms, but it was a gesture that served not one whit to distract me from my only aim at the time—to fall into a deep and undisturbed sleep.

CHAPTER 7

WHEN I AWOKE IT WAS WITHOUT THE PROMPTING OF ANY
hand and to a smell of fish that inserted itself into my
nostrils like dirty fingers. Sunlight was streaming
through the cracks above my head, but although I
could hear the sound of waves there was no movement
to suggest that we were still at sea. I stretched my
cramped limbs, all of which seemed to have been extended slightly further than the tolerance allowed for
by nature, and hauled myself to my feet.

The vessel was pulled up on the shore and the position of the sun indicated that it was approaching mid-
day. Scattered around were boats of a similar nature
and before me a collection of dilapidated dwellings
raised on piles, suggesting that we had returned to the
small fishing village from which our vessel had put
out. A collection of almond-eyed urchins gazed up at
me inscrutably and amongst them stood Kushoni mus-
ing reverentially over the muskets neatly piled together like stooks of corn. He addressed me without
looking up, which I suspected was a calculated gesture, intended to impress me with is prescience.

"You do well, Englishman, to sleep until the work is
finished," he said in mock reproach.

I informed him that by my own reckoning my
labours of the previous—it was previous?—night had

constituted a sufficiency of work to earn me a few hours
sleep, especially since lying trussed up like a chicken
had hardly been the best preparation for my change
into a pack-mule. I further enquired if the muskets
were stacked ready for me to bear them a further few
leagues toward their eventual destination. To this he
replied haughtily that I should direct my eyes towards
the dwellings. This I did and was pleased to see Somi
riding a small but spirited looking nag. The pleasure of
the sight spilled over on to a veritable pack train that
she was leading, two equipped with saddles. These
were so high, both before and behind, that they resembled wing-back chairs and could have supported a
corpse in an upright position. I surmised that these
might have belonged to Kushoni's fallen comrades
and this was confirmed to me, with the additional
information that we were now in the Kingdom of Figo
and but two leagues ride away from the Daimyo's
palace. To this destination we were bound once the
muskets have been loaded. These was no suggestion
that Somi and I might have alternative plans and after
a quick review of our situation, I had to concede that
this seemed a realistic surmise. Better to recoup our
energies and see how the land lay at the Daimyo's
palace. Our reception could hardly be hostile, arriving
as we would be with the highly prized muskets and,
by his own estimation, the equally highly prized Kushoni.

I clambered down and said goodbye to the urchins,
who remained totally unmoved. I found this a trifle
irritating, as most of the juvenile natives I had met en
route to Japon had responded with comforting enthusiasm to my presence. Of the crew of our vessel
there was no sign and I was informed that these
worthies had been thanked for their assistance and de-

parted to a well-earned rest. There was no mention of payment and it occurred to me that the lot of the lower orders in Japon was probably richer in experience than currency.

Now, one of my skills about which I have remained manifestly modest, so far in this narrative, is that of horsemanship, and having helped lash the muskets to the lack-lustre sades that had been supplied for the purpose of transporting them I leapt into the saddle with as much grace as the singular design of that article would permit. If I had hoped that this action would elicit some favourable reaction from Somi—and I had—I was disappointed. She was in one of her melancholic moods and replying to my greeting with the miminum of enthusiasm required to refute a suggestion of actual rebuff, she reined in her mount and took up a position with the pack animals. This action I put down to a recurrent preoccupation with her father's death and as such totally understandable. I therefore decided to let her come to terms with the tragedy in her own time before paying her further attention. To this end I attached myself to Kushoni who was hunched up on a mount caparisoned like a rood screen and together we rode into the interior.

The way was through the rice fields which in many ways resembled a marshly extension of the reed-strewn sea. The Japons submerge their fields in water and ordure and wade through this mixture to tend their rice crop, in which pursuits I say good luck to them. The green shoots extending away in orderly lines presented a pretty enough picture, but the whole mounted a monstrous assault on the nostrils. It occurred to me that good arable land must be at a premium in the kingdom if this exposed coastal region had to be cultivated. Only a stone barrier separated the rice fields

from the sea and I felt that this could easily be
broached by a storm half as intense as that which had
put pay to the Mace. The land was crossed with narrow causeways and along one of these we rode with
Somi bringing up the rear. The peasants working in
the fields wore flattened conical straw hats and these
they speedily doffed at our approach. One fellow on
the causeway removed his sandals and lowered his
head like an embarrassed child until we were past.
Kushoni made no acknowledgement to these salutations and I think that they were so much a convention
of the populace that he was scarcely aware of them.

I was soon in no doubt as to where we were bound
for a low swelling began to thrust itself above the
perimeter of my vision and turn slowly into the mound
surtopped by a high wall and beyond that a jagged outline of buildings. As we drew nearer I could see that
the walls were composed of high stones forty spans
high and dovetailed neatly into each other as if fitted
by a carpenter. In their midst stood a great gate surmounted by a cedar arch like the spread of an eagle's
wing and in front a drawbridge straddling a deep
moat. It was an imposing edifice and Kushoni was
quick to detect my admiration.

"A fine sight," says he.

"Fine!" I agreed.

"And impregnable."

"How can you be sure?"

Kushoni smiled with the satisfaction of a man who
has made you say what he wants you to say and has
more to impart.

"The foundation stones of that wall were laid on
living men."

"I am disgusted, as I am certain you hoped I would
be. Such barbarism in unknown in my country." I ac-

cept this as something of an exaggeration.

Kushoni leaned forward in his saddle earnestly. "You have no conception of our ways. Any of a Daimyo's followers would consider his life well spent if it was sacrified to ensure his master's future safety."

"You mean that a man would volunteer to have the life squeezed out of him by one of those stones?"

"Willingly!"

"Then may I ask why I have the pleasure of your company at this moment?"

"What mean you?"

"I had thought my meaning must be obvious. Surely such a loyal servant of his Daimyo as you, would have been first to have his bones crushed beneath those ramparts?"

Kushoni looked at me disdainfully.

"My relationship to Taisake is such that his interests are best served by the retention of my body in an upright position, and anyway—" here his voice lost a little of its composure—"some captive Satsumas were in hand to prevent us having to call upon our own resources."

I did a tolerable imitation of a snort.

"Brilliant. So you forced your miserable captives to lay down their lives." The pun was unintentional and in any case went unnoticed by Kushoni, who like most of his race that I had so far encountered, gave little indication of possessing a sense of humour. "The lost opportunity must have cut you to the quick."

Kushoni's face relinquished none of its hauteur.

"It was as good a choice as lay before them, and, although I do not understand why I should have to explain myself to you, I did make my own personal contribution."

"And what was that?"

"Momentoes I picked up, whilst on the great Hideyoshi's Korean campaigns."

My heart softened a trifle as I imagined some much prized sword, or other trophy, lost for ever.

"Namely?"

"Two score of Korean ears and noses that I had been keeping for one of my own building ventures."

"Your munificence overwhelms me." What more was there to say. I presumed that ears and noses created less problems when laying the foundations of the smaller dwelling, but did not press Kushoni on the matter. Sometimes I felt I would never fathom this fellow.

As we approached, the drawbridge was lowered and we passed through the gate in silence. Inside the walls the central feature of the castle was a square tower of seven storeys commanding a view of the countryside. Each storey grew from the curved eaves of the one beneath it and was its inferior in size, so that there were nine windows in each wall of the lowest storey and but three in the highest. The walls of each storey were painted a different colour—red, white and blue with the uppermost one entirely gilded. The windows were varnished black and the roof covered in bluish tiles rising like cobble stones, with the corners of the gables rounded and gilded. It was like nothing I had seen before, Although I was becoming accustomed to the strange curved roofs which looked as if they had been warped by the rain. The whole structure was raised above a man-made escarpment of stones, dovetailed with precision and rising to a height of thirty spans. In the whole of this front elevation there was only one narrow entrance, obviously intended to deny easy access.

"What is this building for?" I asked Kushoni.

"It is an armoury and is where the Daimyo and the

royal family will retire if the castle walls are breached. If necessary they will cut their bellies rather than capitulate."

"You mean kill themselves?"

"That is right. We call it seppuku and a way in which even the most unworthy can die with honour."

"And we call it a mortal sin for a man to take his own life. Anyway, I do not see why you have need of such a place. Did you not tell me that those flattened Satsumas rendered the castle impregnable?"

I waited with interest to see how he would deal with this remark, but, as usual, when faced with any question that implied a criticism of the Japonian code of ethics, he chose to ignore it.

"It is not polite for a guest to ask too many questions," he said, "it would perhaps be better if you let your eye do some of the work of your tongue."

I accepted the rebuff with easy fortitude and continued to look about me.

One surprising feature of the castle was that although obviously geared to the needs of war, it was fitted out with such elegance and style as to seem more like a private house. Tall trees graced the courtyards, and beyond the keep there was an ornamental garden, laid out in a series of shallow pools fed by a clear stream flowing over white sand. Small fish abounded in the pools and the whole was rich in sweet-smelling plants and tiny trees, the miniatures of those that rose above the castle walls. In the centre a fountain played and the water was channelled towards the apartments, presumably so that it might be used for household purposes.

Near to the garden was a long graceful building approached by a flight of stone stairs, and it was here, I was informed by Kushoni, that the Daimyo was waiting to receive us. Inside the entrance chamber the beauty of the fittings and the extensive use of gold for decoration fair raped the eye, and I could not help thinking that with a hatchet, a sack and five minutes alone, I might be able to set myself up for life. Brocade tapestries depicting scenes from nature adorned the walls and there were numerous balconies leading off each, made of polished wood and affording views over the surrounding countryside. The first room led into another, equally sumptuously furnished, and I began to wonder how much more ostentation was to be broached before we came into the presence of the Daimyo. Kushoni informed me that these rooms were called zashiki and the gold-painted screens with which they were decorated, byobu. Three more rooms were passed through before Kushoni stopped to ease off his sandals, and indicated that I should do the same. A door slid open, as is the habit in this country, and we were ushered through by an elderly man in a long white robe, who had been fussing about us ever since we entered the building.

At the far end of the room was a dais and on it two men squatted cross-legged like tailors. A dozen elegantly dressed retainers were also present, and, near the dais, a party of women whom I assumed, with heightening interest, must comprise the female members of the household. It was they who made the first salutation. Folding their fans and clapping the right hands against the left, they dropped their arms and moved from side to side, at the same time as shuffling sideways in unison and uttering a hoarse cry as if afflicted by a desire to cough. My previous acquaintance with womenkind had not prepared me to deal with a gesture of this sort, but Kushoni merely inclined his head in their direction so I did likewise. Beside us the white-haired old fellow took a step towards the dais, knelt down, sat back on his knees and bowed forward so deeply that his forehead was pressed against the matting. He then extended his arms with his palms downwards so that he could not have seen his master even if he had raised his eyes.

I hoped that these gymnastics were not expected of me and was relieved to see that Kushoni contented himself with making a deeper obeissance to the dais than he had to the ladies. I therefore did the same.

The man who sat in the middle of the dais had his head shaven like a priest and was wearing a robe of peacock blue silk bearing a design of leaves and flowers. The sash at his waist was also of silk and in it he carried a Katana—this being their name for the long sword—and a wakizashi, or dirk. He held a fan of ostrich feathers which he waved gently as if the motion formed a distraction whilst he examined us. His face was fat and round as a butterball and well endowed with lip spread out on a platform of teeth that looked as if they had narrowly avoided being totally expelled from the mouth by some explosion emanating from the back of the throat. The man who sat to his right and further back in a slightly subservient position was dressed in the same style and also carried two swords of the country in his obi. The front of his skull was shaven and he wore his hair in a long pigtail which was brought forward and tied in such a way as to rest upon the shaven part of his head. It occurred to me that Kushoni's hair might once have been dressed in this fashion but allowed to go to seed. His expression was sullen and preoccupied and it seemed to me that my own person was singled out for special scrutiny. Even in a squatting position it was obvious that he was unnaturally tall by the standards of his country-

men and as lean as a bean. The contrast between him
and Butterball who I took to be Taisake, the daimyo,
was almost risible.

Taisake folded his fan and inclined his head towards me: "You are welcome, good Kushoni," said he,
"and also the European who we hear has been of service to you. We are glad that your venture has met
with some success." Here, the other occupant of the
dais allowed himself a sneering smile which did nothing to abate the instant dislike I had conceived for him.
"It is something I would discuss with you at greater
length. Let us take tea as I am certain that you have
need of refreshment."

I did indeed, but would have appreciated something a little stronger, not to mention a square meal
to soak it up. "Matsumota will join us and we will
retire to the cha-no-yu."

I think I have already mentioned the Japonian passion for this drink and my own lack of enthusiasm. I
had not considered that they might have special
rooms in which to indulge the habit, but this was clearly the case. The womenfolk shuffled deferentially and
we withdrew by a door so narrow that I could hardly
squeeze through it. Along a corridor and up a fine cedar
staircase and we were in a small courtyard twelve
foot square abutting on a verandah beyond which lay
the tea room. Inside, the place was sparsely furnished
by contrast with what we had been through, with a
black earthenware hearth in one corner, on which
stood a tripod bearing a handsomely wrought kettle
above a charcoal fire. The Japons are sticklers for
etiquette and ritual and to my mind the ceremony of
tea drinking represents the ultimate in tedium that
such occasions can inflict. The powdered leaves are
decanted from a canister or caddy into small porcelain

vessels with a cane spoon while the coals that heat the
kettle are lovingly tended. When the water is boiling
the lid of the kettle is carefully placed on its own tripod and water added to the ground-up leaves, this
mixture then being stirred with a whisk until any
lumps disappear. The resultant steaming green liquid
is the highly prized cha or tea. Each step in the operation is carried out with reverential care and attention
to detail, and for what comes out of it seems to me
like eating three plates of green figs and achieving
but a small fart at the end of it. Could you imagine
anyone in England going through such a rigmarole
without being considered a lunatic? Still it is hardly
possible to go into a Japonian dwelling without being
offered a cup of the brew and the most imposing list
of restorative and curative powers are attributed to it.
They say that it aids digestion, clears the head, soothes
headaches, cures stomach upsets, clears up bowel trouble, relieves the stone, cools fever, leaves a pleasant
taste in the mouth, aids continence—the list might go
on for ever. What is more, the utensils used in its con-
coction—kettle, tripod, bowls and caddies—are often
of considerable age and change hands for quite ridiculous sums of money. I have seen a battered old tripod,
twice resoldered, which I would hardly deign to scrape
my boots on, and which I was told had been bought
for the equivalent of a thousand ducats. Still, in fairness, as the Japons themselves point out, these objects
can be put to a purpose, whilst the emeralds and dia-
monds which we revere have no real use whatsoever.

In this particular ceremony Taisake himself served
us which was obviously something of a rarity and an
expression of esteem for Kushoni near purred with
pleasure whilst the Matsumota fellow could scarce
conceal his irritation as we held out our bowls. At first

we sipped in silence and if an attempt at good manners had not led to me adopting their fiendishly uncomfortable squat I think I might have fallen asleep. Eventually Taisake placed his cup on the low table before him, using the very tip of his fingers in a gesture of excessive refinement and sat back on his haunches.

"Now tell me in more detail," says he, "what befell you with the pirates and why"—here he glanced quickly at Matsumota as if seeking his approbation—"why the number of muskets obtained fell far short of what we had paid for."

Now it was the turn of Kushoni's face to cloud over, for I think he perceived that the question was being asked by Matsumota rather than Taisake and there was obviously no love lost between the two of them.

"As you know, my lord," he said, "as you both know," here he looked hard at Matsumota, "a messenger came from the pirates to say that there were matters to discuss regarding the muskets and we took this to mean that they had arrived. It was your wish that I should go to the island and oversee their transport to Figo. It was to this end that I set sail twelve days ago."

He then went on to describe how he had found the pirates' stronghold sacked and no sign of the weapons, his search and meeting with me and our ensuing adventures. I took it upon myself to recount the taking of the Mace and my belief that the pirates had intended to thieve the muskets thus keeping the monies they had been given for their purchase, as well as laying hands on our cargo. Also, how the typhoons had disrupted their plans and how a part of the shipment had found its way ashore when the Mace broke up, and had been secreted by Perez.

To all this Taisake nodded and seemed quite content with our explanation but if Matsumota was intent on keeping an expression of contemptuous incredulity from spreading across his narrow features he made a poor job of it. When we were finished he shook his head slowly and looked expectantly at Taisake, like a dog waiting to be slipped the leash.

"It is with regret that I listen to your tribulations good Kushoni," said Taisake, "and even greater regret that I hear of the loss of the muskets. Still, one must give thanks that you are still with us and salute your valour and that of our subjects who perished so bravely for their daimyo."

Kushoni inclined his head and I permitted myself the same gesture as I felt I deserved a share of any praise that was going.

"What say you Matsumota?"

"I share your gratitude, my lord, that the life of my brave and loyal friend has been spared and would only ask if he was able to recover any of the ten thousand silver taels that were paid to the pirates in expectation of the muskets?"

"No, my lord, I found no trace of a living pirate, let alone the money."

"It is unfortunate," said Matsumota, allowing a thin, small smile to moonlight across his face.

"What mean you?" Kushoni said, bridling.

"I mean of course that the recovery of the money would have seen some profit in the enterprise despite the loss of our brave subjects to which our master has so rightly alluded, but more important, it might have served to still the rumours which certain no doubt worthless, people have seen fit to conjure up around this whole unhappy business."

"I have heard no rumours." Taisake's voice became shrill when it was angry.

"No, my lord, I have considered them mere tittle

tattle and not worth relating."

"Until this moment," said Kushoni.

"Until this moment, indeed, when I felt that the presence of our loyal subject would serve to dissipate them in an instant."

"What form do the rumours take?" said Kushoni. I noticed that his hand kept stealing to the place where the hilt of the sword would have been resting had it not been kept with all weapons outside the tea chamber.

"They take various forms, all of which, of course, I find it loathsome to relate."

"Of course," said Kushoni. Matsumota smiled away the interruption and continued.

"I cannot find words soft enough to paraphrase the calumnies and so had best repeat them as I heard them begging that you excuse the directness."

"I would be grateful for it," snarled Kushoni. "Speak on."

"Very well. Some say that you have informed the Satsumas of our plans and now bide with me—" Kushoni's fist had shattered the tea vessel as if it was a wren's egg—"and assisted them to overrun the pirates' stronghold so that they might take the arms and you the ten thousand taels."

"A lie, a monstrous lie." Kushoni addressed himself to Taisake. "Must I sit here and listen to this debased slander?"

"Others look at your kinship with the Englishman and say that a bargain had been made with the captain of the ship he sails with and that he is here merely to give some credence to your story."

"Rumour must have wings," says I, 'to speed so fast and in so many directions and in so short a time. We are scarcely arrived in Figo."

"Time enough. News of your coming preceded you from the coast."

"I wish you would tell me the source of these rumours," growled Kushoni, "that I might make the speakers' heads sit ten paces from their bodies."

"I can point to no individual source. Those that I heard them from are common people passing on what they have been told. What a relief it is to hear how boldly you sweep aside these imputations. I am certain that if you persist in this fashion your detractors will soon cease their mutterings. The threat of your sword arm is one that most men fear."

"You imply that I am guilty yet able to avoid committal because of my prowess with a sword."

"My lord," Matsumota appealed to Taisake, "I intended no such thing, I meant to compliment my loyal brother on a skill which is much admired. I think he becomes too testy on the whole subject."

"I think your words were poorly phrased," said Taisake, "and liable to give offence."

"In that case I beg forgiveness and hope that I may be granted indulgence for my clumsy tongue."

"I have never thought your tongue less clumsy than an eel," said Kushoni, "I hope it does not tie itself in knots and choke you by the throat."

"Really, my lord—"

"And one more thing. I will be your guardian against slander, Matsumota. When I hear men say that it was you who informed the Satsumas of our plans so that they might seize the arms I will scold them like wicked children. I will say that it was quite unremarkable that Nomura and his band should have decided at that moment to sack the pirates' stronghold. I will say that the diligent scouring of the mainland was occassioned by no more than a decision to gather nosegays to be home to their master. I will say—"

"Enough," Matsumota rose to his feet as if the word was a charge exploding in his vitals, "you dare to draw me into your guilt. Then find your sword!"

"Willingly and look upon it well for you will never see it once it is in my hands."

With this exchange they were moving towards the door so fast that they might have locked shoulders in it.

"Stay!" Now it was Taisake's turn to shout. "Remember where you are. Have you no shame. This is the cha-no-yu where men discourse with wit and sensibility, not conduct themselves like drunken savages. How dare you talk of bloodletting. Do you think that in our parlous state we can afford to squander each others' lives. That I can see two of my ablest samurai squabble to the death like crazy children?"

The effect of the words was quite remarkable for both Kushoni and Matsumota froze like Lot's wife the moment the first syllable had passed his lips. As he went on their heads fell lower and they stood shame-facedly, in every respect like children, both wilful and repentant. I realised then just how powerful was the authority of a Daimyo, even vested in the person of this little man whose only claim to height rested in the pitch of his voice.

The two samurai fell apart mumbling apologies and Taisake waited until their voices had died away into contrite silence before continuing.

"Let us have no more accusations. There is a pre-sentiment of treachery but there are servants who have passed amongst us and may have overheard our plans. Perhaps you Matsumota, since your ears seem so at-tuned to rumour, might make investigation in their quarters. Inform me swiftly if your inquiries reveal anything and you have my assurance that any traitor will only live long enough to regret his action. Now withdraw and I suggest you meditate until your blood has cooled."

Matsumota said no more but bowed and went out pausing only to let his eye burn on Kushoni for a second so that I thought my friend's flesh might start to smoulder.

Taisake waited until he had left before indicating that Kushoni should be seated again.

"Be not too offended by his words," said he, "I believe that the man's only fault is over-zealousness. Jealous perhaps of your high standing in the kingdom, but in the main a loyal subject and a wise counsellor."

Kushoni grunted and looked down at his empty tea cup. "I bow to your judgment my lord," he said grudgingly.

"And now our Englishman," Taisake smiled and gave me a fine view of his exploding teeth which I would gladly have foresaken. "He eats better than the Jesuits, does he not?" With these words he clapped his hand upon my upper thigh testing its plumpness in a gesture not un-reminiscent of some I had met upon the Mace. Kushoni looked embarrassed.

"Given the opportunity I do," I allowed myself, "but my labours of late have given little time for feasting."

Taisake withdrew his hand regretfully. "Of course, I forget my duties as a grateful host. You will be taken to your quarters and given food which I hope will meet with your approval. Later perhaps we can talk as I would like to hear news of your country. I feel that we might well be able to entertain each other over a cup of wine." He accompanied this intriguing proposal by narrowing his eyes, which presented no great difficulty, as nature had given him a fair start in that direction.

"I look forward to that moment," I said diplomatically, "and would only ask that it might take place when I have recovered sufficiently to ensure that I am not too dull a companion." With these fair words I rose quickly to my feet and with Kushoni beside me made my way to the door which opened magically before us.

I wished to enquire further about Taisake and when I might expect to continue my journey to Nagasaki but my friend was in no mood for conversation and grinding his teeth set his legs in motion and stalked away out of the courtyard. I watched his characteristic gait bear him from my sight and followed the white haired retainer to my quarters, eager for some food and Somi—in that order.

CHAPTER 8

MY CHAMBERS, FOR THERE WAS MORE THAN ONE ROOM, were hardly inferior to anything I had seen in the palace and made the manor of my late protector outside Plymouth seem like a carpenter's shop. Not honest oak and pewter here but a variety of sandalwood and cedar, polished and carved as if it had been a brief to the craftsmen to cover every inch with intricate embellishment. It was as if a million termites possessed by an artistic inspiration had been earnestly chewing at the woodwork for a thousand years.

In one corner lay a bed, or rather bedding, for the Japons seem to have no height in any article of furniture, possibly because being so small of stature themselves it makes them feel taller when they rise. At the head of the litter was what I could only imagine must be a wooden pillow, but it looked far too like a chopping block for a man of my sensibility to want to put his head on it.

I looked around hopefully for the food that had been mentioned but there was no sign of it and I was advancing hungrily into the next room when a delectable little slant-eyed minx came out of it. She was more simply dressed than the women in the Daimyo's chamber and wore a short kimono revealing what I was pleased to recognise as a pair of shapely legs. Smil-

ing sweetly, she enquired if I would like a bath. Silently
cursing the Japonian addiction to time consuming rigmarole, I thought it best to accede to her suggestion,
both out of politeness and because, even by my own
generous reckoning, I was beginning to smell less
wholesome than a leper's armpit. I followed the girl
into the chamber and was surprised to see a bathing
place sunk into the middle of the floor like a stone pool.
What is more, the water in it was steaming and must
have been heated somewhere in the foundations of the
palace, before passing into the chamber, because the
pool was too large to have been filled by hand and
there were no signs of any utensils which might have
been used for that purpose. I paused and smiled at
the girl, waiting for her to withdraw but she gave no
sign of doing so and set about collecting some earthenware flasks which I imagined contained bathing un-
gents. Thinking that she was merely curious, like so
many of her kind that I had encountered on the voyage, I stripped off my clothing hoping that what was
revealed would shock rather than disappoint her. This
done I descended the marble steps that led into the
water and to my amazement the girl followed me. Not
only followed me but approached me and began washing my body. I thought at first that this must be the
preliminary to some amorous exercise, but although
never abandoning her smiles and eager-to-please demeanour, and sparing no part of my anatomy her diligent attentions, the girl was obviously most interested
in scrubbing me clean. This may have been the limits
of her desire, but I soon aspired to better things and
found that my hands, always prompt servants of my
appetite for dalliance, were unable to prevent themselves from foraging across her neat, wet body. This
she took in good part, or I might say parts, and I was

just beginning to relieve her of the encumbrance of her clothing when three more succulent little moppets suddenly appeared from nowhere and came tripping down the steps into the bath. This was a surfeit of riches I could have done without. Being washed by any woman other than one's mother is arousing, being washed by four is something of a chore. Giggling and chattering amongst themselves they rubbed, lathered and tweaked until I had no other impulse than to escape from their attentions. This was only achieved when I had been led from the bath and rubbed soundly with a variety of oils which I must confess did induce a feeling of well-being into my tired flesh. Their duties completed the girls lined up, bowed deeply and were gone as suddenly as they had arrived.

I returned to the sleeping chamber and was grateful to find that at last some food had materialised. And most excellent it was too. Some kind of fowl to supplement the inevitable rice, and a jug of wine. As for the dishes it was served in, they were of a quality that surpassed anything I had ever seen. Porcelain, translucent as a pearl and decorated with a hunting scene—noblemen on horseback attacking a wild boar. But it was the contents of the bowls I was most interested in and eschewing the damn chopsticks I fell to with my fingers until an ant would not have found a square meal in any of my platters. My belly filled with good victuals and sake I was of a mind to slumber for a few hours when it occurred to me that I had not found out where Somi was accommodated. No sooner had I decided to seek her out than there was a knock on the door and the white-haired retainer entered. Having apologised for the incomparable squalor of my surrounding and the inexcusable vileness of the food and wine as is their habit in Eastern climes, he explained that 'my lady' had a fever and would be pleased to see me as she was in a state of some alarm.

Some Japonian garments had been laid out for me and I was speedily into these and following the retainer down the corridor. Somi's chamber was no great distance from mine and inside it I found her in a poor state with eyes closed and a lather of perspiration on her brow. All the physical hardships she had endured and the horror of her father's torture and death must have been responsible for this condition. No doubt she had been ailing on our journey here when I had put down her silence to illhumour. She was being attended by two ladies, or so they appeared by the quality of their robes and the ornamental pins in their hair which was swept up into frozen waves.

"Here I am," I said unnecessarily, taking her hand. "I was on the point of coming to find you when the messenger arrived."

She smiled a slow disturbed smile, and tried to squeeze my hand although the pressure was woefully weak.

"It is of no matter. I am sorry that I was so distant on our journey here but my mind is possessed by ghosts and demons. Now with the fever they swirl before my eyes so I can hardly see you. I beg you, do not leave me now until—until . . ."

"Of course I will stay with you until you are quite recovered and then you shall come with me to England. I thought that it was already decided."

I tried to thrust a cheerful note into my words for I knew what Somi was thinking, she believed that God was punishing her and that she would die like her mother and father. I must confess that I was a trifle uneasy myself. Perhaps there was some substance in her fears. I tried to talk to her and racked my brain for things to tell her about England, in which she had always shown great interest, but I could see that her mind was elsewhere and it was becoming damned hard work by the time her head fell back against the bedding. Still clinging to my hand she relapsed into an uneasy sleep. I disengaged my hands from her damp fingers and pulled up the sheet which was wringing wet where it had pressed against her body. It was sad to see the poor child in this state and remember our more moving moments together. I took my leave of the ladies in waiting, asking that I should be summoned when Somi awoke or anything untoward occurred, and made my way back towards my own chamber.

I say towards because my guide had disappeared and in that maze of richly decorated corridors I soon found myself hopelessly lost. This was confoundedly irritating because there was still some sake left in my chambers and my bed was calling out for the imprint of my body. I looked around hopefully for someone to direct me and espied at the end of a passageway a wench reminiscent of those who had been scrubbing me an hour before. Reminiscent because to me the Japons have a tendency to sameness, though in fairness they may well think likewise about us. Anyway, I started after the creature who no sooner saw me advancing than began to play the coquette, and pressing her hand to her mouth skipped out of sight down another passageway. I lengthened my stride and turned the corner just in time to see her disappearing round the next. I must confess that my irritation was now becoming tempered by a sense of enjoyment in the physical chase. It was remiss of me I knew, so soon after leaving the stricken Somi, but I began to feel a rare desire to catch up with the slender nippon. I rounded the corner at a gallop to find the corridor empty. But all was not lost because I had the distinct impression that I had seen a door slide shut half way down it. I scampered forward and gave the door a few discreet taps. No sound. One more tap from the impulsive Adam and I was sliding back the portal and ushering in my friendly idiot grin.

The room was huge and vaulted with a carved ceiling full of dragons and demons lowering down upon me as if resentful of my presence. Two huge chests like tombs stood against the walls and the atmosphere was sombre enough to make any quickly rehearsed banter dissipate itself at the back of my throat. Not that there was any need of it for the object of my chase was nowhere to be seen. I was about to withdraw speedily when I heard a low sigh and what I took to be the rustle of clothing. Ever the optimist, I pressed forward to where the shuttered windows cast more light, and found myself nearly stepping upon a figure stretched out on a litter of richly worked bedding. One glance was sufficient to tell me that I was in the bed chamber of my benefactor Taisake and that it was his plumb body that was stirring at my feet. No prompting was required to make me realise that my presence in the royal bedchamber could lead to a number of unfortunate interpretations. Not least of them being that I might return some of the interest Taisake had evinced in my person. I was therefore doubly strengthened in my resolve to escape and straining towards the door when, damn me if I didn't hear a gaggle of female voices approaching it from the outside. I contemplated standing my ground and trying to bluff my way out of my predicament, but force of habit and the pressure of hands on the door sent me darting behind the nearest tapestry from where I held my breath and viewed their entrance undetected.

There were five of them, making up one of the fairest bevys of female beauty I have ever wished to lay hands upon. Long dark tresses, heavy as oiled silk and eyes delicately rimmed with lines of black to accentuate their almond shape. Their bodies were slim as young boys and they moved with the shy uncomplicated grace of fawns. As for their mouths, they were as delicate and succulent as ripe buds. There was not one of them the inferior of her fellows.

Four of them carried flasks and cups and the fifth a thick hempen rope so I was soon developing a crick in my neck to see what would take place. I was not left in suspense for long. As one they fell upon their knees and began to arouse the Daimyo with kisses and nibbles along the length of his body, like piglets searching for their mother's teats. I think it fair to say that they aroused me before their master and I was in some fear that the tapestry might not yield an adequate hiding place. What an old rogue Taisake must be. Certainly his tastes were catholic enough. I felt almost envious of somebody whose several proclivities could so easily encompass both genders and wondered if I might not be lacking some fundamental physical spark, or perhaps I had merely mininterpreted his squeezing of my thigh and effete appearance. Perhaps it was no more than a friendly Japonian gesture. I wish Kushoni had stayed long enough to be questioned about it.

Not surprisingly Taisake was no sluggard in sitting up and he promptly snatched one of the flasks and rewarded its bearer with a smacking kiss on the lips. The other settled down about him and there was much jostling and tactile roguery with his podgy hands shooting out to squeeze, pat or pinch a favourite. Even as an observer I was getting a fair measure of pleasure from the goings on and was craning for-

ward as much as I dare when the Daimyo set down
his cup and looked about him ruminatively.

"Now who will try me today?" says he, almost to
himself. "Sigushu." Out shoots his arm and he pulls
my particular fancy on to his mouth. The old satyr
was wearing a sort of nightshirt but not for long.
The girl and her helpmates turned him out of this like
a steamed pudding and looking at the rolls of fat almost swamping the toadstool between his legs I
could not help wishing that they were grappling with
a foe worthy of their attentions. Once naked he lay
back and his chosen one began to run her fingers lightly all over him in a way that brought me out in a rash
of goose pimples. Shortly her mouth went down and
the Daimyo's hands began tugging at her baggy pantaloons.

I was so engrossed in this spectacle that I hardly
noticed two of the other girls exchange a nod that directed one of them towards my hiding place. My first
reaction was that I had been discovered but passing
near enough to be touched the damsel stopped beside
me and opened a small cupboard built into the wall.
From this she withdrew a handsome piece of ivory,
unmistakably carved in the shape of a male member.
This was remarkable enough, but what was downright
terrifying was the close up view of the maiden's hand
that this presented. Her nails were black and in some
cases bitten half way down to the quicks; the backs of
her fingers were covered in a fuzz of fine black hair.
Hair? My eyes veered back to the bed where my fancy
was now disrobed and revealing, unmistakably that
she was a he! His bunch of grapes dangling about
Taisake's mouth and that worthy like a successful Rey-
nard, engulfing them. My senses were turned upside
down by the shock and nausea of it. So my suspicions

had been true, and I had been gulled into squandering my manly lust on a spectacle fit only for my base shipmates on the Mace.

What ensued I will not run the risk of disturbing pure minds with. Suffice to say that the dildo and other devious instruments were plunged into service by the assembly as a mass orgy revealed all my erstwhile loves as no more than craven catamites. No multiple practise was too vile for them to perform with squeals of relish, but for all that they could achieve amongst themselves Taisake remained flaccid as a frost-bitten snowdrop. It was not until the hempen cord was brought into play and he was lashed by every youth in turn that he eventually spent himself in a flurry of wrist-wrenching orgasm. To do him a kindness I can only imagine that a surfeit of licentiousness, with every whim indulged, had dulled his sense to the point where there was no new sensation left to titillate his jaded appetite. A sorry end, both literally and metaphorically, and one that I hoped might be denied me, though I suspected I would be dead in six months given his opportunities.

Sweating behind the tapestry I endured these goings-on until I thought my aching limbs might start groaning out loud, but there was no speedy relief to my fatigue. When the protagonists of the orgy had received their individual fulfillments they fell to carousing until they were insensible. I had to wait where I was until the last pederast had slumped to the floor in sodden slumber before I could tiptoe out of the chamber and breathe clean air. My God, but it was a relief to rub the circulation back into my cramped limbs and stride down the corridors.

I found my way back to my own chambers with irritating ease, considering my earlier blunderings, and there waiting for me was the old retainer, looking agitated. His face cleared magically as I came through the door.

"My lord, I am relieved to see you. I had thought that you might have taken offence at your poor accommodation and gone to seek better."

"My chamber is very adequate."

"Or departed in search of more satisfying food. You must excuse the poorness of our repasts."

"I have no quarrel with the food."

I could see that this old man was going to play havoc with my nerves.

"There must have been something that your lordship sought?"

"I went to open my bowels," says I, emphasising the words with the most descriptive gestures I could summon up. "Would it be politic if I asked you to accompany me in future?"

"Oh no, my lord."

"Right. Well perhaps you would be good enough to take me to mistress Somi. I am certain you would not want me to walk alone."

He hurried out and I let him wait a few moments whilst I drained the last dregs of sake before following and ushering him ahead with an imperious wave.

Somi was still sleeping but sweating so profusely that the perspiration ran down her face like rain down a window pane. Her flesh burned and her skin had taken on an ominous waxen hue. All the signs alarmed me greatly and I turned to the two female attendants.

"What ails her?"

"A fever, my lord."

"I had some inkling of that. Can you not say more?"

"No, my lord."

"And how serious is her condition?"

"Grave, my lord."

"What can be done to save her?"

"Her fate is in the hands of Buddha."

Buddha is one of their gods, and to a man of my religious persuasions, or lack of them, this offered little
solace.

"Is there no medicament that can be given her?"

"Not for this fever, my lord. The bonzes offer up
their prayers."

"May much good come of them," said I, turning on
my heel, "summon me if her condition alters. I will
be in my chamber."

"Yes, my lord."

I had the feeling that the poor child was near to
death and though not renowned for compassion this
disturbed me. We had been through much together
both in lust and adversity, and with her father dead I
felt a particular responsibility for her. It was ironic
that having survived so many hardships she should be
struck down when we had reached temporary sanctuary. I stood by the window in my room and puzzled
as to what action I could take. There must be some
physician in this damn country who could do something for her. I considered finding Kushoni and enlist-
ing his aid but dusk was deepening into night and
perhaps it was better to leave her to the natural remedy of sleep and see what might be effected in the
morning. This I resolved to do and was on the point
of bedding down myself when I observed movement
in the ornamental garden which presented a pleasing
aspect from my window.

Three females were walking slowly by, taking an
evening stroll. They were all ladies of quality, that
was clear, but one, by virtue of her dress if nothing
else, surpassed the others. She was slight as is the

rule and wrapped up in her long kimono as if it was a blanket designed to shield the contours of her body from the most inquisitive eye. I could not make out the design clearly but it seemed to feature all the fitments of the universe, stars, moon and sun, gold on a black background. Her hair was piled high upon her head with a large bun behind and dressed with jewelled combs and dangling brooches cleverly arranged to produce the best effect. She twirled a folded fan about her finger as if bored, and occassionally stopped to comment on a feature of the garden or pet a small monkey that one of the ladies with her was carrying. Normally she would have received a good deal of my attention for she had an air of spirited aimlessness which I have always found appealing in women. However tonight my mind was on other matters and when our eyes met I did no more than hold her gaze coolly and incline my head as a mark of respect to her imagined rank.

"Who is that lady?" I said to the old man who still clung to my side like a burr.

"The daimyo's mistress my lord."

"You mean his concubine?"

"No, no my lord," the tone was shocked, "I mean his wife."

"And does he have but one wife?"

"Oh yes my lord."

"And children?"

"The union has not yet been blessed with issue."

Little surprise there. I could imagine that the lady passed very peaceful nights. Probably why she looked so bored. I watched her out of sight and yawned loudly to prepare grey beard for my words.

"And now I would like to be left to sleep."

"Yes my lord. I will be near at hand if you have need of me."

"I have no doubt of it. Good night."

"Good night my lord. I hope your sleep is sound."

"I hope so too."

I pushed the garrulous old windbag out of the door and lost no time in committing my body to the bedclothes. The sheets were of pure silk and soft as a maid's belly compared to what I had been sleeping on of late. Snug in their embrace I should have been in the Kingdom of Nod within seconds but my contrary mind persisted in choosing that moment for an unwelcome examination of my situation.

If this was the court of a poor kingdom in imminent danger of attack from its more powerful neighbour then I wondered what degree of affluence pertained in the other sixty odd states. Certainly Ieyasu must be a man of power if he could hold them in check. Kushoni had repeated to me Somi's account of how this man gave his tacit support to the Satsumas and was equally convinced that he would give his blessing to their annexation of the Figo kingdom.

If some large scale conflict was imminent then that was as good a reason as I needed to be somewhere else—in the hold of a Portuguese merchantman sailing out of Nagasaki harbour for instance. And neither Taisake nor Matsumota persuaded me to stay. I had no wish to become the latest addition to the daimyo's troupe but knew that a downright refusal would hardly endear me in a land where personal affronts invited swift reprisal. Matsumota was no more reassuring. A sinister figure who wasted no love on Kushoni and would have none to spare for me as one of his associates. All in all, apart from the bath girls, there were few inducements to overstay my welcome. Few inducements, yes, but now an obligation—Somi. What scant sense of honour I possessed demanded that I remained with the girl until she was recovered or dead,

in the morning I would buzz about to see what could
be effected to secure the first alternative. Things must
be resolved quickly so that we, as I hoped it would
be, could be on our way to Nagasaki before more
bloodshed overtook us. Even as I lay there Nomura
and his hordes might be stealing across the mist-hung
ricefields. Listening to the silence, I could trace the
outline of his dreadful face in the darkness. I swear
that if he had suddenly loomed out at me I would not
have been surprised. Such thoughts were poor heralds
of rest and I tossed and turned for hours before eventually falling into a troubled sleep.

CHAPTER 9

I WOKE UP IN THE MORNING IN BRIGHT SPIRITS, AS IS my habit, for I seldom carry the worries of one day into the next, and pulled on the suit of clothes that had been laid out for me. These were quite different to what I had worn the previous day and a much better fit. So good in fact that I suspected my diligent hosts might have set to with needle and thread in order to encompass my generous frame. Catching a glimpse of myself in the mirror, as I was inclined to do whenever the opportunity presented itself, I had to confess that I cut quite a dash in my Japonian garb: the loose jerkin held casually with a broad sash, the long baggy pantaloons meeting my sandals bound high to the knee. I withdrew my arm from the drooping sleeves as I had seen Kushoni do in his quiescent moments, and folded them across my chest. The effect was imposing and could only have been bettered by a couple of swords in my belt. The absence of these I would have to remedy shortly, both for ornamental and protective reasons, though as I have said before the sword is not my favourite weapon.

I should mention, for lovers of such details, that the weapon I had been issued with on the island had been discarded in my flight to the junk, an act which had won the contempt of Kushoni who I felt probably slept with his katanga in his hand.

Preening myself, I could not help but wonder what my old mother would have made of her first born —if that were indeed my true identity—and for that matter my erstwhile comrades on the Mace. I had the feeling that the effect achieved might have been the downfall of my virginity. The thought made me wary of my next meeting with the daimyo, but further reflection was disturbed by the sound of movement outside my window.

Looking out I saw a strange procession passing. It was led by a scruffy fellow with a pick axe on his shoulder, followed by another bearing a shovel. Behind them came an official of some sort bearing a scroll and in his wake an unhappy wretch with his hands bound behind his back and a scrap of paper dangling from the knot. Behind him and secured to the prisoner, for that is clearly what he was, by a silken cord, was a brutish fellow with a long sword at his side. He was flanked by two soldiers with insignia like our archery targets on their chests, each resting a pike on the prisoner's shoulder, in case he felt a compulsion to escape. I would not have been in that man's shoes for my own weight in gold but resolved to follow and see what took place.

I had no sooner cocked a leg over the window than Masumota hove in sight and, roundly abusing all in the procession, ordered the men with shovel and pick axe to fall out. I tried to address him civilly, deeming it best to try and win his favour, but his scowl had lost none of its sourness since our previous meeting so I held my tongue.

The procession continued to wend its mournful way beyond the confines of the palace, passing amongst some handsome many coloured buildings, until we reached the castle walls and another gateway. Through this we passed, with me lagging behind and feeling rather foolish. Before us was a jumble of crude bamboo dwellings making a marked contrast to the ordered spaciousness we had left behind. Through these we marched, and although I saw no one beyond a mother who ran out to snatch up a child playing in the dust, I had the feeling that we were being watched by a hundred pairs of wary eyes.

Beyond the houses we were on open ground and my nostrils began to be afflicted by a monstrous and familiar stench. A large dog padded silently towards me with something gripped between its teeth. I took little notice of it until it was nearly abreast of me, and then, looking down, saw that its prize was a human hand. This sight disturbed me, somewhat especially as this limb seemed only recently to have parted company from the rest of its body. Ahead of me the party had come to a halt in the presence of three large crosses and I wondered if I had come to a burial ground. In part I had.

Drawing nearer I could see that the crosses were smeared with blood and that the whole area was stained with that commodity, so that a dark syrup seemed to be seeping from it. The smell was such as to send the hand across the mouth to stop the stomach lining jumping out of it. Scraps of human flesh and bone littered the scene and the one concession to order was a huge dung heap sprinkled with human heads in various stages of putrefaction like plums in a pudding.

If I had any doubt about what I was to witness, these were swept aside as the prisoner was pushed down upon his knees and obediently extended his neck. The official then began to read from the scroll

which I realised must contain a statement of the condemned man's crime, but he had got no further than a
few words about 'most heinous treachery' when Matsumota cut him short and ordered the executioner to
do likewise to the prisoner. In all this time the poor
creature had not said a word, but conducted himself
with such composure that the proceedings might
have been taking place without him. I wished that I
might have such courage.

The executioner stepped forward, measured his
blade against the man's neck and raised it. At this
point I turned away for I thought the man deserved
some privacy as he died. I heard the blow fall and
when I turned back the head was half a dozen paces
away, still wearing its expression of repose and with
the eyes open. The blood flowed from the severed neck
as from a breached dam.

The sight of this poor fellow, so recently alive, now
struck into infinity, filled me with awe and self disgust,
as if I had been a party to his killing, but worse was
to follow. Creeping up from behind like mist from the
ricefields had come a gaggle of urchins, some of them
sporting katangas longer than themselves. No sooner
had the corpse stopped twitching than they were
streaming towards it and beginning to hack it to
pieces before my eyes. I was reminded of Kushoni
selecting a weapon for me after the attempted ambush.
That had been sickening enough, but to see mere children perform in this fashion was unnerving. Glibly
they shouted the merits of their individual blades and
when the corpse was thoroughly dismembered even
conducted a competition by piling pieces of flesh one
upon the other and seeing how many could be cut
through with one blow. All the while their elders
looked on indulgently as we would at children cock

fighting. I later found out that this sword testing on the corpses of criminals is an established Japonian custom and that they even have a name for it: Tame-shigiri. What a people!

I had seen more than enough and stole away with a decidedly queasy stomach. I was puzzled by the dismissal of the gravediggers but assumed, and this was later proved correct, that some crimes were considered so heinous as to forfeit the right to burial. Quite a number of them it seemed, if the pile of heads on the dung heap was anything to go by.

I retraced my steps through the settlement where every nook and cranny seemed to mask a pair of watching eyes, and re-entered the castle. When I returned to my room it was to find more food laid out and my guardian in an advanced state of agitation.

"To save your breath," I said, holding up my hand, "let me tell you that I have been attending an execution. Do you know anything of the matter?"

"I believe that the man was a traitor, detected by the lord Matsumota."

"He moves swiftly, the lord Matsumota."

Swiftly indeed. Little more than twelve hours had passed since our audience with Taisake and already one head had rolled. A pity, one felt, since he achieved results so fast, that he had not made his inquiries in the right quarter earlier.

"Your lady has awakened."

Somi! Not a thought of her had passed through my mind since I awoke. Zounds! But I was a heedless fellow, though callous might be a better word. Sometimes my lack of feeling disturbed even myself. Trying to make amends I bustled down the corridor towards her.

If I had expected a discernable improvement I was

disappointed. She seemed to have shrunk during the night. The pallor intensified, the light in the eyes dulled. I took her hot, damp hand and mumbled the unhelpful words that one uses on such occasions. A smile plucked at her lips but she was like some small, frail bird dying on the shore.

Determined to do something, I gave her hand one last squeeze and went in search of Kushoni. When I found him, he was standing in a patch of open ground with a sword in his hand slashing away at the empty air like a madman. He went on in this fashion for a few moments, emitting the occasional grunt, and then sheathed his weapon.

"Very elegant." This remark was accompanied by a lightning assessment of my person and a faint smile.

"I did not come here to talk about myself," I said, somewhat nettled. "Somi is dying and I would ask you to use what influence you have in this place to help her. Surely there must be a court physician, or some such."

"Not any more. The last occupant of the post turned one of the Daimyo's ailments into an affliction."

"Where is he now?"

"I think you attended an execution earlier today. You probably saw him."

"You mean—"

"He is lying out there somewhere."

"You mean everywhere, do you not? My God, there must be someone who can help us. What happens in this country when people catch a fever?"

Kushoni thought for a moment. "They either recover or they die."

"As Buddha decrees?"

"Perhaps!"

At this I started to rant and call down all manner

of imprecations upon the Japonian race, labelling them callous and inhuman and, in fact possessed of most of the vices that have been attributed to me at one time or another, but Kushoni merely rode my words and stroked his jaw ruminatively.

"There is a woman," he said eventually, "that I have heard tell of, who deals in potions and physics. I knew a man who held her in great awe and said that she had brought back his wife from the dead. When I looked upon her I could believe it."

"Where is this woman?"

"She dwells in a village about half a day's ride from here."

"Take me to her I beg you, or send someone to guide me."

"You care about this girl do you not?"

"I care that she lives."

"Very well, I will ride with you myself. I had thought to go hunting, but that can wait, and there is a most excellent swordsmith in this village, so the visit may be to our mutual profit."

I thanked him profusely and went to tell Somi where I was going, but she had relapsed into a fitful slumber, and deeming it unwise to disturb her, I returned to meet Kushoni. Two mounts were provided in an instant and though splendidly caparisoned this did not entirely hide their deficiencies. The Japonian nag is much smaller than our own and though game like its riders, is a creature of little elegance. I hauled myself into the damned uncomfortable saddle and we were off.

At first the way led through the ricefields and we proceeded by the narrow causeways that bisected them, but almost imperceptibly the ground began to rise, and though still hugging the ricefields in its swelling contours, started to form a natural progression to the distant hills. These hung before me like one of the tapestries in the Daimyo's palace, but lost some of their pleasing aspect as we drew nearer.

It was in one of their sharp undulations that the village lay, and a poor place it was. All crudely thatched houses and not a tile to be seen. One puff of wind would have carried it away. The inhabitants grovelled before us, removing headware and sandals, when they had either to wear, and scarce daring to raise their foreheads from the ground. Kushoni took this very much as his due, but I found their protestation of love and fidelity bordering on the absurd and not a little embarrassing. I also noticed that the population of the village seemed to be comprised of men, old women, and children. I could conceive that living in such a place must be a pretty ageing process, but hardly sufficient to account for an instant progression from infancy to dotage amongst the females. We were taken to the headman's hut and given cha, and I had hopes of bringing the conversation round speedily to the purpose of our visit, but the pesky fellow went rambling on in the most obsequious manner about the high taxes that his people had to bear and whether it was not possible for the noble Taisake to send troops to guard them against the Satsumas. I had not realised that the hills marked the border with Satsuma and that the village we were in was constantly being raided and its women carried off. Quite why, puzzled me, unless the Satsumas had a predilection for maturity, but perhaps they had already borne away the more spritely specimens. Kushoni listened patiently and explained that he played no part in assessing taxes, and regretted that the villagers had to sell their rice and live on maize, in order to survive. Moreover, he was careful to point out that, as they well knew, there was a state of hostilities between Figo and Satsuma and the conduct of a war required money. He was certain that none of them would wish to be accused of not doing anything in their power to lengthen the life of their Daimyo and make every moment of it more sweet?

To these stirring words the headman nodded grudging assent, as he could hardly do otherwise. On the question of soldiers, Kushoni said that these too were fully committed to the defence of the Daimyo's palace and that there were not enough of them to support garrisons throughout the country. He then had the temerity to observe that their situation might be remedied if more young men presented themselves for military training, and asked if there were any in the village who would like to return with us. The headman said that though all his young men could aspire to no greater heights that serving their Daimyo in battle, to their eternal regret their services were required in the fields. And so their conversation might have gone on till my hair started to fall out, had I not rudely thrust myself into it and stated the purpose of my visit.

The headman contented himself with a final word on the subject of the rice crop, saying that since it had recently been gathered in he was doubly affeared of an attack from the plundering Satsumas, and then put himself at my service, expressing wonder that I should have come from another continent for such a purpose. I did not disillusion him, but merely stated that the reputation of his soothsayer had indeed spread far.

We departed from the headman's hut—through a huge crowd who I am certain had never seen a European before, for their curiosity nearly got the better of their manners, and this is most unusual amongst the Nippons. We were led towards a dwelling that stood somewhat away from the others and had a loftier bamboo construction lending it a faint aura of distinction. The crowd at our heels hung back respectfully as we approached it and the chief cleared his throat and tapped on the door, dislodging a couple of large spiders. There was no answer, but a further tap led to the door sliding back a few inches, with a difficulty that suggested it was seldom opened. A gust of smoke billowed out sending the onlookers back another couple of paces and a voice as dry as a cinder bade us enter.

Once inside it was difficult to see anything through the smoke and gloom but my eyes eventually settled on what I at first took to be a pig, so vast and glistening was its body. Further probing revealed that it was a huge woman, quite bald as far as I could make out, and squatting on the floor like a mound of rancid butter. Her flesh hung from her in folds and her eyes were almost obscured by her fat cheeks. Though not particularly sensitive to strong odours, I must confess that to be in her presence was not to be reminded of roses.

"Hail," said the Chief brightly, and a little afraid, "this gentleman has come across the ocean to seek your council."

"More fool him," said the shapeless old crone who was now looking like a lizard so many were her wrinkles. "Does he wish to take the edge off his growing?"

"If I did, I would not seek a remedy in this quarter," says I, wishing at the same moment that I had held my tongue.

"Ei, ei, you have no respect for age young man. What is your ailment?"

"I have no ailment. I came here on behalf of a girl who is dying of a fever."

"Do you love her?"

"I do not see what that has to do with the matter."

"I am interested. It must be love that brings you on so long a journey. Where do you come from?"

"A place called England. But I would mislead you if I said I had come all the way from there to seek a remedy. The girl is part Japon."

"And do you love her?"

"I have no knowledge of what love is so I cannot say. I care that she should not die."

"Fairly said. Perhaps to care that people do not die is to love them. Now, of this fever. What is the colour of her skin, and does it bear many blemishes?"

I described as well as I could Somi's condition and the old hag grunted in a fashion that I hoped indicated comprehension. She scrambled to her feet like a cow getting up and started to poke about in the darkness behind her. I could scarce see anything for with my eyes watering so much from the smoke and my nostrils screwed up against the stench, I was in something less than total possession of my senses.

When she turned back to me it was with a small flask in her hand which she pressed into mine. Now for the first time since I had landed on the mainland I felt that some money should change hands, but despite all their attentions, the Daimyo's entourage had thrust none of this commodity upon me. I was forced to resort to words of thanks, which I myself have never found an adequate substitute.

"Half in the morning, half at night," barked the crone, ignoring my effusion. "If that doesn't save her nothing will."

I thanked her again and stepped outside with some

speed. Kushoni was standing there with his sword
across his shoulder and hand on hip so I asked him if
he had a few coins that I might give to the old woman. At the word money his demeanour changed from
easy lassitude to outrage.

"Money!" he bellowed. "Money! You think that I
would contaminate myself with money. I am Samurai!
I would not let the stuff touch my fingers. Do you
take me for some measly merchant, some base grub
seeking to purchase men's good opinion. If I ever have
a son, and God forbid, I will not let them teach him
how to count. It is the path to ruin."

I was amazed at this outburst but as I knew more
of the Japons I found that there were in fact three
classes, Samurai, farmers and those in trade. Even
such poor fellows as we were amongst were held in
greater favour than the merchant class who were uni-
versally despised and found it nigh impossible to im-
prove their status, unlike their ilk in Albion. I started
to remonstrate with Kushoni and then gave it up for
experience had proved that there was no budging him
on Japonian custom.

I hoped that he had forgotten about the swords, but
I was disappointed. Like a ship under sail he strode
back through the village and up to a rude shelter fash-
ioned like a cow byre with one side exposed to the
street. The fire was fanned by a giant bellows and the
scene not unreminiscent of an English smithy's. Small,
sweating men with pincers moved around like imps in
hell, and showers of sparks leaped as if from a man
pummelling a glowing length of metal. This fellow
Kushoni greeted in a manner bordering on the respectful, which rather surprised me, and was shown a range
of swords, all of which he weighed carefully in his
hand and made a few passes with. I could not help

thinking of the scene at the execution ground and hoped that a supply of corpses was not kept at hand for potential purchasers to test their weapons on. Whether this was the case or not I never found out for a great clatter rang out above our heads and running into the street I saw that it was produced by a man sitting on a small platform atop a tall pole set beside the road. He was beating a length of bamboo for all he was worth and gesticulating towards the hills. There, could be seen a plume of dust rising from eight riders who were clearly sweeping down upon the village. I imagined the watchman must be issuing a call to arms, but if this were the case his signal was misinterpreted for men scattered in all directions and Kushoni and I were soon left alone listening to the hiss and crackle of the smithy's fire.

"Where is the granary?" shouted Kushoni after some fleeing wretch, but the man dived through a window without checking his stride. The watchman might have followed him, for comprehening that his message had been received, he came down the pole with his body hardly touching it. Kushoni stretched out an arm and seized him by the collar.

"Where is the granary?" he repeated, "come, show me you fool or I'll split your head open."

This message was also understood and the watchman gesticulated to the centre of the village before bequeathing Kushoni the collar of his kimono and racing away in the opposite direction.

"Peasants!" exclaimed Kushoni bitterly. "Come, we must go to the granary."

I felt unprepared to argue with him but my own preference was to follow those who had clearly learned from previous experience. It was unlikely that we would find the granary a rallying point, and two against eight have never been my favourite odds, even when taking the considerable attributes of Kushoni into account. I scuttled after my mentor who could move with uncommon speed when the mood took him, and after stumbling into a few households and terrorising the inhabitants out of their half empty minds, we came upon the granary. Our blundering had served some purpose for it provided me with a bow and a quiver of arrows which I felt their erstwhile owner was unlikely to use. This thought I derived from the sight of him lowering himself into a large chest as we came through the door.

At this point I think it worth mentioning that I have always been a prodigiously fine shot with a long bow and since the weapon in my hand was nothing inferior to what I had been used to, it was unlikely to adversely affect my performance. This fact will be clearly seen as I resume my narrative.

The granary door was secured but Kushoni burst it open with a blow from the hilt of his sword and we stepped inside. The rice was piled up upon trays which rose above our heads to a loft practically groaning with the stuff. Kushoni drew the door shut behind us and applied his eyes to a crack in the bamboo shutter.

"What are we going to do?" I asked, wondering if this was the ideal position from which to defend ourselves against the eight men bearing down on us.

"You do nothing," he said. "When they arrive I will deal with them. You stay here until I tell you otherwise."

"Willingly," I said, and took up a position beside him with my bow at the ready.

We did not have long to wait. There was a clatter of hooves and a party of armour-clad horsemen reined

up in a cloud of dust before us. I covered them with a
glance, but as the horses stamped and reared I suddenly became aware of the man in their midst. Even
with a horned helmet that hid most of his face and
flowed down in ribs of steel over his neck I had no difficulty in recognising him. Nomura. It seemed there
was no shaking off the fellow and my stomach muscles tautened like the string of the bow in my hand. I
felt Kushoni stir beside me and grunt his irritation.

"What now?" I murmured.

"No change."

Nomura leaned forward on his horse's neck and
breathed in deeply through his truncated nostrils. The
scar across his face glowed red. It was a hideous
countenance, made more awful when registering emotion or physical effort. He gazed around the empty
street and yelped at one of his followers who slid off
his horse and moved towards the granary. I could
hear only the jingle of the horses' bridles and the swish
of the chain mail on the man's shoulders. Kushoni
slowly drew his sword. I felt myself near to death and
a great tide of self pity flowed over me finding kinship
in my stomach which was fast turning to water. Two
strides and the man was at the door. He pushed
against it, seeming surprised to find it open, and
stepped inside. Kushoni took a pace towards him and
lopped off his head. It was done so swiftly that I stood
transfixed—but not for long.

No sooner had the head touched the ground than
Kushoni booted it through the door and marched out
after it. It was a stirring exit and even Nomura's face
registered surprise as he reined in his startled mount.
The head spun to a halt in the middle of the street but
no sooner had it stopped than Nomura had recovered
his composure. Rising in his stirrup, he urged his horse

forward bent on riding Kushoni down. The nag was
well protected by armour, but Kushoni rolled backwards so that he was actually underneath it when he
struck upwards with a most vicious blow that opened
up the belly like a pea pod. The poor creature went
berserk and there was blood everywhere before it collapsed on its knees and hurled Nomura to the ground.
I had strung an arrow and was prepared to loose it in
him when I saw another of the band riding at Kushoni. I instantly changed my aim and sent a shaft
through the man's neck so that he was yanked from his
saddle as if snatched by a rope. It was a brilliant shot
and I could not stop a shout of triumph bursting from
my lips. Nomura was still stretched out where he had
fallen and as Kushoni closed with him I thought the
bastard must be finished. However he was the most
cunning and resourceful fellow, for with Kushoni almost above him he rolled to one side and springing to
his feet seized hold of the fleeting horse and vaulted
into its saddle in a manner remarkable for a man of
his outlandish girth. I loosed an arrow at him but for
once my aim was faulty and it struck his shoulder
armour and was deflected harmlessly aside. One hin-
drance he had to contend with was the body of the
man who I had shot which still had one of its feet
trapped in the stirrup. Nomura was equal to this
problem. With one blow he calmly amputated the limb
and galloped off leaving the mutilated corpse behind.
The others fought to win control of their mounts and
follow him but in the confusion of snorting beasts,
made worse by the death agonies of Nomura's
mount, they were slow to rally and Kushoni had unseated two of them before the remainder escaped.

I felt elated at our delivery but Kushoni was quick
to chide.

"You let him escape," he moaned.

"Let him escape," I shouted. "Did you not see the shot that saved your life? Look, look, skewered at full pitch. Can you not recognise a marksman when you see one?"

"Yes, yes, but you missed Nomura. No marksman misses the important shots. Still, we have no time to argue. They will be back."

"You think so? Having lost three men?"

"Pride will bring them back. They dare not lose face before these peasants. Come."

He led the way back inside the granary and no sooner had we slid the door to, than there was a clatter of hooves outside and an object thudded against the side of the building. We waited for an instant as the hoofbeats faded away and no sounds came in their place and then, suddenly, there was the tell-tale crackle of flames. It was obvious what they were up to and I pressed back a shutter and leaned out attempting to brush away the fire-arrow with my bow. I had just succeeded in dislodging it when a musket shot rang out and the ball parted the hairs at the end of my nose and narrowly missed Kushoni. I nearly tore my arm off struggling back into the room and we both dropped to the floor.

"There must be more of them. I saw no muskets."

"Unobservant fool," snapped Kushoni, "it was the first thing I looked for. There is but one. Stay here and make a show of movement whilst I seek him out." I was keen to say that we had taught the Satsumas a lesson and now was the time to withdraw, before we became the meat supplement to a large dish of roasted rice, but Kushoni was already stealing towards the back of the building. Minutes passed and I started at every creek and whisper that ran though the building

but nothing happened. Still crouched low I picked a
hole in the wall to give me a field of view, hoping that
my action could not be observed by the man with the
musket for the walls were not over thick. Of him there
was no sign but I had hardly established this fact than
there came the drumming of hooves and another rider
came into view. If my first effective shot had been brilliant I must concede a measure of luck to its successor.
I leaped to the still open shutter and unleashed a shaft
which miraculously struck my attacker beneath his
raised arm as he was on the point of loosing another
fire arrow. He buckled in the saddle and fell forward
with the flaming arrow playing against the horse's side.
The terrified beast sprang forward and for all I know
is running still.

Four down and four to fall.

Minutes passed and there was still no sign of Kushoni
and then—the sound of movement from the rear of the
granary. I levelled an arrow at the opening but when a
figure appeared it was Kushoni bearing a musket. I
did not have to ask him how he had got it for there
was blood on the wakizashi at his waist. I seized the
musket eagerly and found to my relief that it was
primed. Now for the first time I began to believe we
had a chance. Such confidence was, as is usually the
case with me, premature. There was a commotion
above our heads and before I could turn an arrow
thumped down transfixing Kushoni's arm. A man or
men had crept into the lot. I saw a shadow and let
fly with the musket. But—in my panic—too soon. Even
though the hellion was nearly on top of me I missed.
It was a grievous error but as usual Kushoni was equal
to the situation. Lashing out with his sword he severed
a rope which I had barely noticed stretching dust-
covered to the roof jambs. This was in fact but one

securing the great trays of rice which had been hauled aloft to dry. With one corner sagging the Satsuma lost his footing and came plummeting down beneath a torrent of rice. Before he could move Kushoni had slashed through three more cords and I stood ankle deep in the stuff. All that could be seen of our attacker was a couple of flexing toes protruding from a mound in the middle of the granary. Kushoni looked at them and gave one of his rare smiles.

"At least he will not starve to death," he said.

"Indeed," I observed, wishing I could find the sight as amusing.

"Do we continue to wait here?"

"No, there are two left if my calculations be correct and we will take the fight to their quarter. I do not wish to lose Nomura."

I would have lost Square Root at the first opportunity but in this situation my fate was bound to Kushoni and there was no gainsaying him.

I broke the shaft which had transfixed his arm and drew it out. Luckily it had pierced the soft flesh above the elbow and there was more blood than damage. This done we took up our weapons and ran hard for the houses opposite, in case there was anyone waiting for us. We need have had no fear for there was only the mournful head of our first victim watching us from the middle of the street. Round the back of the houses we found our horses waiting patiently where they had been tethered. Still the streets were empty and there was not a soul to be seen. The peasants were obviously not given to acts of foolhardiness. Kushoni, who did not possess my respect for the musket had not thought to bring any balls or powder with the captured weapon and I persuaded him that it would be wise to go back and retrieve them. We had reached the end of the mean

street, little more than a kennel, when we suddenly
came upon Nomura and the last of his band sitting
pensively on their mounts and obviously deliberating
their next move.

The revelation was mutual and for a second we
gazed at each other before Kushoni spurred forward
with a hideous scream that sent my nag's ears back
near into its head. I followed in his wake uttering my
own pallid squeak and wondering what I was going to use for a weapon at close quarters, as I was still
without a sword. The problem was deferred because,
to my surprise, Nomura and his fellow took off down
the village street as if all the hounds in hell were after
them. We followed in a cloud of dust and I settled
myself low over my mount's neck and abandoned myself to the chase. When the dust had cleared we were
in open country with the gap between us unchanged.
Not unnaturally the Satsumas were riding towards
the crest of the hills and I wondered where the boundary with their kingdom might lie. The way now became
peppered with outcrops of rock and I noted that the
two riders in front were splitting up. Kushoni, to my
relief, peeled off to follow the unmistakable bulk of
Nomura and I pursued his minion who dashed between two rocks which rose like the portals of a door.

The sight beyond near tipped me out of my saddle.
Flanked by high rocks was a pool and in and around
it were two score of naked wenches displaying every
charm that God had given them. Our precipitous arrival threw them into a rare panic and served my prey
scarcely better for his mount dashed into the shallow
water and unseated him. I was close behind but managed to preserve my seat—and well I did. Hardly had
the Satsuma hit the water than the doxies converged
upon him like ants and proceeded to hold him down

and drown him by sheer weight of numbers. As I
watched in amazement I suddenly felt hands reaching up to pull me down and the prick of a dagger being wielded by a fair temptress and aimed at my groin.
In a panic I near pulled the bit out of my horse's mouth
and wheeling round galloped out of that hell-hole as
fast as I could.

I had no sooner come to the conclusion that this
secret place was where the cunning villagers hid their
daughters from the Satsumas—and probably the likes
of Kushoni and myself—than Kushoni himself came
thundering down the hillside urging me to ride for my
life. I spurred alongside him to be told that, with his
devil's luck, Nomura had cleared the hill to find a
party of Satsuma cavalry four hundred paces in front
of him, thus forcing Kushoni to give up the chase and
flee for his own life.

I was nothing loath to leave this place and so with
Somi's precious flask still pressing against my ribs we
skirted the village and struck out through the ricefields
for home. Many times I looked back fearfully but there
was no sign of pursuit.

CHAPTER 10

IT WAS DARK BY THE TIME WE GOT BACK TO THE DAIM-yo's palace and I hurried to Somi's quarters gritting my teeth in trepidation. To my relief she was alive and seemed little changed from when I had last seen her. The silent ladies in waiting still fluttered deferentially at the end of the bed and the air was heavy with un-exploited time. It was as if everyone was waiting patiently for the girl to die.

She was asleep when I came in but we propped her up and poured some of the potion down her throat. She barely stirred and certainly did not recognise me which was a change for the worse. I could see too that the ladies in waiting had little enthusiasm for the remedy, and so went to my chamber much cast down and wondering if she would greet another sunrise.

It was, therefore, a vast relief next morning to find some colour stolen back into her cheeks and her eyes open and smiling at me. She was able to speak coher-ently and actually confessed herself desirous of food, which was a considerable change for the better. I gave her the rest of the potion and took the hand she of-fered.

"Dear John," said she, her eyes moist with grateful tears, "I hear that you endured great hardships to pro-cure this medicament. I thank you with all my heart."

" 'Tis nothing," I said, all modest clumsiness. "I

could not abide to see you suffer. Anyway, your thanks are properly due to our friend Kushoni, who led me to the physic."

"I will be glad to show him my gratitude."

She raised her hand and touched my cheek as if to confirm that I really existed. "It seems strange now, but when I awoke and you were gone I believed you had deserted me."

"Zounds. How could you have thought such a thing?"

"You know how melancholy I have been of late. I believed that fate was poised to strike me down as it had done my mother and father."

"Nonsense," said I, not revealing that I had flirted with the same surmise, " 'twas but a fever and you will soon be recovered."

"Thanks to you, I can now believe that. You have relieved me of much anxiety." She looked upon me with so much affection that I felt almost uncomfortable. If I had cured the wench's mind as well as her body I might have taken on more responsibilities than I was prepared to discharge. It occurred to me that I must give some thought to the whole question of my relationship with Somi. With Perez alive I would have felt few qualms about abandoning her when we came to Europe, but now I was her guardian as well as her lover. Perhaps it would be better if I left her in Japon. She herself had expressed fears about quitting what was, in truth, her native land.

"Now you can start preparing for our journey to Nagasaki," she said, as if reading my mind. "I am certain that you are anxious to be on your way."

"When you are fully recovered," I murmured considerately. "Now do not tire yourself with too much chatter. I will return later."

And so I went on my way ruminating on what I

should do. But as is so often the case with me, I could think of no satisfactory solution to my problem and so thought of something else. In the following days this course of inaction was helped by Somi's unexpectedly slow recovery which presented me with the time to indulge a number of new interests.

Kushoni, although saying nothing to me, had obviously voiced abroad my prowess as rider and archer, and I found myself participating in one of their sports called Yabusame which necessitated galloping past a garland suspended from a pole and loosing an arrow through its middle. This I was passing good at and I noticed that the Daimyo's wife was not slow to single out my efforts for special plaudits. I felt I could have benefited from closer connection with the lady, but at the time there was little opportunity for it. Taisake, himself, I hardly saw because he was smitten with a mild fever and when not on his litter was frisking in the company of his transvestites, or Tobiko as I heard them called. Matsumota, also was a rare sight. Since I was mostly in the company of Kushoni this was understandable, but I was told that at any time he was a secretive fellow, retiring for long periods to pray and meditate. He also arranged flowers in bowls and vases which struck me as a strange thing for a man to do, but in this he was in no way exceptional for the Japons, as a race, are gluttons for embellishing nature.

Nearly every day Kushoni and I went out hawking, which I found good sport, but his greatest service was to teach me the essentials of sword play. I have already alluded to my dislike of the katanga, but under Kushoni's skilled tuition and rigid discipline I began to acquire some aptitude for the weapon.

It was at this time that I witnessed one of the most remarkable feats of swordsmanship that any man might imagine, let alone hope to see with his own eyes. On certain days in their ridiculous calendar, which was a thing quite imcomprehensible to me, being composed of the names of animals to signify hours, these lasting for two of ours, as well as the same animals indicating the years in cycles of twelve—I once tried to compute my imagined birth date in the Japonian manner and never completed the task—a market was held outside the palace and a variety of beggars and performers went through their paces. There was one fellow who impressed me particularly for he did tricks with a sword. He could stand atop a small platform balanced on a pole, and bending with the most supple movement, cut through the pole beneath him, without disturbing his perch. He was also able to split the thinnest bamboo shoot clean down the middle, and throw an apricot over his shoulder and cleave it in two before it touched the ground.

As I have said I was much impressed and once, as we watched with our hawks upon our wrists, I began to chide Kushoni as to whether he could emulate this performance. At first he took my joshing in good part, but it had been a frugal afternoon and I confess that slightly more sake had slipped down my throat than I had the mastery of. Imagining myself much more the intimate of Kushoni than sober judgment would have told me I was, I began to subject him to good-natured abuse, meaning none of it, for I could conceive of no man who might best him, but nevertheless being as provocative as I could.

Suddenly, he slid from his horse and drawing his sword stood before me barring my path. His teeth were gritted and his gaze venomous.

"Right," says he, "step down from your horse. If you would see tricks, you shall have them!"

I began to assure him that all my remarks had been in jest but he cut me short with an imperious wave of his hand and I dismounted quickly. He surveyed me coldly for a minute and then picked three small limes from a tree nearby. He sheathed his sword and stood before me weighing the limes in his hand. Then suddenly—one, two, three—they were thrown high in the air, and would have fallen behind him. "Arrhaa!!" With this self-enthusing shout he whipped out his sword, and whirling round, struck at each of the limes in turn; so fast that I saw nothing, but only felt the juice sting me across the face. He then beckoned me forward and indicated the six pieces, each a perfect half.

"You have a marvellous eye," says I respectfully.

Kushoni smiled grimly and beckoned me towards a small thicket of saplings. He selected one which stood a little away from its fellows, and coolly topped off its top, leaving a stump that stood three feet from the ground. The sapling was four inches thick so this was no mean feat, but what was to follow made me question my eyes. Hopping up on the stump Kushoni bent double and with a rhythmic swing sliced through it so that his perch toppled slightly. I began to murmur my plaudits but he told me irritably to be silent, and then, with a loud grunt repeated the blow further down, again cutting through the stump, so that he was now balanced on three logs. As I looked on in amazement, he adjusted his foothold and twisted down once more. This time, he knocked aside the middle log with the flat of his sword, but preserved such a miraculous balance that the log on which he stood dropped in its place with him still on it. I knew not what to do I was so stunned by the performance, and to this day I could totally accept the incredulity of anyone who had not witnessed the deed with his own eyes.

Kushoni stepped down with perhaps a suspicion of sweat on his brow and advanced towards me with that peculiar rolling gait of his that I knew presaged trouble.

"Now," said he, all heavy menace, "perhaps you would have me slice some blades of grass to satisfy you?"

I assured him that this was not necessary and that I was well content, but his sword darted before me like a lizard's tongue picking up flies, and I fell back against a tree very adequately silenced. Suddenly, his hand shot out and seizing a small blossom, he pressed it into one of my nostrils. My hands rose instinctively but at his warning bark dropped down obediently to my waist.

Kushoni stepped back and surveyed me grimly. "If you would smell again the like of that which adorns you you so prettily," said he, "I would advise you not to move."

His arm came back, and realising what he was about to do, I closed my eyes and near split my mouth in tight-lipped trepidation. The blade hissed through the air and my heart stopped to listen to it. The next instant the blossom was sent spinning from my nostrils and I could breath again. I opened my eyes to see Kushoni sheathing his sword, and gingerly felt my nose which seemed much as I had always remembered it.

At that moment relief was replaced by rage and I felt furious that any man should have humiliated me so. Shouting at him to defend himself I drew my sword and charged forward. I was inviting death, which is much against my nature, but I do have some pride and at that moment it got the better of my judgment, no doubt assisted by the sake. Kushoni waited until I had committed myself to a blow, and then, stepping inside my swing brought up the hilt of his sword to strike me squarely against the side of my head. My own weapon hurtled harmlessly over his shoulder. I went down heavy and helpless, waiting to be despatched but there was an almost commendatory look in his eyes as he gazed down at me. He fetched my sword and handed it to me.

"Impetuosity is a swordsman's worst defect," he said over his shoulder as he walked towards his horse, "you had best remember that when we resume our lessons tomorrow."

And that was that. The incident was never alluded to again and in no way was Kushoni's attitude to me affected by it. I think in fact he respected me the more for drawing a sword on him because, as I have mentioned before, the Japons despise a craven spirit.

It was about this time that I attempted to draw him out about himself, but with little success. I gathered that he had once been married and that his wife had died in tragic circumstances but these facts were revealed with enough reticence to suggest that further information would not be gladly given, and my recent experience was a warning against probing too deeply. Certainly his attitude towards women, or lack of it, suggested someone scarred by misfortune rather than a creature with the Daimyo's leanings.

As the days passed and Somi's condition improved visibly I realised I must face up to the question of our impending departure. To live so regally was something I could never aspire to again once I returned to Albion, and many the morn I lay abed feeling the silk beneath my chin and contemplating enrolling as a mercenary in the Daimyo's service. In this way too I might resolve my problem with Somi. But it seemed an act so irrevocable and—most important to a man of my temperament—foolhardy if the Satsumas were as powerful and predatory as they were labelled, that I did nothing about it. Of the Satsumas there was no word except that it was rumoured that Nomura had grievously injured his arm which, if true, accounted for his precipitous flight. Our escapade was talked of throughout the Kingdom and did much to enhance the respect in which I was held and hence occasion my impulse to stay.

It was ten days after we had returned with the potion that two events took place which were to affect my future plans materially. The first was when two emissaries arrived from Shimazu, the Daimyo of the Satsumas. With banners streaming they spurred through the castle gates and galloped to the palace, presenting as haughty an appearance as they could muster. Though not at the audience I soon learned that they brought with them a missive from their master which challenged the Figos to a Dakyu match and offered them safe conduct to the Satsumas Kingdom where the match would take place. Of this game I will speak later; suffice it at this moment to say that it is played by a number of men on horseback.

The emissaries were entertained with cha and hypocrisy whilst it was decided that the challenge must be accepted since to refuse would be more abject than the risk of defeat. I was surprised that two Kingdoms on the brink of total war could consider the idea of playing games, but such is the Japonian temperament that no man should be amazed at anything they do.

The second formative incident occurred one day after I had taken my bath. It so happened that on this occasion I had also taken one of the bath maidens

and was comfortably settled aboard her broad little
hips when Somi slid back the door of my chamber.
She had chosen that moment to surprise me with her
first faltering steps but I think the element of surprise
was fairly evenly distributed between the three of us
and she retired wailing piteously. It occurred to me, as
I coolly finished the job in hand, that this glimpse of
my true nature might well serve to make me a less
desirable property in her eyes and that it would be in
my interest to provide her with more evidence of my
unsuitability as a spouse. I was considering this excellent plan a few hours later when Kushoni paid an urgent visit to my chamber. He informed me that six
riders were required for the Dakyu team and that
with Matsumota sick, they required a rider of his stature as a replacement. Would I make myself available?
Willingly, said I, for it occurred to me that to absent
myself so soon after slighting her would give Somi
further reason to become disenchanted.

It was to this end that I pulled on my clothes and
was soon bound for Satsuma. Our retinue was large,
too large thought Kushoni, and in its midst sat Taisake
resplendent in a massive palanquin, or sedan chair,
carried by horses. To the rhythmic beat of drum and
gong the procession pursued its stately path through
the rice fields and it was not until nightfall of the same
day that we had crossed the hills and dropped down
towards the castle of the Satsumas. This had a ram-
part, two moats and two walls, one of stone, and so
was to the naked eye, the superior of the Figos'.
Torches blazed from every wall and there were vast
numbers of armed men guarding each access point.
Perhaps they were all posted for our benefit, but I
was impressed. My prime concern was to keep a wary
eye open for Nomura whom I expected to emerge from

the shadows at every second, but there was no sign of him and we were shown to our quarters without incident. These were no whit inferior to what I had enjoyed at Figo, but unequipped with female company which was perhaps a good thing if I was expected to give my all to the Dakyu match the following day.

The field of play was like a military parade ground and might well have been one for there were many soldiers amongst the crowd surrounding it. There were high banks on three sides and these were flanked by a variety of gaily coloured standards, all deeper than they were wide as is the Japonian custom. We were all accoutred in the same style wearing wide brimmed hats which sat very high on the head—very high on mine—and were of a uniform redness. At one end of this terrain stood an upright wooden fence with a hole in it about the size of a pumpkin, ten feet from the ground. Another much lower fence stood eighteen feet in front of it. The game, inevitably, was complicated, but in essence it required propelling a number of balls through the hole in the fence by means of a bamboo pole with a small net fastened to the end of it. Each team had twelve balls of its own to see away and once these had been dispatched a further ball was thrown into the arena which both teams competed for. The winning team was that which first goaled all its twelve balls and then the extra one.

Needless to say, there was no restriction on preventing the other team scoring, and I noticed, even in a couple of practice games, that the contest had a tendency towards roughness. My role, in fact, was a defensive one because I found it extremely difficult to net the ball and quite impossible to flick it into the goal. The greater the motion I engendered the more precipitous was the ball's descent to the ground.

I was quite content in this position because the physical hurly burly was not indistinguishable from the football matches in which I had played as a boy.

After our game little mounts had kicked their heels for a while the Satsumas took the field to resounding cheers and the banging of gongs. Conspicuous amongst them was Nomura on a nag as broad as he was wide which was no mean compliment to its girth. Obviously his arm must be recovered.

They made obeissance to their Daimyo as we did to Taisake who sat stiffly, or as stiffly as his physique would allow, beside him, and took up a position in the centre of the field. We joined them and bowed to each other without a trace of emotion passing across our faces and then retired to form up in line abreast at the end of the field.

A silence came over the crowd and I must confess to a feeling of excitement as the great moment came closer. The horses seemed to sense it too and snorted and pawed beneath us. I looked at Nomura who was gazing steadfastly to the front and then at Kushoni who was similarly preoccupied. Only Taisake's wife seemed to have eyes for me and though she was some distance away I read a smile on her face. I could have looked longer but my attention was attracted by a lonely figure stalking imperiously to the centre of the terrain. It was one of Shimazu's samurai wearing full armour and bearing a small wicker basket. A gong sounded, the basket was upturned, and two score of red and white balls scurried across the ground. The contest was on.

As instructed I galloped hard for the low fencing in front of the goal but I was left behind in the headlong rush for the balls. The skill of some of the riders was quite remarkable for three of them each picked up a

ball at full gallop and had shied for the goal before
I was within twenty yards of them. Doubly distress-
ing was the fact that two of them were Satsumas
and successful, whilst our man missed. I joined the
scrimmage in front of the goal and lunged hard into
another Satsuma who was setting himself to score. He
cursed and flung out a fist which struck me across the
bridge of the nose making my eyes water. Bastard!
Fortunately retribution was at hand as I had thought-
fully sharpened the handle of my bamboo for just
such an eventuality. A jab in the withers and his mount
had shot him over the fence like a pail of slops. I
wheeled about and looked for new challenges. Nomura
was wielding his net like a whip and riding down
friend and foe alike but he was on the other side of
the hurly burly. Kushoni swept past, rose in the saddle,
and coolly flicked a goal without checking his pony's
stride. Another Satsuma was beside me and I struck at
his net so the ball dropped over the edge of the fence.

It was then that I noticed how the host team was
favoured. If one of our balls went out of play there
was hardly a move towards it but no sooner had the
Satsumas been forced into error than a servant near
ruptured himself to return the ball, if not actually
place it in a proferred net. Realising that this might be
the end for us I galloped away to where Taisake's
squires attended upon their master and shouted at the
mincing fools to run and redress the balance. Turning
back I could see that we were already in a parlous
state. Soldiers were stationed behind the goal to raise
a standard of the appropriate colour each time a score
was made. There were six white raised and but three
red. It was also obvious that Kushoni was the pillar of
our team and the rest of them little better than I.
Nomura needed three men to hold him in partial check

and it was here that I regretfully decided to apply
myself, believing, without much conviction, that he
could hardly slaughter me under a flag of truce. I
went for him gamely, but when I was at close quarters he unleashed such a jab with his elbow that it
knocked me clean off my horse. The Satsumas shouted
and jeered and I felt a fool, until I suddenly saw a
white ball lying nearby unattended. I glanced round
quickly and, with everybody seemingly engaged elsewhere, swept it under my robe. My mount stood by
obediently and I charged back into the fray resolved
to revenge myself on Nomura. The flags now stood at
nine to five in favour of the Satsumas but with the ball
in my robe I felt less alarmed. As I came through the
horde Nomura was before me balanced for a shot.
Quick as an Arab's cock I had my stick reversed and
sunk the shaft into his horse's rump. The beast rose upwards, but not so far as Nomura, who must have
made the birds envious before he hit the ground. With
him out of action we rallied and three more shots
found their mark. Nine eight to the Satsumas. By now
the horses were wild eyed and their mouths lathered
with blood and sweat. They were brave little brutes
and well-disciplined but the constant wheeling demanded of them and the battering they were exposed
to was beginning to take its toll. Much the same could
be said of the riders whose snorts and honks were now
almost louder than their mounts'. With Nomura on
the ground I set to trying to keep his nag away from
him, but then a new thought occurred to me. Coming
close to the creature I leaned down and swiftly loosed
its girth. This accomplished I let it find its master, who,
all eagerness to resume the contest, seized the saddle
like a drowning man and took the most awful tumble
as he attempted to vault into it. My God! His curses

would have warped unborn children and I spurred into the fray to be away from him. Now it was ten all and I felt almost secure. Only two more goals and the clinching ball would be introduced for us to secure and seal the match. The Satsumas could never win whilst their twelfth ball nestled against my chest.

It was at this moment that base treachery was introduced into the game. As we jostled against the fence a Figo ball dropped over. All was confusion but I saw a Satsuma groom secrete it and return a white ball into play. I attempted to shout out to our retainers but was knocked aside and by the time I had pulled round it was to see the rascal stealing away from the arena. Even as I struggled to compose a course of action a white ball winged through the board and the Satsumas were in possession of a twelfth.

It is in such moments of desperate peril that the natural resourcefulness of an Englishman is supposed to be seen to best advantage and I was pleased to find that this was the case with me. If no red ball was available then I would have to make one. Casting about for a spur-gouged flank I found one and forced the nag hard against the fence. In this position I extracted the white ball and rubbed it against the beast's bloodsodden side until it was a passable red. A roar from the crowd told me I was not a moment too soon for the Satsumas had goaled their twelfth ball. No sooner was it through the opening than a yellow ball came sailing into the arena. I cunningly let my ball slip to Kushoni who was standing slightly apart from the hurly burly and in an instant he had swept it up and flicked it through the opening. Twelve: twelve. Now both sides were free to contest the yellow ball and battle was really joined.

When competing for twelve balls there was some

room for personal manoeuvre but now the twelve riders converged like carp nibbling a piece of bread. Any
man who could sweep up the ball soon had it dashed
from his grasp and there was no opportunity to pass
to a team mate. It was in this situation that Nomura
was most dangerous both because of his physical
strength and unflagging zeal. It always seemed likely
that he might break clear especially as his team mates
were lasting the pace better than our brave but un-
trained band. Inexorably the Satsumas held possession
and drove towards the goal holding off those who challenged their ball carrier. The crowd, sensing victory,
bayed their delight and my heart fell. We had come
so near and now the tourney seemed to be slipping
away from us.

"We must disrupt them," panted Kushoni into my
ear, "come, fall back and we will charge at them."
I nodded for I could not find the strength to speak and
we peeled off the struggling phalanx and drew back
about forty paces. A word from Kushoni and our gal-
lant mounts sprang forward and launched themselves
at the six Satsumas. Their outriders swung at us with
their nets but we brushed them aside like flies and exploded into their midst. Immediately all was confusion. Men, horses, shouts, blows. I lashed about me
with the best of them and noted that the marksman's
net was empty. Where was the ball? I gazed about me.
Nothing. And then—a flash of yellow beneath me. I
scraped my net along the ground and—miracle—I had
it! But for how long?

Our impetus had taken Kushoni and myself free of
the pack, but now as one man the Satsumas were in
pursuit. I raced for the goal with Kushoni by my side
to lend support, but Nomura burst between us and
rode me out towards the mound, with the crowd shout-

ing for my blood. I struggled to veer round but my
teammates had been left behind and sheer weight of
numbers forced me further away from the goal. Blows
hurled down about my shoulders and it was almost a
relief when my horse stumbled and the two of us were
sent sprawling in a cloud of dust. The crowd whooped
and the Satsumas cast about for the ball. For my part
I looked beyond them all to where the lone figure of
Kushoni rode unchallenged to the goal and rose in
the saddle. It was at this moment that the crowd's
roar died away to silence and even the Satsuma riders,
sensing that something was amiss, pulled up their eyes.
In one easy movement Kushoni flexed his arm and
the yellow ball flew clean and sweet through the centre
of the hole.

If it had not been common knowledge that I had
changed nets with Kushoni, it was then. I heard
Taisake's delighted chuckle one second before Nomura's roar of rage. Seizing his net like a lance he hurled
it at my head hard enough to have clove it in two had
he made contact, and screamed that he had been
cheated. I was exhilirated and our modest band of
supporters cast themselves into each other arms in a
delirium of joy. Our team, all being of the samurai
class, was not wont to such excesses, but their satisfaction was scarcely less demonstrative.

Quite what took place after the contest is, I fear, obscured in a mist of sake but I recall being under no
constraint to remain in the Satsuma capital, and leaving under a hail of stones and abuse from the multitude, who had taken their defeat in very bad part. My
companions were in rare good spirits and we made
our way to a port which stood on the boundary of the
two kingdoms and was under the control of neither.
Here I was promised an entertainment and I remem-

bered feeling that the remedial pressure of a woman's loins against my own would do much to take my mind off my aching limbs. However, two things conspired to deny me complete satisfaction. The sake already alluded to and the initial nature of the entertainment.

When we set foot upon the broad verandah of the house there were girls in plenty and I believed myself in a high-class brothel. Excellent, thought I, and prepared to loose my loin cloth but with untoward ceremony we were ushered into a long low room, all screens and lanterns, and I espied the dreaded tea pot boiling away merrily in a corner. In no time we were on our haunches and being served by a bevy of overdressed maids with faces white as flour. This effect was especially hideous on those that had black teeth—a fashion usually followed by married ladies of breeding. Seeing them I thought immediately of Taisake's wife and wished that I could be lying with her—a thought that any of my loyal fellows would probably have slit his belly rather than entertain. The tea ceremony dragged on with an excess of mannered conversation on all sides, so that I was nearly asleep before a flurry of movement made me perk up. It was wasted motion because we were then entertained by a troupe of actresses who performed what I was told was a traditional piece. This attained a new apogee of tedium as far as I was concerned and my eyes were soon firmly closed, a facility which my ears envied. Music was much in evidence in the play and in this department the Japons are singularly lacking. A stringed instrument called a samisen was plucked like a chicken and the notes made a horrible discord which set my teeth on edge.

At last it was over, but by this time I had consumed

another flask of sake and would have been better left to sleep than led away by a couple of wenches as I was.

I am loath to report what happened next for it did little to enlarge my reputation, but I imagine that nearly every man has experienced the same problem at one time or another, so I will not shirk it. The circumstances, at least, are worth recording.

As I have intimated we were each led away to a separate chamber and even in my fuddled condition I noted that two girls attended each man. 'Little butterfly' and 'Brightness of the flowers' were the names of mine as I recall it. I was soon to learn that one was the assistant of the other and actually introduced the member as if mating a stallion. I fear that, carrying so much sake as I did, this service was one I was in frequent need of. Another of the maid's chores was to stand by with a supply of paper tissues which were applied whenever they were needed. My whore had so many clothes on that I had to unroll her like a bandage and it was a fact that her breasts were so firmly thrust into her chest that she was the only woman I have seen with recessed nipples. She tried gamely enough to arouse me but my heart was not in it—with the inevitable result that nothing else was. Still, neither of them would give up, and mirrors were erected so that I might titillate myself by an examination of our conjoined privy parts. When this brought no result scrolls were produced which when unravelled showed a multitude of sexual interchanges obviously intended to stimulate the appetite. Unfortunately they had the opposite effect on me for the sight of mighty members breaking through doors only served to make mine droop more shamefully. One thing that intrigued me about these shunga—as I afterwards learned they were called—was that the greater the degree of sexual passion depicted, the more prevalent were the paper tissues. Obviously when they covered the floor like rose petals this signified a successful copulation.

I think my memory is my friend when it does not recall how my participation in the evening ended. Suffice it to say that I have only a clear recollection of being shaken awake by my fellows who were, by now, in no better shape than me. Weaving an unsteady course to the entrance we struggled onto our mounts and acknowledged the obeissances of the whores. I vomited immediately, which made me feel much better, and we struck out for home.

CHAPTER 11

THE SMOKE COULD BE SEEN FOR MILES. AT FIRST IT seemed like a cloud permanently anchored above the castle but as we drew nearer its true origins were unmistakable. Part of the wall was scorched and black and behind it a thick column of smoke rose steadily into the air.

In the general alarm my thoughts sped to Somi and by this very action alarmed me still further. Could my resolve to discard her be serious when the possibility of her death caused me so much concern? Could it be that I actually—I tried to confront my outraged sensibilities with the word—loved her?

We spurred our tired mounts forward and were within hailing distance of the castle when the gates opened and disgorged two horsemen who rode out to meet us. They were grimy and bloodstained and so exhausted as to be hardly able to gasp out their story.

It appeared that on the day after our departure there had been a market outside the castle walls. As was the custom, traders had come from all parts of Figo and a group of Satsumas had taken advantage of the hustle and bustle around the rear gate to steal through it in ones and twos without being challenged. Once inside they had formed together and, at a signal, drawn their weapons and charged for the keep, cut-

ting down everyone in their path. The muskets had
obviously been their prize but luckily the narrow entrance to the building had defied even a charge of
gunpowder and the raiders had fallen back on to the
royal kitchens and servants' quarters. There a furious
battle to the death took place in which the Satsumas
had evidently set fire to the building they were defending. Whether this was to create a diversion, or, as
it seemed likely to any student of the Japonian nature,
to sell their lives as dearly as possible, was not completely clear. It was only reported that when the buildings were well ablaze the Satsumas had burst out and
fought to the last man without asking for quarter.

Their downfall had not been occasioned without
great loss, as we saw when we entered the courtyard.
Two piles of bodies awaited burial and it was noticed
that some of the Figos who had perished were little
more than children—boys who had been passing and
snatched up a weapon perhaps. I looked with some
anxiety at the corpses in case I caught a glimpse of
Somi's fair form, and asked of her whereabouts from
the first servant I recognised. The man shrugged his
shoulders and said that for all he knew she was in
her chamber, so that was where I went with all speed.

To my alarm the room was empty save for a lady
in waiting I had not seen before, standing by the window.

"Where is the lady Somi? Has she been spared from
injury?"

"Your concern surprises me." The voice was cool and
well known to me.

"Somi!" The creature turned round and it was in-
deed she. But I would hardly have recognised her.
She was dressed entirely according to the fashion of a
Japonian lady of breeding and her hair, which had

been so fine when laying about her shoulders, was now piled up upon her head and beset with combs and pins. Her face was powder white and it seemed that she had made some attempt to pluck her eyebrows.

"Thank God you are alive," said I. "But what is the meaning of this attire?"

"The meaning is quite simple. I have decided that I am a Japon and that believing this I should adopt the ways of my countrywomen."

So Somi had thrown in her lot with the nippons. I should have been delighted for it was the fruition of all my recent plans, but of course, in my contrary way, I now became determined that I should not lose her.

"I wish I could say that I found you a mite as appealing in those robes as I was wont to do," I said.

"Your interest is touching but I hardly find it plausible."

"Faith, but you treat me badly. Did I seem uncaring when I entered your chamber?"

"Speak not of treating badly. First I find you dallying with some strumpet and then you go away without leaving me so much as a word."

"Think nothing of it. It was but my base appetite—and poorly fed in your absence. I only behaved so because your more pleasing person was denied me. As for my going as I did, I was ashamed of my conduct and could think of no mending words."

I sensed that she was weakening and laid my hands gently on her shoulders but she brushed them aside.

"Do not think to move me with your honeyed lies. If you could treat me like this in my own country what hope is there for me in England?" True words which I was hard put to answer, so I ignored the question.

"Why do you speak of 'my country?' Have I not

told you before that you are not a Japon? You do not look like them, or behave like them. Even in those clothes, with all the effort you have made you cannot disguise yourself. You are Somi and nothing else—My Somi. . . ."

So saying I tilted back her downcast head and kissed her gently on the lips withdrawing the combs from her hair as I did so. I must say it was well done and would have been better so, had not my white-whiskered dotard come panting in, saying that Taisake wanted me.

These were ominous words at any time, knowing that gentleman's propensities, and doubly so just as I was beginning to bend Somi to my purpose. It appeared that Matsumota had been summoned to explain his conduct at the time of the Satsuma attack and for some reason my presence was required at their confrontation. I bade farewell to Somi, who was now halfway returned to her earlier petulance and made my way to the conferring chamber.

Taisake and Kushoni were already squatting on the dais and the former waved me to a place beside him. I was surprised that I should be shown such favour but the reason for my presence was soon made clear.

"I have summoned you," says Taisake, "because I believe you are a cunning fellow who has our interests at heart. Do not look so surprised, the emotion does not suit your face. Any man who had seen you playing Dakyu could be witness to your guile."

I averted my eyes modestly.

"Also," he continued, "since you will soon be leaving us you can carry the secret of what takes place at this meeting with you. Your opinion will be impartial and your departure will prove that it was not given in the hope of future favour."

My respectfully lowered head was no sooner raised than Matsumota had strode into the room. He was scowling, which was not unusual in my experience of him, and crossed the room in great strides before sinking gracefully to his knees before the dais. As before I was stuck by the risible contrast between his own great height and that of the average Japon. He was as tall and supple as one of their bows.

"Allow my unworthy and undistinguished self the privilege of congratulating your Lordship on his great victory," he began in typical courtier fashion but Taisake cut him short with an admonishing wave of the hand.

"We may be in the mood to receive your tributes later. For now we would know what part you played in the defence of our castle against the Satsumas."

"Unfortunately, none my lord."

"How come?"

"It has been my practice, of late as you know, to spend much time in meditation, and on the day of the attack I was praying for your victory at the shrine of Kebuki."

"Most praiseworthy. But why so far afield? The castle is well equipped with places of worship."

"I am a man of simple tastes my liege. I find that my ascetic spirit is best served in humble surroundings."

Kushoni snorted. "Yet you were left to conduct the defence of your master's property. How did you imagine that this might be achieved from a distance of two leagues?"

"The castle was secure. I had no reason to suspect treason."

"The position you hold demands that you suspect everything and everyone."

"I believed that I had uncovered the traitor. I as-

sure you that after this incident I will be more ruthless in my surveillance." Here he granted me a piercing look which bore no good will.

"That is an assurance I have heard before," said
Taisake, "and I command that this time no man is
executed without my express consent. It seems to me
that perhaps an innocent man may have perished."

"He was guilty my lord, have no fear of it, I heard
him confess with my own ears."

"There are ways of making a man confess to anything," said Kushoni, "and I believe that Matsumota
knows all of them."

"I must protest, my lord," said Matsumota, becoming agitated. "Am I being accused, and if so, of what?
I have discovered one traitor. Am I to be blamed for
not having seized all his accomplices? What have
these gentlemen achieved, and why should they be
free from the imputations that are levelled at me. This
European—" he turned to me and I saw his teeth—
"this creature from another world who now nestles
close to your breast like a new born babe. He brings
the muskets to our land. He mingles with the pirates
and the Satsumas. Why does no one think of accusing
him? Why should I who have always been a faithful
servant of your majesty, albeit an unworthy one, come
under suspicion."

"Silence!" snarled Kushoni. "To accuse the Englishman is to point a finger at me. He is my friend and
to dispute with him invites the intervention of my
sword."

"Brave words," sneered Matsumota. "I might expect
two dogs to bark with the same voice. One steals whilst
the other watches for the master's return."

Kushoni rose to his feet. "By Buddha, you have
tried my patience too far. One of us will die 'eer we

have taken twenty paces from this hall, or I am not Kushoni, unworthy son of Maniko, governor of Banduki Province."

"Best ask your mother to confirm your lineage," responded Matsumota. "I fancy she may have a surprise for you."

At this insult I expected blood to flow for Kushoni's features contracted like a fist and he took a step towards Matsumota which as a guarantee of his intentions would have made any apothecary reach for his bandages, but, as at our previous confrontation, Taisake's intervention was swift.

"Be seated, both of you," he shouted. "My judgment is what matters and it is made on facts, not conjecture. You, Matsumota, were absent from your post at time of need and thus responsible for the demise of numerous of our subjects. You know the penalty for a samurai who, in error, slays one of his own company. That man shall lose a finger from his right hand and this is my judgment on you."

"But my liege—"

"Silence! How dare you raise your voice to me. One more word and your head will be on a stake outside my bed chamber. Adam, enact my sentence."

"Me?" I was horrified. I am nothing loath to wield a sword in battle but to lop off a man's limb in cold blood filled me with repugnance.

"My lord, I—I—"

"Proceed! Or I will summon an executioner and set him a two-fold task."

There was nothing for it so I gritted my teeth and accepted the wakizashi which was thrust into my hand by an attendant who emerged wraith-like from the shadows. Matsumota, with a lack of concern which I envied, extended his right hand and laid the fingers nearest to the smallest on the edge of the low table before me. To add to my discomfort he looked at me straight between the eyes and smiled. It was a smile that would have dried up the milk in a mother's breast. I turned my glance away and held my arm above the table conscious that it was shaking. I thought of appealing to Kushoni but knew that it was worthless. The sweat was bursting from my forehead and my eyes were blinking. Now!

My arm fell and the finger hopped across the table pursued by a pool of blood. Matsumota did not move his hand but continued to look at me with an expression that presaged more bloodshed. I laid the sword down beside me and watched it taken away. The severed finger seemed already to be turning blue but perhaps it was the work of my imagination or the colour of the table.

"Now you may leave us," said Taisake coldly, "and take your property with you."

"Thank you my liege but I have no need—"

"Take it!"

Matsumota inclined his head and picking up the finger stalked from the chamber.

"I think you are still too kind to him. If it were me I would have his head sitting on that table. You will live to rue your charity, mark my words."

"The man has behaved foolishly but I cannot conceive that any of my samurai bear me ill-will. The very thought is painful to me."

"Painful or not, my lord, you must examine the facts. There have been many cases where the sacred fielty that exists between a samurai and his Daimyo has been broken."

"But not in my own experience. Say no more of it, your words wound me. I accept that your intentions are good but I believe that your opinion is coloured by your personal feelings for this man and that you will never concede his merits."

"My lord—"

"I said 'no more.' Let me not speak again upon the matter."

Kushoni scowled and then grimaced as if to admit defeat. He was pulling himself to his feet when one of the household servants arrived considerably flustered.

"There is an emissary outside from the lord Ieyasu," said he. "He says that he has words to impart to you."

"Let him be brought in forthwith," said Taisake. "I'll warrant he does not bring fond greetings from his master."

"More like an increase in tribute," groaned Kushoni. "It becomes more impossible each day to wring a tael from the peasantry. Their crops are mortgaged three years ahead."

"Ieyasu is the ruler of this country is he not?" I asked.

Kushoni snorted again. "He would have it so if he could. No, by treachery and force of arms he has brought many kingdoms beneath his thrall and lords it over us in Edo. The Satsumas make war on us with his blessing. Surely you know of this?"

"I have heard you speak of it."

"Silence, both of you," snapped Taisake. "I do not want your prattle borne to Ieyasu's ears. We suffer badly enough in that quarter as it is."

It was at this point that the emissary was ushered in. He was a dashing fellow, well accoutred in a heavy patterned material that enveloped him like a sheet of lightning. A white band was worn around his forehead bearing the device of a black scorpion. He was of a haughty demeanour and extended a scroll to Taisake with the minimum of deference, although his words dripped from his lips like honey in typical Japonian fashion.

"My master, the great Ieyasu, has placed in my unworthy hands this missive which he bids me present to you with his best wishes and hopes for a long and happy life, blessed with a plenitude of children each as gifted and brave as its father."

"Your master does me too much kindness. I reciprocate his wishes and beg you to take him shortly a humble gift as a heartfelt but inadequate symbol of my respect." Taisake continued to look at the emissary indulgently. "It is fitting," he continued, "that the messenger of one so mighty should himself be one of nature's favourites."

At these words I was glad to see the emissary evince some of the discomfiture I had experienced in the past. Really, I believe that Taisake was a persistent enough pederast to win the respect of even my comrades on the Mace. I was fortunate that fate had kept me out of his clutches. With one more admiring look at the emissary he broke the seal on the bamboo scroll and unrolled it. All was silence for a moment and then he sucked in his breath sharply.

"We go to Edo," he said.

"Edo?" Kushoni's voice was incredulous. "Why should we go there?"

The emissary was only too ready to supply the answer to this question, albeit a lengthy one.

"My master, the great and incomparable Ieyasu had deemed it in the interests of all who dwell upon these islands that he should assume the title of Shogun. This he will do at Edo before a score of days have passed. He asks all those who number themselves amongst his friends to attend upon this happy occasion and will know them when he sees them."

"This invitation is extended to all Daimyos?"

"To each and every one of them throughout the length and breadth of the sixty-six kingdoms. One of my comrades is even now attending upon the Lord Shimazu of Satsuma. I think you know of him."

"Almost too well," said Taisake. "You may have noted the condition of our castle?"

"Certainly, my lord. But I thought it bore witness to some unhappy accident."

"I fear not. Still, we must not subject your noble ears to the tedium of parochial disputations. Let us entertain you 'eer you bear our acceptance to your mighty and most beloved master."

And so the evening descended into a mighty carousal from which I woke with my head ringing and the insides of my mouth dry as baked dung. With the departure of the Figos imminent the time was also ripe for me to take my leave and I realised that I must resolve the question of whether Somi went with me. Being a mere woman she had not qualified for a place at the banquet and so the next morning as soon as I could place one faltering foot before the other, I took my fuddled head to her chamber. Exactly what was said my condition precluded me from remembering but I do recall the substance of her final words.

"Very well," she snapped, tossing back her hair which had now settled down to something of its old glory, "I will accompany you, but with the conviction that I am a fool and offending against everything that my conscience and intuition tell me to be right. An amiable rogue you may be, but if I had ever believed your ways to be a substitute for the discipline forced upon me by my upbringing—I sorely deceived myself. I will come with you because there are still questions which I wish to answer about myself and because I believe that their solution may lie in the world beyond these shores. Do not think that a repetition of your recent behaviour will escape unanswered. You will find me a good learner and not prepared to entertain your knavish tricks without reply."

She spoke with spirit and I think I admired her then as much as I had ever done. Certainly, I was convinced that whatever befell her she would not be happy in Japon. She did not possess the subservient temperament that was so much a feature of their women.

I sought out Taisake and thanked him as profusely as I was able for his hospitality. He seemed preoccupied with plans for his journey and giving my arm one last intimate squeeze granted me the use of two horses for the trip to Nagasaki, and returned to selecting the material for the cushions in his new palanquin.

Everywhere I went there were men polishing harness and refurbishing equipment and it was rumoured that the Daimyo's entourage would include upward of a thousand men. This seemed to me to be folly, bearing in mind the status of the Figos, but it was generally reckoned that the Satsumas would take even more men and thus be at no advantage in terms of the garrisons left behind.

Kushoni I found in the ornamental gardens flicking idly at the cherry blossom with his katanga.

"I came to bid you farewell," says I.

Kushoni sheathed his sword and coming towards me placed an arm on either side of my shoulders.

"It will take me time to adjust to life without my squire," said he. "If you had been with us longer I could have made a worthy Samurai of you."

"Or a worthy corpse. And that thought alone makes it easier for me to take my leave of you. My gratitude

for all that you have done for Somi and myself. I am
certain that Taisake could not wish for a more gal-
lant champion."

"My thanks to you also. I do not forget the debt I
owe you for saving my life. In fact I ask you to take
this, both as a symbol of my friendship and of my gratitude."

And with this he drew his sheathed sword from his
belt and held it out to me. I knew that the weapon
was like a child to him and tried to hold back saying,
quite truthfully, that my prowess was not worthy of it,
but he would brook no denial and thrust it into my
hands. It was certainly a beautifully balanced weapon,
and, though not finely worked, beyond a sharkskin covered hilt, worth a small fortune—the equivalent of five
hundred English pounds was a figure I had heard
mentioned. Eventually I took it and after a few more
niceties we bowed respectfully to each other and I
went to find if Somi was ready to leave. Beneath all
the stilted words lay a very genuine regard for the man
and a wish that I had the language and the opportunity to express it. But farewells, in my experience, are
always stumbling, mumbling occasions, even between
two scholars, and so I went on my way sad but re-
signed.

The sight of Somi was cheering. In my absence she
had changed her vestments and there was a bloom on
her like fruit ripe for the plucking. All light and trim
with sparkling eyes and her neat little body lending
an eye-catching outline to her kimono. I was glad that
she had thought better of her slavish imitation of Japonian dress for, with the exception of bath girls and
those who toil in the rice fields, the female Nippons
wrap themselves up far too much for my liking and
seem quite ashamed of their breasts, if they have any

at all. Perhaps this is because they are milk containers, as the Japons abhor the stuff and probably do not like to be reminded that they once existed on nothing else.

To reach Nagasaki it was quicker to ride back towards Satsuma and hire a boat at the open port I had visited on my return from the Dakyu match. This being due to the particular configuration of the coast which on a map looked as if a multitude of mice had been gnawing at the shore line. The small armada of Figos was assembling at a point not far distant and as we took a final leave of the castle the Daimyo's retinue was being brought into file. They made a handsome spectacle in their multicoloured vestments. Lancers on horseback with long-flowing pennants billowing behind. Infantry, with villainous looking pikes and halberds. Musicians with fifes and drums so large that they obscured the man behind them, and seemed to be proceeding on their own legs. The Daimyo's palanquin, borne between four horses, and looking like a house designed by God and woven in gold thread by tiny birds. It was a brave sight to make me almost sorry I was not riding with them. Almost.

Somi and I rode out and the exuberant beating of the gongs followed us across the rice fields until it was almost fainter than the image of the castle on the skyline.

It was dusk by the time we reached the port and having been in the saddle all day, I thought it best that we found somewhere to stay the night, putting off our search for a vessel until the morn. This decision was also prompted by a desire to find Somi beneath me, rather than a horse. An entertainment which I felt might be less easily and pleasantly effected on the deck of some malodorous fishing junk. How I would fare in this resolve I was not certain, as Somi's manner had been somewhat less than affectionate on the journey.

"I hope you will grant me the indulgence of a separate chamber," said she tartly as we approached a pleasing lakeside inn on the edge of the town.

"It had not been in my purse's mind to do so," said I, "I have no conception of your own resources but mine do not extend to the provision of more than one room."

"A pity, for I had quite set my heart on a night of slumber uninterrupted by your snores."

"Since when have you had occasion to endure my snores?" I said showing her the savage grandeur of my profile.

"For myself, never. But I have heard the bath girls chattering, and they say that you are much prone in that direction," she paused, "perhaps too much."

I held myself in check with difficulty. "I am certain," I said icily, "that you have within you somewhere, the means to spare yourself from that discomfort."

"I know not to what you allude. Let me remind you of my earlier words. I am not here as some bauble of your lust and I have abandoned all hope of finding in you some code which might guide my own existence. Therefore—and please heed my words—you are here solely as my guardian and protector. And I have scant confidence in you in that rôle, let alone any other."

"You have the fault of all your sex that you burden yourself with too many words for your wit to bear."

"And your faults are so legion that there is nothing singular about them—ah!"

The last exclamation was occassioned by my toe sinking a couple of inches into her rump as I put the full weight of my foot behind it. She was still clucking

like an outraged hen as the door of our room was slid
open and we were ushered in. It was a pleasing enough
chamber but having ordered some food I ignored
Somi's squawks and strode out on to the balcony.

There was a small fishing vessel on the lake and
I noticed with increasing interest that it was full of
birds—shags and cormorants—who seemed to dive
for fish and then return to the boat. I watched them
for a while before realising that the birds were secured
by a string, and that another was fastened round their
throats to prevent them from swallowing their catch.
I found later that this mode of fishing was much practised in Japon, especially at night, by lamplight, with
the unfortunate birds occasionally allowed to enjoy
one of their prizes.

When I returned inside, food had been brought and
Somi sat on her haunches before it. The sight of her
made me bite my lips for she wore a simple dress cut
deep between the breasts with her silken hair flowing
over her shoulder to reach her waist. She did not
meet my eye but sat back all sulky and irresistible. I
slunk to her side, contrite, and attempted to nibble
her cheek but she brushed me aside having the effrontery to say that I stank like a pig. There was a fresh
bloom on her skin bred from washing and so I took the
hint and stripped and sluiced myself down with a
pitcher of water no doubt provided for that purpose.
This done I settled down before her, naked, excusing
my condition with the information that I had no other
clothing than that which she had taken exception to.
This statement she ignored and, preserving her dis-
dain, picked at her food whilst I sought to ruffle her
composure with remarks calculated to make her smile.
My object was achieved in a way I had not intended,
for my enthusiasm for her person became so intense

that it reared above the table and threw her into a fit
of charming giggles. Not slow to follow up his breach
in her defences I took myself across the table and as
our mouths met, and hers repaid my pressure with a
vengeance, I savoured the exquisite anticipation of
what was to come. Overflooding with ardour I let my
lips stray down her stomach and sent them to browse
amongst the softer pastures of her thighs. This action
turned her into a wild beast and though I would have
stayed longer her urgent fingers implored me up and
into her. I felt my feet brushing the food from the
table and heard the clatter of platters but I cared not,
for as one appetite was being denied so another was
achieving satisfaction. Somi beneath me was in a
frenzy and I felt like a man in a small craft riding out
a dangerous sea. Writhing, groaning, moaning, tearing, wrenching, scratching, she struggled as if striving
to capsize me; but I pinned her down and finding a
rhythm in our motion, attacked her with it until she
let out a scream, composed of pleasure and surprise,
and fell back gasping. I was not in much of a mood
for speech either at that moment, so we lay together
panting and listening to our hearts pounding like
drums.

It was a sound that soon had company for a door
slid back in the chamber next to ours and we could hear
a number of people entering. Japanian walls are not of
the thickest and my first reaction was one of irritation.
My second was of fear because the rasping voice I
heard demanding sake was well known to me. Nomura! The fellow dogged my footsteps like a shadow.
Somi's recognition was less immediate but when the
ogre spoke again her exclamation of terror forced me
to put a hand over her mouth.

"And bring three women," he bellowed, "clean ones,

not your usual crutch-weeping hags. One scab and I'll have their bellies open."

To this remark one of his companions replied in an even coarser vein and they all set to splitting their sides with laughter. Nomura's laugh was easily recognisable for it sounded as if it was scraped off the back of his throat with a spoon handle. Somi and I sat quiet as church farts and hardly dare move lest they all come tumbling into the room. Our prudence was exaggerated but to anyone who knew Square Root it would have been understandable. Every time their conversation slackened I feared that we were on the brink of discovery.

From what we could hear it seemed that the Satsumas were also on the point of embarking and that Nomura and his cronies were celebrating their last hours ashore much as I might have done myself. I had almost stopped paying attention to their words and was starting to search surreptitiously for any food that had been spared our passion when I thought I heard someone mention the name of Matsumota. Immediately my interest was aroused and I pressed my ear to the thin partition.

"When will the deed be done?" said one of the voices.

"The night before they reach Edo," replied Nomura.

"And how will it be effected?"

"Faith. I do not know. Ask the man yourself if you can find him. Poison perhaps, or with the sword. He will be close enough to choose any way he likes."

"But what will the Figos do then?"

"They will be thrown into confusion and run to Ieyasu saying that their leader has been slain—"

"And he will soothe them and grant their lands into the keeping of our lord Shimazu."

"Precisely."

"And what of Matsumota. He will be given some high office I suppose?"

"So he has been led to believe. But it is a heinous crime to slay your daimyo, even one such as the pederast Taisake, and I believe that Ieyasu may well demand his death as an example to those who might be tempted to espouse a deal of equal treachery."

"And so Shimazu will be duty bound to have him executed. I like this idea vastly."

And here they all set to laughing again whilst I expelled my breath through tight-clenched teeth. So Kushoni was right in his suspicion and the vile Matsumota was to play the assassin before defecting to the Satsuma ranks. Someone must warn my erstwhile comrades. With a heartfelt contempt for the profligacy of my own good nature I realised it would have to be me. Even as I was thinking I was pulling on my clothing and Somi was quick to see what I was about. She came close and threw her arms about me. "You're not leaving me now?" she whispered, passion and outrage mixed.

It was, of course, an understandable gesture on her part but a foolish one. To be clung to thus only hardened my resolve to be away. I lose interest speedily when women make too much show of their emotions. In affairs of the heart, if you would preserve your lover's affections, give not too generously of your own.

"I have no choice," I hissed irritably, "you heard what was said. Matsumota is going to kill Taisake. I must warn them! I wish, believe me, that there was another way out of this matter."

"But what of me? What manner of man are you to leave me like this? I had thought our travels together might endure longer than this. My misgivings are soon proved correct."

"Heed my words you inconsiderate wretch. Do you not recall that your life was saved at the Figo court? Do you not reckon that you owe them some obligation? I assure you that I will not be away one moment more than I have to. Now for God's sake lower your voice and let me be gone."

She placed her hands across the door, barring my way.

"Take me with you."

"Impossible, I will have to ride like a demon to reach them 'ere they embark. Now step aside."

"I will not. Lay one finger on me and I will raise such a shout that Nomura and all his band will stand behind me within seconds."

I was grateful to the girl for making it so easy for me to strike her. I half turned away as if in resignation and then brought my fist swiftly to the point of her chin, so that her triumphant smile seemed to jump in the air before it disappeared. I caught her falling body and placing it tenderly on the litter listened to hear what sounds were coming from the next room. There was no intimation that our disagreement had been overheard and so I slid back the door and crept outside.

Three strides down the corridor and I heard the squeak of female voices. The innkeeper must be returning with Nomura's women. I shrank into an alcove and watched them swish by. Three of the ugliest, broadest-beamed hussies I have ever clapped eyes on, but no doubt selected for resilience and imperturbability; Nomura was no Holbein. I dare not let them see me lest they mention our encounter as a tongue loosener. I could imagine how the brute would enjoy testing his katanga on me. The thought made me feel a slight pang of remorse at leaving Somi so near to him, but provided the innkeeper made no mention of me, and she did not venture from the room, she must be safe. At least so I persuaded myself as I slid from the building and went to find my horse.

Of the next few hours there is little I can remember. Suffice it to say that I lost my way several times, thrice blundered into a paddy field—once nearly fatally— and was in a worse state than my nag when I eventually arrived at a wide ribbon of sand which seemed, in the intermittent moonlight, most like that on which I had first set foot when coming to the mainland. I searched the calm ocean for light but there was none. Praying that I had been directed to the right point I spurred my gasping mount towards the tattered dwellings standing back from the shore and battered on one of the doors.

At first—nothing. Then the door slid back fitfully and my nostrils were invaded by a stench I remembered from other days. On seeing me the creature whose home it must be shrank back in alarm but I thrust in my arm and snatched him out like a fox cub.

"The Lord Taisake and his men," says I. "Have you seen aught of them? I believe that they plan to embark near this place."

"You are too late," said the evil-smelling one, a certain satisfaction colouring his voice. "They sailed on the evening tide."

"All of them?"

"I cannot tell but I saw Taisake and his nobles embark but forty paces from here."

My grip slackened and the fellow twisted away and was disappeared into his house in an instant. The door slid shut and I was left searching the horizon as a cloud covered the moon.

CHAPTER 12

NOW I MADE A DECISION WHICH WAS TOTALLY AGAINST my nature and which, even in the maturity of later life, I find it difficult to explain or excuse.

I decided to follow the Figos to the mainland.

What prompted this ill-considered and foolhardy gesture I cannot conceive unless it might have been a secret desire to escape from Somi. Anyway, once this wretched notion formed itself in my mind there was no budging it. I knew that Edo was some days march from where the Figos were landing and that this would afford me the opportunity to ride after them, were I able to get a prompt passage to Osaka. To this end I flogged my slavering nag back to the port and with some trepidation halted at the inn, to tell my plans to Somi.

I got no further than the back entrance for the inn-keeper dropped on me like a spider to say that Somi had taken her mount and was gone, leaving only a scroll meant, presumably, for me. I asked cautiously after Nomura and hearing that he was still sleeping off the excesses of the previous night, paid the fellow and unrolled the scroll.

"Despised ruffian, I leave you these words so that you might have some record of my loathing for you at this moment. That you could strike me with your fists as well as with your deeds is more than my heart and understanding can bear. I go now to throw myself on the mercy of the Figo garrison and pray that I may never see you again."

I was not at all cast down by this, it seeming a pretty typical female communication and was careful to reveal where I might find her. In fact, I was delighted to have avoided a confrontation which I felt certain would have been violent. I would attend to my business on the mainland and then return for Somi, provided of course that no better offer presented itself.

The next part of my story does not repay detailed telling. Suffice to say that I persuaded the owner of a fishing junk to ferry me to Osaka which was where the Figo party was bound. The voyage was made on what the Japonians call the inland sea, it being enclosed by the mainland of Japon and the islands of Kyushu and Shikoku and was an interminably slow one. I had hoped that on a smaller vessel I might reach Osaka before the Figo junks, but this was clearly not to be the case. The only diversion the voyage offorded was the fisherman's daughter who I at first took for a boy. This misapprehension she was clearly at pains to correct and proved herself the most curious creature I have ever encountered concerning the European body. Needless to say, one evening after we had been lying becalmed for hours and had taken advantage of this situation to enjoy a quick bathe, I set to satisfying her curiosity and it was in this position that her father, literally stumbled upon us. Fortunately, perhaps, he was a man whose principles were tempered by self interest, for having at first threatened to throw me overboard—no mean feat for one who stood a head short of my shoulder—he then set to re-adjusting the price of my passage and eventually offered me

the permanent use of his daughter for another fifty
taels. It is a fact that poverty leads many of the peasant class to sell their daughters as servants or into
prostitution, but I think that this man would have disposed of any member of his family had the price been
right.

I declined his offer and the rest of the voyage
dragged by in a state of barely suppressed bitterness
so that I was doubly relieved when Osaka hove into
sight. It was a pleasant port with a multitude of vessels and dwellings and well-wooded slopes from which
the roofs of temples and shrines twinkled in the sunlight. This predilection for things religious was something I found difficult to equate with the bloodthirst-
iness of the Japonians for instance.

As we put in we passed a torii, a wooden gateway,
most handsomely wrought, and standing in the shal-
lows. This, I was told was usually set outside a shrine
so that the wild birds might alight upon it and sing
their morning praises to the Gods. A charming thought
and an elegant structure but I could not help thinking that the hands that shaped it would be nothing
loath to test a sword on a passing dog to see if the
blade was fit for human flesh.

Once ashore I was soon surrounded by a crowd of
gawpers, who had clearly not set eyes on my like before. I immediately set to asking about the Figo retinue and was soon informed that they had landed two
days before. This cheered me, as the loneliness of my
condition and the idleness I had been subjected to had
left my mind prey to fears that I would never find
them and only succeed in cutting myself off from any
hope of return to England.

As for the town, I had never seen one so great, and
was thankful that the fisherman's daughter led me to a
place where I might buy a horse. To find this we went

through many markets, some selling fruit and vegetables and another fish—dried, salted and fresh—until we came to a street where there were nothing but horses to be hired and sold. I selected one and was soon on my way towards Miyako, which I was informed was where the great road to Edo began. My inquisitive helpmate was sad to see me go, but I gave her a sum not much less than that her father had tried to sell her for, and she departed in better humour than might have been the case.

As I have already said, I was much impressed with the town and especially with the great bridges crossing a river in its midst. These were high and all of wood, beautifully carved and with the main supports mounted in copper. There was also a castle which made that of the Figos seem like a child's toy. Stone walls, twenty feet thick, and trenches outside so deep you could lose a church in them. A mighty place, and one that I could not have conceived of existing, a few months before.

With the Figos so recently arrived, and most of them on foot, I believed that I would close the distance between us swiftly, but it suddenly occurred to me that in my haste, I had made no enquiry about the Satsumas. It was conceivable that they might have landed before me and I was not of a mind to ride up Nomura's backside, if it could be avoided. This thought made me look out carefully, but although the road carried an abundance of travellers, there was, thankfully, no sign of the Satsumas.

The number of people on the road, and the size of Osaka, made me feel that Japon must be a far more populous country than England and this thought was substantiated when, towards evening, I came upon Miyako.

This town was handsomely set on a spacious plain,

surrounded on three sides by high mountains. Its
streets were wide and laid out at right angles to each
other so that the whole appearance was very orderly.
Palaces and fine buildings there were in profusion and
the town was scrupulously clean, with covered pas-
sageways before the shops, many of which had curtains in front to keep out the dust. I afterwards learned
that the town had more than 800,000 people living in
it, which must have made it the largest in the known
world. Also 5,000 temples and 50,000 whores, which
seemed to me the right proportion. It was also where
the now powerless emperor resided and famous for the
refined speech of its inhabitants.

I would have tarried there longer, but conscience
urged me along the road and I soon found myself on
the Tokaido, the great highway, a hundred leagues
long, that led to Edo and the Shogun Ieyasu. The way
was mostly sand and gravel, and at the end of every
league pine trees had been planted on mounds at each
side of the road, so that a fair reckoning could be made
between porters, horse hirers and travellers. At each
stage along the way there was considerable traffic in
horses and I reckoned that those in control of it had
their hands on the means to a considerable fortune.

By the time I had travelled a few leagues along the
road it was becoming dark and I was tired and hungry.
I still reckoned myself a day's ride behind the Figos,
but so far short of Edo that there was as yet no danger
to Taisake—provided that Nomura was right about
the timing of Matsumota's treachery. With this in
mind, I was haggling about the cost of a night's sleep
at one of the stopping points, when I suddenly noticed
Kushoni's favourite mount hobbling nearby. There was
no mistaking the beast, for it had a distinct V-shaped
scar above the nostrils. In response to my eager ques-

tions I was told that the Figos had passed through
but an hour before, changing Kushoni's lame nag in
the process. With night falling fast, this meant that
they must be but a few miles ahead, and probably
had already made camp. My informant confirmed this
view by saying that a mighty river lay close at hand
which no man would attempt to cross at night. I
thanked the fellow and galloped on, trying to plan my
best course of action as I went.

Wisest, I felt to find Kushoni and pour out my tale to
him, provided that I could reach him without alerting Matsumota. If this could be achieved and Taisake
informed, then Matsumota, if he had closed his eyes
in sleep, might never open them again.

I was indulging myself with these thoughts when
I came to the top of a pass, and looking down could
see a profusion of lights and fires. This must be the
Figo camp. I came off the road and picked my way
slowly through the trees that lined it in abundance.
Soon there was a chatter of voices and a blaze of
sparks soared up before me. I dismounted and, tether-
ing my nag, crept towards the fire. Around it squatted
half a dozen men and I immediately recognised the insignia of the Figos which gave me some comfort. I
skirted them without announcing my presence and
moved on through the trees. Baggage and weapons
were scattered everywhere and I had to step warily
to avoid stumbling over those who were already set-
tling down to sleep. This must be the quarter allotted
to the common soldiery.

Further along the slope I could see lanterns and
they in turn revealed the tent like dwellings of the
nobles. Finding that of Kushoni presented no problem, for every man of quality in Japon has his own
badge which he displays on his dwelling and his vest-

ments, and so it was merely a question of moving along
the line of tents until I recognised that of my friend.
Hoping that I would find him alone, I moved swiftly
from the shadows and darted through the entrance.

He was not alone. He was lying on a litter of blankets with two women and none of them looked overjoyed to see me. Kushoni sprang to his feet like a sapling which had been bent back and suddenly released.

"How dare you," he stormed, "do you not know that
he who enters a Samurai's chamber unannounced and
uninvited forfeits his head?"

"I understand your consternation and I humbly apol-
ogise for my impulsive entrance," said I, "but I bring
you news of the most vital nature and it is imperative
that I speak with you. Can I—"

I was about to ask if I could speak in front of the
women, but they had drawn blankets over their heads
and were now invisible. Kushoni snatched up a robe,
for there was nothing to prevent me enjoying an uninterrupted view of his flesh, and drew me outside. I,
in my turn, pulled him towards the trees and cutting
short his questions about why I was not in Nagasaki,
told him what I had overheard at the inn. This he listened to with his usual mixture of gasps and grunts
covering the gamut of outrage to incredulity before
bidding me wait two seconds whilst he returned to his
tent.

In fact it took him only a little longer to attire
himself and lay hands upon his katanga and the restless way he ran the weapon through his fingers suggested that it would not stay much longer in its sheath.
He indicated that I should follow, and stalked ahead,
his paces measuring men for graves. I had thought he
might be going straight to seek out Matsumota, but a
few strides brought us to a palatial tent, which must

clearly have been Taisake's. This was divided into chambers and in one of these we were eventually brought into the presence of the Daimyo, passing as we went in a cherubic boy, which perhaps accounted for the Daimyo's flushed and breathless manner. He was not called on to speak much, however, for after an introductory word from Kushoni, I was launched into another account of my eavesdropping.

Taisake listened in silence, his eyes narrowing to slits. When he spoke, the words were spat out like cherry stones.

"Bring me his head."

Kushoni needed no second bidding and rising from his haunches was out of the chamber before I had found my feet. I stumbled after him, feeling the night grow cool about me and scenting death in the air. Soldiers were called, bearing pikes, and together we tramped to the tent which bore Matsumota's insignia.

All was silence, save for the sound of Kushoni's katanga sliding from its sheath. No light crept from the tent and the door flap was securely closed. Kushoni despatched men to surround the structure and advanced towards the entrance. I drew my sword and followed him, feeling beside the normal emotions of fear and excitement, a slight tinge of guilt that I myself had turned informer. I did not have long to dwell upon the paradox because Kushoni suddenly let out an ear piercing squawk and slashed a great vent in the side of the tent. He was through the gap almost before the sound of torn cloth had penetrated my ears and when I followed him it was to find a young man blinking up at the point of Kushoni's sword. He lay on a pile of bedding and was presumably Matsumota's squire or catamite, or both—the Japons see no harm in sodomy, saying that a boy has no virginity to lose.

"Where is your master?" said Kushoni brusquely, "we would have words with him."

"The most honoured Matsumota does not confide his every movement to one so unworthy as myself," replied the youth, haughtily.

"I advise you to reflect upon my question," said Kushoni. "I will not ask it again."

"In that case you save us both breath," said the youth. "I have no knowledge of his whereabouts and if I did, I would not tell you."

Kushoni nodded and then suddenly lashed out with his sword taking the fellow's head clean off his shoulders. I found this a most callous deed and said so, but Kushoni would have none of it and I afterwards learned that the Japons carry their vengence over to the victim's family, often putting women and children to the sword when the mood takes them. It is also usual for the squire to perish with his master and to take his own life if his lord perishes in battle. Such deeds being commonplace and Matsumota having no wife or issue, Kushoni was doing no more than his duty and might even have been congratulated on sparing the squire the painful experience of cutting his belly.

Nevertheless, I felt pretty sick as the blood flowed towards my toes and asked Kushoni how this act would help us lay hands on Matsumota. He did not see fit to reply but addressed a few words to the soldiers before marching off into the night with two of them at his shoulder. I followed on and had barely caught up with them when I heard the sound of fast running water below me. Looking down I could see patches of silver flashing amongst the trees which clearly indicated the course of some great river. At that instant we came out into a clearing and I saw a sight that nearly drove me back into the trees. A giant seemed to be poised above a bend in the river with blazing eyes like those of a wolf. Crosslegged it sat and its outline was sharply etched against the night sky. If it had suddenly risen and stalked forward to grind me underfoot I would not have been surprised, but luckily with this surmise came the realisation that it was a great idol, an image of Buddha or suchlike, and that there must be some chamber behind the eyes from which the light was coming. It was an awesome sight and the river at its foot narrowed into a gorge so that the water burst through like cannon fire.

"I believe we will find him here," said Kushoni, "trying to find a God to whom he can excuse his perfidy. Come."

He led the way across rocks, slippery with spray, until the idol towered above us like a cliff face. An entrance there was in one of its toes, which gives some idea of its size, and we crept along a passageway until we were in the hollow interior. The exterior seemed to be covered in gilded brass or copper but understandably the inside was less well-finished and a rickety wooden stairway lurched from side to side up the uneven walls. In the middle of the dimly lit chamber knelt a figure and I saw Kushoni tighten his grip upon his sword. But it was not Matsumota. The man in the white robe with a shaven head and a curious two-cornered hat perched upon it was a priest of bonze. He rose and came towards us asking that we remove our weapons in this holy place, but Kushoni bade him hold his tongue and asked who was above.

Surprised, he said one of our number, an unusually tall man. No sooner were the words fallen from his lips than Kushoni had his foot on the stair, hissing at us to be silent. The bonze began to raise his voice in protest, but a pike presented itself against his throat so

fast that hardly a word was formed before it died
away to a whimper. Scarce knowing why, I set my
footsteps after Kushoni's and clambered upwards until there was but a faint glow beneath. I have climbed
church towers but this seemed like a cathedral spire,
so infinite were the twists and turns. And all in darkness with no sound other than the flutter of unseen
bats. I was so close to Kushoni that I could smell him
and our feet pressed the same boards. At last there
was a glimmer of light above and Kushoni took his
sword firmly between two hands. I followed suit
with less enthusiasm and we crept on at a snailpace
until an oblong of light reared up before us and we
could peep towards its source.

There was a chamber, its ceiling shaped to the contours of the idol's head, and in the midst a brightly
burning brazier. Despite this it was well draped in
shadows and amidst them knelt a man with his back
to us. It was still easy to identify him for his height
knew no equal amongst the Japons—Matsumota. He
seemed to have no weapon with him, but still I held
back as Kushoni introduced himself into the chamber
with no pretence of silence. Matsumota must have
heard him but made no movement, which contributed
to my uneasiness. The wind from the eye vents rushed
in and fanned the flame of the brazier making the
shadows dance against the wall. It was an eerie sight
past all description.

"What brings you here to disturb a man at meditation?" said Matsumota, without turning round.

"Retribution," said Kushoni coldly. "I would advise
you to commend yourself to the Gods for you will
shortly be in their presence."

At these words Matsumota turned round slowly and
the brazier threw such a light on him that it made his

head seem like a skull full of dark cavities. When he saw my face I thought his eyes opened a fraction wider, but perhaps it was my imagination.

"I know that you would like to kill me," said he, "but you cannot do it here. I am unarmed and this is a shrine. Even your jealous spleen could not goad you to an act so vile."

"You deceive yourself," said Kushoni, "we have heard of your intentions towards our noble lord Tai-sake."

"May I ask what you have heard. It seems to me our lord listens too much to those who would do him most harm."

"To do that he would need an ear inside your mind," said Kushoni, and straightened his arms so that his sword was pointing at Matsumota's shoulder. "We know of your dealings with the Satsumas and there is no gainsaying that you are guilty of the blackest treachery. That being said it only remains for you to choose how you would die. I would take it that you would wish to perish by your own hand as benefits your station?"

Matsumota drew himself up and folded his arms across his chest. I should have become wary as he moved round behind the brazier, but my suspicions were lulled by the sonorous pitch of his low voice.

"At least I am allowed a choice by my executioners. I had thought that starting as you did with my finger," he held out the hand I had been forced to maim, "you might choose to lop off my limbs one by one. Well, there is nothing for it . . ." His voice dropped with his hands and I felt almost sorry for him—"But . . ." With the word he bent double and I heard his hands sizzle as they touched the hot metal of the brazier. Picking it from the floor he hurled its contents

towards us so that the air was full of flaming coals.
Some struck my face and became lodged in my
clothing, and I screamed out in pain. Kushoni bore
the full brunt and fell back cursing while Matsumota
streaked towards the eye vents. I could not believe
that he meant to cast himself out, but without slack-
ening his pace he ran into the night so that for an instant he was framed against the sky like some great
bat, before disappearing from our sight. I rushed forward but looking down saw only the silver torrent,
hundreds of feet below as the wind tore at my face.

"He must perish," said Kushoni at my elbow, but
the words were uttered with more hope than conviction.

"Think no more of him," said I turning round. "We
have troubles of our own."

Never had I spoken truer, for the strewn coals had
fed hungrily on the wooden timbers of the flooring
which was now blazing merrily. Worse, some of the
brazier's contents had found their way through the
floor opening and started a fire on the stairs below.
Even as we ran back flames reared up hungrily to greet
us and looking down I glimpsed clouds of sparks exploding like fireworks. The stairs were impassable.

"We must follow Matsumota," I urged. "Can you
swim?"

"To save my life, I can do anything," said Kushoni
grimly. "Who goes first?"

"It makes no matter to me," I said all easy noncha-
lance, though in truth I was near fainting with terror.

Great billows of smoke were now invading our nostrils and snakelike tongues of flame snapped up at us.
Looking down I felt like some God peering through
the clouds. Two paces away I could hardly see
Kushoni through the smoke.

"We must jump," I shouted, but he was gone. I hurled aside my weapons and balanced on the very edge of the eye socket tried to summon up the courage to jump. Somi had said she did not think we would ever meet again. I wish to God I had listened to her. Never have I felt nearer death. I trembled, wavered— and then a presumptuous shaft of flame darted between my legs and launched me into darkness. Over and over I went trying to tuck myself behind my shoulder. I hit the water an age later and the impact near stunned me. There was a roaring in my ears which I felt might be my brain rushing out of my head and I was snatched, plucked, hurled along without a modicum of control over my destiny. This battering continued until suddenly the pace slackened; I touched a rock beneath my feet, my head rose above the turbulence and I could snatch a lung-full of air. I struck out wildly and fought myself free of the all-powerful current. My hand found a rock which I could cling to, and then another. Slowly I pulled myself towards the bank until I could stand and stagger the last few yards to safety.

Above me flames now belched from the great idol's eyes and as I looked up it seemed more than ever like some malevolent giant furious at being baukled of his prey. I cast about me for some sign of Kushoni or Matsumota, but there was only the thunder of the water and the shadows that did not move.

CHAPTER 13

BUT I FOUND NO SIGN OF MATSUMOTA. KUSHONI I CAME upon cursing amongst the rocks at the water's edge. I thought at first he was looking for me but though he greeted me warmly he was in fact searching for his precious sword which in typically stubborn fashion he had clung on to until almost ashore. I felt a trifle guilty at this because, of course, I had cast aside his precious gift to me without a second thought.

We were not long alone for the soldiers who had accompanied us came stumbling back amazed to see us alive. They said that the bonze, who had fled with them, was vowing all manner of retribution for our sacrilege, and promising to enlist the aid of the lord of the province we were in. Certainly I could imagine that the damage caused to the idol would hardly endear us to the well-ordered Japons and this surmise was made before I saw it by daylight. The intense heat had in many places quite melted away the copper and the face looked particularly horrible being lopsided and scowling, a marked contrast to the serene countenance of the normal daibutsu. This menacing expression was construed as an evil omen by many of the Figos and Taisake was as much put out by it as by our failure to account for Matsumota. Not a sign there was of that rascal and though his body might have

been swept downstream I had my doubts of it as
there was no reason why the devils spawn should have
been any less fortunate than Kushoni and myself.

Now that I had fulfilled my contract with my conscience there was nothing to prevent me returning to
Figo and Somi, but so impressed had I been with
Osaka and Miyako that it seemed foolish not to expend
a few weeks more viewing the splendours of the country, the like of which I might not see again in the rest
of my life. There were also the Satsumas coming up
behind and though I could probably skirt them I felt
a more sensible fellow in the midst of the Figo party.

The next morning, therefore, found me crossing the
river with the rest of them and it was but one of many
such hazards we met on the road to Edo. As I have already said the Tokaido carried a multitude of people
and a majority of these seemed to be not travelling
anywhere but making their living from those that
were. Beggars, friars, conjurers, fortune tellers and
strumpets littered the way, and besides the farriers
there were also men whose sole purpose was to assist
in the fording of the streams. According to the depth
of the river these fellows would assign two or more of
their number to each side of a horse and support its
passage across the torrent. In the winter I can imagine
it being beastly work, but they demanded a high
enough price for their service, so perhaps it was worth
it. The road wound its way through a progression of
lofty mountains and none was more impressive than
Fuji-yama, the Peerless Mountain, which rose to a
height of twelve thousand feet above the sea. It
was in one of the temples, not far distant, that a most
unexpected and entertaining experience befell me.

The matter began with me being told of the festival
of Zakone which entailed the devout attending an all

night vigil at the local Shinto Temple. This description hardly endeared me to the occassion but I was informed that the temple itself was a particularly beautiful one and worth a visit, so nightfall found me joining the trickle of well-wrapped worshippers going through the gates. I thought I might take a quick look at the building before going to my rest and had no intention of seeing the night away there. The entrance to the temple was most impressive being by way of a cedar-lined avenue with fine stone pillars surmounted by lanterns every ten yards. At the top was a wide terrace flanked by all manner of gilded statues and high archways falling back one within the other to the interior of the building. Inside there was a great altar with an open space before it and more statuary set into alcoves in the walls. There were a few bonzes about the altar and the entering worshippers took up their positions on the floor before them. I stood back in the shadows intending to tarry for no more than a few seconds, when I noticed a small procession approaching from the rear of the temple. It was comprised of three priests bearing lanterns on poles and in their midst an exquisitely dressed girl seeming more like a doll than a woman and wearing a profusion of combs and ornaments in her coiled hair. I watched with increasing interest as the maiden stopped before the altar and was helped up on to it. She placed her hands on her breasts and lay on her back, so that she might have been a corpse, awaiting burial. No sooner was she still than a young priest stepped forward, his shaven head gleaming, and began to pluck the ornaments from her hair. This he did with an actor's range of expansive gestures and tongue-clicking.

What was more remarkable was the effect these activities had on the audience. They themselves began to lay hands on each other and their mingling was not confined to couples who had arrived together. Many people I saw wandering about and making physical contact with hardly the exchange of a word. To be not engrossed oneself was to invite approach.

The couple on the altar had now passed the ornament removing stage and the priest was loosing the bands of cloth that secured the girl's kimono. Tugging them aside he exposed her breasts and then set to unknotting the obi about his waist. Less experienced eyes than mine would not have been slow to see the way things were going and I was not a whit surprised when the saucy rogue hopped up on the altar and covered the girl with his body, his rope draping them both like a bird's wings. Once again I felt an immediate call to the priesthood, and could see that the spectacle was having its anticipated effect on the proselytes below. I myself was responding in a very straightforward manner and cast around the assembled company for a possible mate. There seemed nobody not engrossed with a partner and I was on the point of turning away disappointed when a figure came towards me from the shadows. I say figure for its outline was so obscured by a cloak as to render it difficult to sex. Suffice to say that it was not comely and that a pronounced limp did nothing to enhance its appeal. I was therefore amazed when this creature, coming abreast of me whispered my name. "John!"

I pretended I did not hear but the voice was female and persistent. "John, do you not recognise me?"

Against my will I braced myself and peered into the creature's cowl. What I saw there scarcely left me breath for an exclamation. "My God!"

"Not him," replied the stranger coolly, "but one who has the same remedial power and the desire to use it in a worthy cause."

It was the Daimyo's wife. At least it seemed to be

her! I looked again to be certain.

"What brings you here, my lady?" I said, thinking what a damn fool question that was, as soon as the words were past my lips.

"I have already told you. Being married to my lord Taisake, I am not over indulged with opportunities to enjoy the pleasures of the nuptial couch. He is a man who finds small comfort in the company of women and, being of such a disposition, leaves a void within me that needs must be filled."

The last words were spoken with a delightful dropping of the eyes that left me with no doubt as to their meaning. One small thing still disturbed me.

"A most understandable reaction, my lady, with which I readily sympathise. Humbly speaking of my own situation I find I more than counterbalance the Lord Taisake in my slavish adulation of the female form. But—before we converse further on the matter —I am disturbed by what appears to be an injury to your leg. I hope this does not afford you too much pain or inconvenience?"

The fair creature thrust her body against my own and sent a small hand down to caress the greyhound straining in my slips. "Have no fear. You have not found a cripple. It was just a pretence I adopted to dissuade those who might not have suited me. Now, what would you do?"

Typical of all women that I have ever met that she should make all the running but in the end demand to be taken.

I glanced around and seeing a fragrant bush near-by drew her towards it, thinking that beneath its spreading branches we might achieve a happy union. But she would have none of this and in her turn led me towards the heaving mats before the altar.

"Let us not turn our backs on the Gods," she repri-
manded, "remember this is the festival of Zakone."

I am not likely to forget it, I thought to myself, as I
looked round the temple. The couple on the altar were
now hopping up and down like sausages on a griddle,
and the spirit of their coupling was being mirrored in
every corner of the chamber. Taisake's wife was much
affected by the sight for I saw her bite her lips and
screw up her eyes against the tears which welled up
in their corners. She was obviously one of those wom-
en with a predilection for group sex that one occasionally encounters. So be it. She sank down on her
knees, running her open mouth along the length of
my body from lip to thigh, and I was not slow to follow, stifling her moans with my mouth. Her hands
were like ferrets and they savaged my loin cloth away,
gouging the flesh of my belly in their haste. This act
completed, she pushed me back and fell on my member as if greedy for sustenance, making the most out-
rageous sobs and guzzling groans. It was exquisite
agony and I propped myself up on my elbow to watch
her at work, her cowl pulled back and her long black
hair hanging down over her face. Around me, all manner of tableaux were being enacted in the half light
and I found this spectacle of mass lust more titilating
than I would ever have imagined. It was both stimu-
lating and challenging. I felt like an actor eager to
stand out amongst his fellows on a crowded stage.
Freed for a second from the tight encompassing pressure of my partner's mouth, I pushed her back and in
my turn settled myself down to chew her opened fig.
This drove her into such ecstacy that she could scarce
keep her rump on the ground and cried out that nothing so exquisite had ever been done to her. This I
could believe, for the Japons are not over sensitive to

the physical satisfaction of their women and a glance around me showed that most of the females present were little more than adjuncts to the male's pleasure.

Though not wishing to speak too highly of myself as a lover, I would say that I am persistent and wide-seeking in my attempts to give my partner satisfaction, and it seems little to ask of any man to do likewise, especially when his own is so easily achieved. Anyway, after delivering this little homily, back to the present.

Taisake's wife was now shivering like a ship about to break up and her head near twisting off her body. Being the instigator of so much pleasure was pretty affecting, as was the lust-laden atmosphere around me, and when I sensed her nearing fruition, I was not loath to spring into her body and feel the buds popping and myself straining, draining, away, as if every artery in my body was being opened and my whole substance pouring away between her legs.

I lay there panting and feeling for the first time the stone floor cool against my cheek. The moon was now risen whole and perfect and hung like an ornament between the pillars of the temple. The Daimyo's wife snuggled closer to me and I wondered idly what her name was, but could think of no good reason at that moment why I should ask her. There she was invincible and satisfied whilst I lay with the splendour between my legs wilted away to a butter ball and at the mercy of time and nature to restore my ardour. Maybe this is why men treat women so churlishly, because a contented partner only throws into relief their own feelings of inadequacy. I pondered this mighty problem whilst the wench in my arms threatened to suffocate me with her attentions and the couple on the altar were borne away on a litter. Seeing them go reminded me that the festival was to last for the duration of the night and I was beginning to wonder if I would be equal to the demands of the occasion when I suddenly set eyes on one of the court servants who was in the process of disentangling himself from a vast creature built like a female wrestler. At first he looked away, but then deciding to put his best face on it, called out a greeting. Luckily Taisake's wife had her back to him and I was able to hiss a warning into her ear as I saw him make to come over. Like many women before her she responded admirably to the demands of the situation and had her cloak drawn round her before the fellow had taken a step. Without another word she was on her feet and gliding away as suddenly as she had come.

"I see that you have been able to cure her limp," said the courtier, and it was a fact that she had forgotten or forsaken her protective ploy.

"One of my many talents," I observed.

"'Tis a pity she has gone," said the fellow, for I was going to ask if you would care to cure my partner of her fatness whilst I tested the extent of your healing powers."

"It would entail the offices of every man in this temple straining without ceasing for a year to wittle more than a couple of inches off that girth," I said, resisting the enticing glances this mound of blubber was directing at me. "The very sight sends my privates scurrying towards the safety of my rectum."

With these words I bid him good night and fled in search of Taisake's splendid and under-employed wife but there was no sign of her so I returned ruminatively to my bed.

On the next morning we were on our way again with the promise of reaching Edo by nightfall. I took up my station with Kushoni beside the Daimyo's pal-

anquin and was enjoined to catch my lady's eye as she
lolled in her own receptacle behind him. For an instant she fluttered her fan and inclined her head towards me but Kushoni suddenly intercepted one of
our glances and she turned away hurriedly. Kushoni
looked at me quizzically but I gazed through him in
all innocence and we rode on in silence.

I was more forcibly and uncomfortably reminded
of the previous evening when we came upon an execution ground similar to that which I have already described outside the Figo castle. This time the crosses
which I had observed before were decked with human corpses in an advanced state of putrefaction and
I realised that the Japons were wont to crucify mal-
factors by the method that had accounted for Our
Lord. Their crosses were different in a couple of respects, for a short perch projected from the stern and
another cross piece was affixed below it. In this way
the victim straddled the projection with his legs
splayed apart and secured by chains and ropes. No
nails were used.

At the foot of the crosses the hideous Eta, or executioners, scratched themselves and puffed at clay
pipes and I was told that such was their devilry that
they could transfix a body no less than sixteen times
without striking a vital organ. It can be seen that they
could subject the condemned to bear limitless suffering if they had a mind to and in certain cases victims
were left to starve to death and have their eyes picked
out by wild birds, without the remedial pressure of
a spear.

All this and the pervading stench of human remains
were enough to turn the strongest stomach, but it was
the crimes for which crucifixion was the penalty that
disturbed me most. Parricide and counterfeiting wor-

ried me not a jot, but when I heard the word adultery
I could almost feel the cold steel stabbing at my vitals.
My God, to think that I might even now be stretched
out upon a cross. I could see why Taisake's wife appeared to have no surfeit of lovers to take the edge off
her appetite. Turning my eyes away from the vile
sight I rode on, determined that our brief encounter
would have no sequel.

And so, at last to Edo. Similar to Miyako in the
length, breadth and straightness of its streets, and no
whit inferior in its scrupulous cleanliness. It was as if
no person lived there and a marked contrast to the
squalid horror of the execution ground we had recently
passed. The houses were all of wood and some had
two stories. A river flowed through the middle of the
city and its waters were diverted along channels in
many streets so that the dwellers could draw water
from them. It was all most cleverly done and once
again I could not help marvelling at the extremes of
the Japonian nature. That they could seem so civilised
in many ways and so barbarous in others.

Still, we were at our journey's end and I looked forward to our audience with Ieyasu and whatever spectacle his palace could afford. In the last respect I was
not disappointed for the castle which enclosed it was
unlike any of its kind I have ever set eyes on.

To start with it was six English miles in circumfer-
ence and being enclosed within three moats and
three mounds. The first and largest wall was composed
of square blocks of hewn stone set one upon the other,
without mortar, and there were holes in it through
which their few pieces of artillery could be fired. The
drawbridge was huge and the castle gates covered on
both sides with iron bars an inch thick. Between this
and the next wall three hundred paces away, we

passed upwards of a thousand armed men, and it
should be remembered that this was but one entrance
to the castle. Through the second gate, guarded by
four hundred men with naginta, which are like halberds, and we approached a third wall, a dozen feet
in height and surrounding the Shogun's palace and
gardens. On one side were stables containing two
hundred horses and on the other Ieyasu's armoury,
with enough pikes, lances, arquebuses, katanga and
other weapons to equip 100,000 men.

We were housed between the first and second walls
where dwelt the other daimyos who had been summoned to the palace. Between the second and third
walls dwelt the princes and senior court officials and
in the middle, of course, Ieyasu and his women.

Of the Satsumas there was no sign, but such was
the show of armed might about us that I felt there
was no more risk of a confrontation with them than of
two mice beginning to squabble before a lion.

Later that evening, with a good meal inside me and
the gilded eaves of Edo seeming to have stolen their
hue from the rays of the setting sun, I climbed one of
the ramparts and thought myself in some fairy place
almost past man's comprehension. I even experienced
the faintest pang of remorse that I would soon be
leaving it for ever. Luckily, before I had time to further examine this emotion, I saw one of the court ladies approaching me with what appeared to be a missive in her hand. It might well have emanated from
other hands than those of her mistress, but a quick
image of the cross and its grisly burden flashed before
my eyes and I was moving swiftly towards my sleeping quarters.

The next few days were spent in lazing and carousing, for which I have a special aptitude, and during

that time we learned that the Satsumas had arrived
and were dwelling in another quarter of the castle.
Ieyasu did not present himself to our gaze, but remained within the inner sanctum where he consulted
with his ministers. It was on the third day that such a
concourse of armed men moved through to the middle area of the castle that the gates never had an opportunity to close from dawn till nightfall. It was
clearly intended as a show of strength and as such
succeeded, for when the Daimyos and their attendant
lords were summoned the next morning, there must
have been fully 100,000 soldiers paraded in orderly
ranks before them. I have never seen so many men assembled in one place and when Ieyasu and his cap-
tains took their place, the salute that greeted them
would have flattened the walls of Jericho. Trumpets
were blown and gongs struck and there could not
have been a bird left in a tree within twenty miles of
Edo.

I craned forward to see this man who had proved
himself the master of so many warlike kingdoms, but
though his features were severe, there was nothing
about his appearance at all remarkable. His pate was
shaven and his hair pulled back and dressed with ribbons like many of his fellows, and his robe, of yellow
and white, might have been worn by any man of superior rank. In age he was about forty years and
seemed of an ascetic disposition so tight was the skin
drawn across his bones. I had been expecting some
imposing cermony, but Ieyasu did no more than commend the bravery of his soldiers and express gratitude to those daimyos who had made long and irk-
some journeys to be in attendance upon him. His
address was brief, but it took a considerable time to
deliver, for every sentence had to be relayed to the far-

thest extremities of the parade ground and was greeted
by each section of his army hearing it with a roar of
approbation. At last a faint ripple of sound told us that
his final words have been received, and turning to address those Daimyos who clustered about his dais,
he bade that they should follow him to the palace
where he would have further speech with them. This
said he was helped on to his horse and galloped away
to thunderous plaudits of his army whilst the less fortunate Daimyos and their attendants were left to struggle for precedence in his dusty wake.

I was one of their number and together with about
two hundred others pressed through the gates. The
first thing that struck my eye was the beauty of the
gardens. Many delightful trees—cedars, cypresses,
pines, orange trees to name only those that I knew—
all cultivated artificially so that they formed the shapes
of familiar objects like bells, towers, domes and even
boats. There were also many ponds and rocks linked
by hump bridges and a profusion of lilies, roses, violets
and other flowers of diverse colours and scents.

It was in this unlikely setting that we came upon
Shimazu and Nomura of the Satsumas. I saw their
hands move above their weapons as did my own, but
one emotion that did not colour the hatred in their
eyes was surprise. They could well have heard that
Taisake still lived since their arrival in the castle, but
it was equally possible that Matsumota had survived
and fled to them with the story of his failure. Of the
creature himself there was no sign but this was scarcely
a cause for surprise.

We drew apart from the Satsumas and approached
the palace where, perhaps fortuitously, our weapons
were left at the entrance. I have before commented
on the beauty and workmanship of the Japonian build-

ings. Suffice to say that this surpassed them all and
was as if hewn from a solid block of gold, and decorated like the wings of some tropical butterfly. Once
inside we were conducted from room to spacious room,
waiting a while in each in order to marvel at the tapestries and decorations, before finally being led into a
great hall which must have already have contained
upwards of five hundred men. This chamber was surrounded by corridors and balconies and the Mace
could easily have stood in it without the top of the
mast touching the ornate ceiling. The floor was most
beautiful, being composed of tatami or square mats
trimmed with cloth of cold, satin and velvet, embroidered with many golden flowers. They fitted together
so tightly that it would have been impossible to get a
knife blade between them. At one end stood a dais
decked with rich tapestries and on it sat Ieyasu with
his major domo, chamberlain and counsellors standing respectfully behind him.

Around us the Daimyos vied with each other for the
most prestigious position whilst at the same time trying to present a demeanour of the utmost subservience.
They were a motley collection, garbed in a not dis-
similar fashion, but wearing very individual head-
dresses, mitres, three-cornered hats like berettas, hats
like clogs, dressings of ribbons and even turbans. There
was no sound beyond the rustling of their clothing,
but Ieyasu continued to stare down upon us for several
minutes until all was perfect silence. He then raised
his little finger and the chamberlain stepped forward
to inform us that the offspring of the sun and the moon,
most mighty warrior, Tokugawa Ieyasu, having con-
ferred upon himself the title of Sei-i Tai-Shogun, or
Barbarian-subduing Generalissimo, in the best interests of his people, would presently be gracious enough

to speak a few words to us. Having said this the chamberlain then prostrated himself so that his nose must have been near forced back behind his eyes.

Ieyasu waited a few moments more and then began to address the assembly in a cold, flat monotone, which robbed his words of any feeling.

"As I have already said, I am most grateful that you see fit to attend me at this important moment in our country's history.

"Looking around your faces there are many that I have seen before, but in those times it was I who was wont to visit you." He spoke the truth for half the Daimyos present had fought against him unsuccessfully and had their land overrun.

"Now that I have assumed the onerous rôle of Sei-i Tai-Shogun I will be more than ever needful of your support."

"Up go the taxes," murmured Kushoni by my side.

"But," continued Ieyasu evenly, "it has occurred to me of late that most of you are too far away to be easily summoned when I would have need of your advice. This saddens me, for I know that I have much to learn from all of you." He smiled a cold, thin smile that evoked no response from his audience. "The Gods in their wisdom have therefore suggested a solution, which I hope will prove equitable to us all."

I could feel the tremor of suspense that ran through the audience.

"For half of every year you will dwell with me here in Edo and for the remainder you can go about your business in your several kingdoms. And, since I will miss you each and every one when you are gone, your families will reside here always, so I will have a living memento of you." At these words some Daimyos could not withhold their breath and gasped out loud, but Ieyasu seemed to be unconscious of them and went on serenely. "There are many great works that we can accomplish together for the betterment of the kingdom, and looking at the gifts you have so generously given me—" here he indicated a pile of silver and gold bars which would have filled three carts—"I know I can rely upon you and your people for pecuniary aid as well as verbal counsel."

"What did I tell you; we will be ruined," muttered Kushoni despairingly.

"Now I have spoken," went on Ieyasu, "and it occurs to me that there might be one amongst you who has something he would like to say. There might even—" and here he paused meaningfully—"be one who questions my conclusions. If this be so let him speak, my chamberlain will take note of his words—and of his name." Silence fell like a drape on a coffin and the Daimyos hardly dared look at each other as the writing brush was poised above them.

Ieyasu gazed slowly round the hall, his eyes flickering over me, and resuscitated his smile. "So be it, then. My chamberlain will read the list of those who will be first to tarry with me. To the rest of you I say, do not take this to mean that I hold you in any less esteem. I will be equally glad to welcome you when your time comes."

Devious rogue. I wondered that he could speak the words without choking on them. The Japons are truly masters of the honeyed phrase, though in his position Ieyasu could have made them all sniff a turd for a posey had he wanted to.

The chamberlain stepped forward and I primed my ears to catch the name of Figo on the list he read.

"Simoosa, Fida, Kawatsii, Fidsen, Mimasaka . . ." I could see the man's eyes approaching the bottom of

the scroll. "Bidsen, Fooki, Sangami, Surunga. . . ."
Taisake would have six months grace. "Wackasa, Figo." The last name on the list. What cruel luck. If
luck had ought to do with it. And no word of Satsuma.
I glimpsed the proud Shimazu, thoughtful and predatory. His schemes could scarce fare worse in Taisake's
absence.

Ieyasu dismissed us with a regal wave and we made
our obeisance and shuffled out. He was as cunning as
a jungle full of monkeys, there was no doubt about it,
but any man who could hold sixty-six Kingdoms in his
thrall and live in such magnificence had my admiration.

Kushoni and I accompanied Taisake to his chambers and it was clear that our lord was quite cast
down.

"You are right. This man intends to ruin us," said he,
calling for sake to be brought.

"Certainly he intends to keep his daimyos under
strict surveillance. Six months of the year in Edo. That
will cost a pretty penny," said Kushoni.

"Do not remind me," groaned Taisake, "each Lord
vying to appear grander than his fellows. Our retinue
alone will cost a fortune."

"And then there will be your contribution to the
Shogun's good works. What form do you fancy they
will take?" said Kushoni.

"Castles and weapons I would reckon."

"Or perhaps new roads for all the daimyos to march
up and down on," said I.

"Do you attempt humour? If so I find it in poor
taste."

"And some will miss their wives and families,"
blurted out Kushoni, trying to come to my assistance.

"What mean you 'some.' Do you both set out to be

insulting? This man will hold my wife as a hostage. It is iniquitous."

We both agreed with him, but each one of us knew that nothing could be done about it. Ieyasu was too powerful and his new measures were cunningly conceived to ensure that no man could manoeuvre himself into a position to challenge his authority.

"I am more fearful of the Satsumas," continued Taisake ruefully. "The devil might have contrived that I stay here whilst Shimadu returns."

"Perhaps he did," said Kushoni, "we all know that Ieyasu smiles on the Satsumas. I share your fears and believe that I should return with at least half the retinue. We need men at the castle, not here."

"But what of my position—"

"With respect my lord, you are thinking as Ieyasu wishes you to think. He would turn all our soldiers into courtiers and have them parade the streets of Edo rather than our castle walls."

And so they went on into the evening with the sake sliding down merrily and nothing being resolved, until I was glad to stagger to my bed and leave them still at it.

My next recollection is of someone shouting and my eyes opening to the realisation that it was long before my normal hour of rising. Still dark in fact and with the cold night air blowing against my face. I pulled myself up and stumbling over a wench I had forgotten was still there, made my way to the door and slid it open.

Outside, the first grey streaks of dawn were beginning to colour the night sky and by their light I could see the man who was calling out Taisake's name. He seemed in the last extremities of exhaustion but his mount was in worse, and even as I looked, crumpled

to its knees. Reins of saliva hung from its mouth and
its hide was lathered to a froth. I did not know the
man, but he must have recognised me for he sunk
down at my feet and immediately began to blurt out
his story.

"The Satsumas are at the gates," he sobbed.

"Which gates?" I interrupted for I could not immediately conceive that the man could have come all
the way from Figo.

"Figo Castle. The Lord Taisake's castle. The day
after you had sailed they crossed the border and
butchered everyone in their path. All who survived
have fled to the castle. It is the only stronghold remaining. There, thanks to the muskets, they still hold
out—or did when I left. But there are few musket balls
left and with Shimazu and his men returning—"

"Shimazu and his men. But they are here in Edo."

"I think not my Lord. They rode past me as if their
horses' tails were on fire. I would recognise the one
who is thick as two men anywhere."

"How long ago was this?"

"At nightfall."

Nightfall. If they rode flat out all the way and had
no difficulty in changing their mounts, they might be
in Osaka by daybreak of the following day. If the castle had not fallen then their return would surely tip
the scales. And in the castle, god willing, was Somi.

"The lady Somi. She is in the castle?"

"Yes my lord, she is in good health."

I felt a pang of guilt at the words. Whilst I caroused
in Edo she was near to death—might even now be
dead. Well, now I supposed I must try and make
amends. I thrust a flask of sake into the messenger's
trembling hand and went to find Kushoni.

CHAPTER 14

THIRTY-SIX HOURS LATER—OR WAS IT FORTY-SIX, BY THEN I had lost all conception of time—I lay below decks on a Portuguese merchantman and listened to the bilge water sluice to and fro beneath me. I tried to keep my legs apart lest the raw flesh on the inside of both thighs married together, but the legacy of tiredness was too great. Now, like a persistently aching tooth, the pain became almost tolerable by dint of its familiarity. My flesh, near pummelled from my bones, seemed so loose that my body might have slipped out of it with an unkind movement of the ship. I closed my eyes and prayed for the remedial balm of sleep.

We—Kushoni, about fifty Figos and myself—had galloped down the Tokaido practically without a halt. Now we were thirty; a dozen men had been swept away on one of the river crossings, three had been thrown by their dying mounts, half a dozen had perished when we had been forced to fight for new horses at one of the stopping points along the way.

We had rode into Osaka like men marked out for death, a sight to make any grave digger's palms itch. Wild eyed, sweat-stained, salt-rimed, scarce able to stay in the saddle. Down to the port we reeled desperate to lose no time in finding a vessel. But there was nothing. A threatened storm had taken every ship of

substance out to sea. All save one, and this a most
remarkable vessel for me to set eyes on. A Portuguese
merchantman. Standing aloof about the host of junks
which nuzzled against its side like piglets begging to
be suckled. Thank God I had some words in that language from Somi and took myself aboard where I was
very well received, the captain having got nowhere
with his trading and grateful to find even an Englishman who might be prepared to help him. I played on
this desire to great effect, saying that I was military
adviser to one of the most important men in the land
and would use my influence to help in the setting up
of a trading post. This, of course, dependent on us being ferried to a distant province in order to crush an
attempted rebellion. The captain was dubious but
since none of his other plans were anywhere near fruition it was not difficult to persuade him to take us
aboard. We were stowed away among foul smelling
hides, a commodity it seemed not in much favour
with the Japons, while the crew peered at us with considerable suspicion.

As well they might, especially since the Figos had
refused to part with their weapons when coming
aboard. They, poor devils, were for the most part in-
different sailors and added to their tribulations by
puking lustily before we had even cleared the harbour.
Near me sprawled the messenger who had alerted
us at Edo and I marvelled that he should be prepared
to ride a distance equal to that between John O'Groats
and Land's End scarcely without respite. The Japons
are most certainly a tenacious people. This man's only
rest had come whilst Taisake went to enlist Ieyasu's
aide against the treacherous Satsumas, or at least try
and gain temporary release from his attachment to the
Shogun's palace. But Ieyasu had not even deigned to

address him and kept him waiting for an hour before sending a messenger to say that his cousin, Taisake, was too much needed at court to be released on any pretext, and that if one daimyo left others might question why they should stay. Taisake had returned in a squeaking rage made worse by the rumour that Ieyasu had held a private audience with Shimazu shortly after his arrival in Edo.

This suggestion of a conspiracy between the two, supported by Ieyasu's refusal to give succour, had Taisake vowing he would take to the road with all his men, but we dissuaded him from such an act of self immolation and told him he must stay. After more time waiting it was agreed that Kushoni and I would take as many men as could leave the castle without exciting comment and strike out to take command of the garrison and, if possible, harass the retiring Satsumas. Of these there had been no sign, which was not surprising since they had more than twelve hours start on us, though we saw some of their broken down mounts at the stage posts. The condition of these suggested that their riders were driving as hard for Osaka as ourselves.

Now, as I looked at the brave Figos strewn about me, I could not help thinking of my first encounter with the Japons. Clinging to the rudder of the Mace I would never have conceived that a few months later I might be lying in a hold with thirty of their number and on the best of terms with all of them. I tried to give Kushoni an encouraging smile but this man's face was as green and unseeing as a cucumber. I lay back and thankfully my disconnected thoughts made way for sleep.

In the next day or two there was plenty of time for thought. Too much of it. Thought leading to melan-

choly. Action is a great physic for me and those hours
gazing over the side of the Portuguese vessel might as
well have been spent behind prison bars. I thought of
Somi and whether she was alive, the Figo castle and
whether it still stood—and most persistently—of my
vulnerability in this alien land. What I had seen of
Ieyasu's army made me feel like an ant scaling an
acorn to reach a mountain. If we could account for
the Satsumas—and by God that was task enough—
then it would require a miracle for us to avoid annihi-
lation at the hands of Ieyasu. Only by some political
manoeuvre could Figo survive. I wondered what mad-
ness, fate or ill-fortune had thrust me into this situation.

If his trading mission had been ill-fated the captain
of the vessel did at least have good charts and with
them I was able to show him exactly the position of
the Figo castle. By taking a longer route it was possible to approach quite close by sea and this I deemed
advisable so that we might see if there was any point
in setting foot on land before risking our lives. I was,
therefore, cast down when we hove to as darkness
succeeded in blotting out our first glimpse of Figo. It
was still possible to gauge some idea of the situation
for the castle stood out in a veritable blaze of light.
A light that ebbed and flared as if some of the buildings might be burning. Around it and for as far as the
eye could see were the lights of the Satsuma camp
shining out like a million fireflies. The sight of them
made my heart plummet to new depths. What chance
did we have of getting through, let alone of influencing the course of the siege.

All that night I stood beside the Portuguese on
watch and peered into the darkness. Occasionally a
burst of speech rippled out across the calm waters but

for the most part there was no sound beyond that of
the sea sucking against the side of the vessel. I tried
to make conversation with the watchman but he was
obviously wary of me in my Japonian garb and be-
stowed few words, though never taking his eye off
me. It was a long night and at the risk of sounding
soft-hearted I must confess that I spent a good deal of
it thinking about Somi.

I wondered what she might be doing and whether
she thought of me; tried to remember the details of
her face and what we had said to one another. Nothing
so releases the store of sentiment in a man as a cold
night vigil on the eve of a day that might be his last.

I must have fallen asleep for when I next opened my
eyes I was stiff and cramped and the grey dawn light
was turning shadows into substance. The castle was
still standing, that I could see, but there were signs
of breeches in the walls and a fire burning near one of
them seemed to be the aftermath of some greater conflagration. I turnd to Kushoni who had appeared at
my side and mirrored my despair at the hordes of Satsumas.

"Ei, ei. They outnumber the rice shoots. I have not
seen so many since Edo."

"Perhaps they followed us down the Tokaido. How
in God's name are we to get through them."

"I do not know. Perhaps at nightfall we might be
put ashore and creep across the rice fields."

"Another day rotting on this vessel. Heaven forbid.
I had thought that perhaps we might persuade the
captain to train his cannon on the causeways and
create a diversion whilst we landed." The main gath-
erings of the Satsumas were about the paths that ran
through the rice fields to the mound on which the castle stood.

"If the ordnance carries that far. A breach in the sea wall would flood right up to the castle gates."

It was at that moment that our eyes met and I knew we shared the same inspiration.

"Breach the wall—"

"And the Satsumas will be swept aside. By God, is it possible?"

We chattered on like excited children whilst the watch observed us with increasing suspicion. Careful scrutiny proved that it was possible. The land up to the castle mound was scarcely more than an extension of the shore and the thrifty Japons had built a barrier of stones and boulders so that every inch of the precious ground might be cultivated. The pattern of green slime on the bulwark showed that the tide rose about six English feet which was enough to leave a good head's span above the average Japon. And the tide was rising.

Primed with this brave intent I scuttled off to find the captain and persuade him to empty a broadside into the wall at the propitious moment, but here I was to meet an obstacle. As I might have supposed the captain was most chary of instigating an action so overtly warlike and detrimental to his future trading prospects. This attitude was also coloured by his observation, for a betting man would hardly have wagered on the defending Figos. I set to with every verbal muscle I possessed but the most I could wrestle was the gift of a barrel of gunpowder.

"Take this and my good wishes," said the captain, "and I will put out to sea and return in twelve hours to see what has become of you." I thought it unlikely that I would see the man again, whatever happened, but thanked him most profusely and threw him an expansive promise about the gold that might come his way, which made his eyes glitter sympathetically.

Now my course of action was clear. I had to ferry the barrel of gunpowder to the barrier, blow it up, and ride a tidal wave to the castle. All without being seen and in double-quick time. Even now our presence was causing a gaggle of inquisitive Satsumas to gather on the sea wall and I could see men forming themselves into battle order on the causeways.

I went below and explained this plan to the Figos who accepted it with phlegmatic resignation—as they would if I had asked them to cast themselves into the sea for their daimyo. We then set to making a sturdy raft whilst the ship put out to sea so that the suspicions of those on land might be allayed. A mile out and this raft was lowered over the side with the barrel of gunpowder securely lashed to the middle of it. Kushoni led the way and the rest of us took up our positions to the relief of every man aboard the merchant-man. We were now alone and I recalled the time, months before, when I had seen the Mace slipping away from me. I felt scarcely less desperate now.

The sea was calm which was both in our favour and against us, for although it made our progress easier, it rendered us more liable to detection. Very soon we took to the water and trailed behind the raft like a shoal of minnows chasing a lump of bread. The thought of sharks was set firmly in my mind and was the reason why I had my hands firmly clamped on the timber. Four hundred yards and there was no one on the sea wall, three hundred and we could hear the occasional musket shot, two hundred and the tide had nearly reached the top of the green slime, one hundred: we held our breaths.

Now the raft was bumping against the rocks and I scrambled up to peer over the wall. The castle was eight hundred yards away and the attention of the Satsumas firmly directed towards it. Even as I watched a company of men were battering at the main gate whilst a hail of missiles fell upon them, showing that the defenders were still in good heart. I say all, but suddenly one aimless rogue loomed into my vision. He stood with some horses fifty paces away and to my alarm detached himself from them and began to walk towards the barrier. I hissed a warning to those below and ducked beneath the parapet. If he climbed onto the wall there was no disguising us. And climb he did. I heard the sound of mounting feet and braced myself against the stones. I had hoped to snatch at his legs but when he appeared it was in a quite unexpected position. I watched him wipe his nose as he gazed towards the horizon end he might even have turned away without espying us had a sudden inspiration not made him decide to piss. He gazed down to trace the future passage of his water and at that moment his mouth dropped open as if pulled by a string. To the best of my recollection it never closed, for Kushoni's wazikashi found a home in his stomach and he toppled down amongst us without uttering a sound. The weapon was retrieved and the Satsuma slipped into the sea faster than blinking and we were free to go about our business.

One of our problems was to secure the gunpowder against the wall and to this end we had brought some spars with which to construct a platform for the barrel. This was not easy since the wall, though disturbingly thick, was smooth and well constructed, so there were few features to which the timbers might be bound. It was for this reason that the structure we achieved was a good deal less than satisfactory and mounting the gunpowder on it a nail biting performance. Twice it was nearly in the sea before we wedged it against the wall and attached a fuse so long it hung down almost to the water. This done the raft was propelled along the wall to a point a hundred yards away from the barrel with one of our number waiting behind to light the fuse.

It was our belief that the powder would, with luck, blow out a small portion of the wall and that we could cling to the remaining section until the rush of water had slackened sufficiently to give us an easy passage on the other side.

This conjecture was to be proved over optimistic. The brave spark whose job it was to light the fuse had no sooner done his duty and started to swim towards us than our excited cries told him that the crude platform was beginning to collapse and the barrel teeter on its brink.

Any man I can think of would have done no more than redouble his efforts to reach us but this Japon trod water for a moment whilst he assessed the situation and then swam back towards the gunpowder. The shouts died in our throats as he pulled himself on to one of the spars, and leaning his puny weight against the barrel pressed it back against the wall. All the time the fuse was burning away merrily above his head but he seemed only concerned with the position of the explosive and made no move to extinguish the fuse. Obviously he was prepared to give his life and I marvelled at such bravery—and stupidity. One instant I could discern the muscles on his flexed arm, the next there was a puff of smoke, the barrier quivered and we were drenched in spray. The noise near drove a tunnel between my ears and the force of the explosion knocked me on my back. At first, peering through the smoke, I feared the wall had not been breached and then I saw a white head of water, like a herd of wild stallions, bursting through the gap. The raft was sucked close to the wall and we all raised a cheer moved by relief at the success of our enterprise.

But our elation was short lived. The smitten barrier suddenly began to tremble as if infested with human life. The trembles turned to shudders, great stones shook loose and dropped into the sea, an awful rending sound smote our ears, the wall collapsed, and we were on the crest of a wave reckoning the duration of our lives in seconds.

We were to live longer than that. Some of us at any rate. With my eyes womb-closed and my fingers growing into the timbers of the raft I was swept along like a frog in a millrace and with as much control over my destiny. I clung so tight that those spars must still bear the imprints of my hands. But it was not tight enough. A sickening buffet nearly jarred me loose, and then another, like a giant hand, knocked me spinning from my perch. I struggled for a moment and then found that the water I was expecting to drown in barely covered my prostrate body. Pulling my bruised and breathless carcass to a standing position I saw that by a miracle we had been grounded on the castle mound. As the tidal wave swept on into the distance so the gates of the Figo stronghold loomed above me like the gates of Heaven. But there was no St. Peter. Rather, a seething mass of men struggling like a plague of rats to reach land. The air was filled with the screams and supplications of those fighting to keep their heads above water and never have I seen such a confluence of human misery. The Satsumas must have been drowning in their thousands.

Looking up to the battlements I saw the bewildered faces of the Figos gazing down upon us, scarcely able to believe their eyes. No God to warn them of this flood. But if surprised by their good fortune, they were not slow to act upon it. The castle gates were opened and a stream of men poured out with lances, swords, shovels—anything their hands could command. They were followed by women—old and young—and even children. All with one aim. To hack down any Satsuma that could stagger to dry land. My God, the slaughter was horrible and so great that the sea about the castle was soon blood rather than water. Only the fact that I was so recognisable saved my life and those of the Figos who still stood with me, for the besieged struck down anything in their path with a cold fury which, when seen in the shape of a toothless old woman disembowelling a half-drowned man with a hoe, was little short of terrifying.

Let these words not be construed as sympathy for the Satsumas, for despite their enormous loss of life they still had the numerical advantage. Even as their men fell so more pushed ashore, over the bodies of their dead comrades, until the whole area around the castle became a struggling, hacking mass of muddy, bloody men, scarcely able to tell which side they belonged to as they swayed back and forth.

I was swept along in this butchery, trying to keep contact with my fellows and catch sight of Kushoni. Just as I had given him up for lost I saw a group of men leaping like hounds at a stag. The object of their attentions circled warily holding his sword out before him with both hands and flicking blows aside contemptuously. I knew the moment well. Kushoni was biding his time and waiting for an opening. The moment came and he leaped inside a crude swing and unleashed such a volley of blows that his attackers went down like stooks of corn. His speed of strike was faster than the eye could see, and as always with him, I could not separate one blow from another. A severed hand hit my chest like a clod of earth from a cart wheel and blood stung my eyeballs. By God, but it was raw stuff.

The battle closed in about us and I struggled to Kushoni's side.

"What now?" I cried above the tumult.

"Back to the castle. We must try and close the gates. The battle goes against us in the open. If we can bring those damn muskets to bear, we can pick them off from the ramparts."

He began to hack his way towards the gates as if clearing a passage through thick undergrowth and I went in his wake. Certainly the tide of the battle was in the balance, for more Satsumas were still struggling ashore and every inch of the land right to the castle walls was filled with men bunched close as grapes. Men who turned the ground beneath them into a morass and with their churning feet dug their own graves. I saw a man go down and be trampled into the mud so he became part of it.

We reached the gates but there was such a wedge of bodies that it was impossible to close them. Even as we strove to turn the course of the battle so a weight of men fell on us like a wall collapsing and we were thrust back into the castle. I lost sight of Kushoni but as I looked about me, above the heads of the combatants I recognised a familiar face. Matsumota. So the treacherous bastard lived! Fighting with cold fury he had rallied a band of Satsumas behind him and was smiting lustily at his erstwhile comrades. Base rogue. I shouted his name like an oath, more to alert Kushoni to his presence than out of any desire to engage him myself, for seeing him in action I could believe what I had heard—that he was hardly the inferior of Kushoni as a swordsman.

My own facility in this department was suddenly put to the test for two Satsumas detached themselves from the general fracas and flew at me like angry wasps thinking, no doubt, to secure my head as a trophy. This prize I was not prepared to grant them and so fell back prodding away as best I could with only my superior reach to save me. I was just on the point of finding out which of us could run the faster when I observed that we were in the area of my erstwhile chamber. This sight did not afford me any immediate relief but it did remind me of Somi and, as if this thought had summoned her, so she magically appeared at one of the windows before me. Any acknowledgement of her presence was denied me by my adversaries who were now raining blows on me like a summer storm and I trundled back once more parrying and lunging for all I was worth—which I felt at that moment was very little. At least there might be some bitter satisfaction for Somi, after all my rebuffs, in seeing me hacked to pieces beneath her window. My arm was nearly dropping off with fatigue and with my back against the wall I felt I must be done for. The deadly Nippons stood off, their chests heaving, and then with a wild scream rushed at me together. I stood my ground until they were nearly upon me and then burst between them as their blades shredded my costume, intending to run until I dropped. This resolve I abandoned when I heard another shriek behind me of an even higher pitch. Somi. I spun round to see my two enemies struggling beneath a great length of tapestry which she must have dropped from the window. It depicted a battle scene, that I recall, and I added to its credibility by donating it a generous measure of

my adversaries' blood. Whilst they fumbled for their
sight I beat them flat as ginger bread men.

"God bless you for that gracious deed," I called up
when the job was done and the tapestry a patchwork
of sodden scarlet, "Let me recover my breath and I
will seek fairer words to thank you."

She made no answer but withdrew into the room
where I was pleased to follow, it seeming a much safer
spot for a man of my disposition. I could see that she
was in no clear mind how to greet me for she bridled
like a bitch priming itself to follow a stick into an icy
flood. So I solved her problem by seizing her to my
bloodied chest and hugging her warmly. In truth I
was glad to see her in one well-furnished piece and
would have been so had she not saved my life.

"See, doubting creature," said I, "I have returned
for you as I said I would. Do you not regret your lack
of faith in me?" Attack is always the best method of
defence with women, for they can easily be persuaded
to exhaust even their best arguments in useless outrage.

"I can only imagine you had no say in this matter,"
sniffed she. "They say that the sky sometimes rains
frogs and it would not surprise me if it was in this manner that you are returned to us."

"Time has not dulled your pleasing wit," I beamed.
"By'r lakin but it is good to see you again. I regret
deeply that I was forced to strike you. I hope you can
conceive that it was only honour made me do so."

"Honour." She snorted. "I am surprised that the
word does not lodge in your throat and choke you."

"Sweeting, strive not to conceal from me with in-
temperate words that melting yearning that finds a
brother in my own heart." I looked at her and felt
again that same uncomplicated lust that had flooded
my loins when we first coupled on the island. Once

again I desired the reward of hazards conquered, fears stilled. Outside this chamber the world could go hang.

"Come. I wish to pleasure thee for being my deliverer." I pulled her towards me again and parted her hair so that my lips could meet her soft, cool neck.

"Base ingrate, liar, rogue, deceiver, scoundrel. . . ." I slid my hands under her robe to feel her buttocks firm and round as apples.

". . . wretch, royle, abject, micher . . ."

Now she was coming down to the floor with me.

". . . villain, helot, coystril, cullion . . ."

"Your slave," I murmured.

The moments that followed were my best that day but had so little affinity with the remorseless tide of bloodshed they interrupted that I will leave it to my reader to imagine the poignant passion of our coupling and pass on to what followed.

When we were friends again I became restless, and once restless, foolhardy to the point of venturing outside. Somi sought to restrain me but I felt a modicum of guilt about my desertion blessed by my conviction that the battle must now be won and that therefore any opportunity to redeem myself by valour must be denied me. Thus primed I bade Somi secure the door after me and was gone.

From the demeanour of the townspeople and what I saw, it seemed that the victory was to the Figos. Small bands of Satsumas still made a fight of it but in the main they had been absorbed like a pitcher of water spilt upon the sand. Outside the castle gates the ground was an open grave and already a stench of death invaded my nostrils. I turned my back on it and walked towards the Daimyo's palace. The sky was darkening and an urgent wind agitated the cedar trees. Now was a time for rejoicing, yet the elements

seemed to match my mood. Despite my reunion with
Somi and my natural relief that it had not taken place
inside a coffin, I was strangely cast down. Even to
such a consummate rogue as myself the slaughter of
ten thousand men was somewhat affecting.

Fortunately, for my peace of mind, further consideration was swept aside by the spectacle presenting
itself in a corner of the square. A crowd of people
formed a ring and as I sped towards it I saw two faces
I recognised. Kushoni and Matsumota motionless before one another with their bodies so close that their
shoulders were almost touching. The sullen wind
tugged at their sodden vestments and wisps of hair
blew down across Kushoni's forehead. Neither of their
faces registered an iota of emotion but their eyes stared
out as if seeing into each other's souls. Both hands
were flexed on the hilts of their swords.

"What does this mean?" I asked one of the onlookers.

"The Lord Kushoni has granted the Lord Matsumota
the privilege of fighting to the death."

"He is a fool then." My informant shook his head.

"A Samurai cannot do otherwise."

We looked on with the only sound the rising wind,
sending dust and debris cartwheeling across the
square. There was no movement from the crowd and
we might all have been statues exposed to the ceaseless
buffet of the elements. I could see into Kushoni's eyes
but there was no malice there, no hatred. They were
the eyes of a hawk that could have seen a mouse move
from two thousand feet. The minutes mounted. And
then, just as I was opening my mouth to speak again,
there was a flash of steel from Matsumota and a great
cry. The blade flew into his hand and hung above Kushoni's head.

And there it stayed.

The blood hitting the ground was the first sound I heard above the wind. It gushed forth as if pumped by a handle. Matsumota's face registered a strain, incredulous surprise and he measured his length in the dust, brushing aside Kushoni's sword as he fell. I will swear to my dying day that I never saw the weapon leave its sheath. Kushoni stepped back as the widening pool probed for his toes and taking one last look, turned on his heel.

It was a finely done thing and a sigh of satisfaction and respect went up from the crowd.

I sprang after him to bestow my congratulations but the minute I opened my mouth he snapped at me like a priest disturbed in prayer.

"Hold your tongue! Have you no respect?"

"I am sorry," I stammered, "I was glad to see you alive."

"No thanks to you of late as I recall it. Where have you been?"

"I went to find if Somi was alive."

"And is she?"

"Yes, thank God. She lives. She saved my life."

"Good, I am glad of it. That she lives I mean—Oh and of course that you do too."

"Thank you. And what of the muskets?" said I, trying to find a subject dearer to his heart, "They are still in our hands?"

"Ay, for all the good they may do. The last musket balls were fired this morning and now there is no powder. But we still have these."

He tapped his sword affectionately.

While we were talking Kushoni was striding up the palace steps and I was hard put to keep up with him.

"Where are you bound?"

"We hold the Lord Shimazu inside," he said. "I believe that he wishes to commit seppuku."

"You mean hari-kiri?"

"When a nobleman slits his belly it is called Sep-puku," said Kushoni wincing.

"Is Nomura with him?" I asked, beginning to relish the spectacle of that blackguard with his gizzard hanging out.

"There is no sign of him. We believe him drowned."

"God grant it so," I breathed gratefully.

All the while we were skipping through the rooms of the palace until we approached one adjacent to that used for the tea ceremony.

"I think I will leave you here," said I, having an inkling of what was to follow. "I have seen enough bloodshed for one day." That a lordly Japon should slit his belly when faced with the stigma of defeat did not surprise me but despite my thoughts on Nomura I had no real wish to witness the proceedings. Kushoni seized my arm.

"I think it is right that you should attend. He has scarcely any followers left and it is meet that the deed should be seen to be well done."

I remonstrated, but to no avail, and so was led into a small chamber all of wood and most humble by comparison with what pertained in the rest of the palace. Sitting on his haunches in an attitude of respect was Shimazu dressed in a simple white robe which must have been provided for him. His armour was laid out before him. This was of a most ornate design with a face armour exactly following the contours of his own visage. This I was later told was so that he might be recognised on the battle field.

Many lords and samurai would only deign to fight with those of equal rank and so might go through a battle without finding an acceptable opponent. Kush-oni was less circumspect.

Shimazu himself was like the ghost of the proud ruler I had seen at the Dakyu tournament. Now he looked grey and old and knelt with an expression of the most extreme contemplation in his eyes. There was one other Satsuma in the room who stood behind his master with a drawn sword, which at first alarmed me, and two other Figo Samurai squatting in front of Shimazu. All the men bowed as we came in and we repaid this compliment before taking our places beside the Figos.

Before us Shimazu untied his obi and let slip his robe to expose his small, fat belly. Removing a silver handled Wakizashi from a stand which had been placed before him, he laid it down carefully on the matting. At the sight of the dagger I began to bite my lip but in doing so I betrayed more emotion than the Satsuma Daimyo who raised his head and looking straight in front of him began to address us calmly.

"I, Akazi Shimazu, most unworthy son of an illustrious father, have, by my craven defeat, forfeited all right to the good opinion of my fellow men and by doing so have only one course left open to me. Unworthy and despicable as it is, I give my life, for there is nothing else to give. I beg you who are present to do me the honour of witnessing the act."

So saying, he picked up the dagger and plunged it into the left side of his stomach. With no more than a tightening of the facial muscles he took the hilt with both hands and pulled it across his stomach so the whole split open and a ghastly mess of entrails was revealed. An upward thrust and the deed was done. The brave fellow jerked his neck forward and he withdrew the dagger and in that movement emitted the first grunt of pain, to hint at the agony he tried to hide. Immediately, the man behind him let his sword fall and the Daimyo's head dropped at our feet. The body came crashing down and all that could be heard was the ghastly sound of the blood escaping from the severed neck. I waited for no more but sped from the chamber even as the second sank to his knees and prepared to cut his own belly.

Now, Matsumota, Shimazu, Nomura, all were dead. Figo was saved and Somi and I lived. Apart from Kushoni there should have been no happier man on earth. But I was too exhausted to be happy. Exhausted and pursued by a strange melancholy that talked to me of death more loudly than the corpses that lay all about me. I took my tired, numb body back to Somi, like a child to its mother. Her hands tore back the door at the sound of my voice and I held her tight in my arms for a score of minutes before letting her bathe me and put me to my rest. With her beside me, a finger tip touch away, I had a mooring in the rough sea of my dreams.

CHAPTER 15

THE NEXT MORNING I AWOKE EARLY IN MUCH BETTER spirits. The sun was streaming through the window and through my half-opened eyes I could see white blossom dancing against the clear, blue sky. It was a fair sight, rich with promise, and one that I sought to introduce Somi to, but she merely stretched like a sleek, smug cat and burrowed deeper into sleep. I let her be and crossed to the casement to examine the state of the flood. What I could see suggested that the level of the water had fallen but this was probably due to the condition of the tide. The sight that snatched my eye was that of the Portuguese merchantman riding gently at anchor beyond the breached sea wall. Even as I watched so a boat was lowered and began its progress towards the shore.

"Somi!" I shouted, so that the poor girl nearly sprang from her couch. "Come, see the means of our deliverance."

She stumbled to my side, still rubbing the sleep from her eyes and peered towards the sea.

"That vessel?"

"Indeed no other. It is the one that brought us hither. I had dared not speak of it before in case it did not return. Now will you come with me? You must see that there is nothing for you here." There was a pause whilst her eyes ranged over everything in the room.

Eventually, after a searching examination of my face she replied.

"I will come, but how will you secure our passage? Will the captain not require payment?"

"No doubt of it, but I believe Kushoni will be easily persuaded to grant us the boon of some gold or silver. Go, gather together those things that you would take with you and attend me here. I will talk with Kushoni and the Portuguese."

So saying, I was speedily on my way. A terrible stench of burning corpses hung in the air and doubtless there were many more rotting without the castle walls but despite all this I felt in fine fettle.

Kushoni I found supervising the burial of dead in a large open grave and the sight of the torn bodies reminded me sharply of Nomura.

"Has aught been seen of Nomura?" said I.

"His carrion corpse has been noted," said he, "on the far side of the castle. But they have been burning the dead there and when I went to look it had been done away with."

"Not without a great deal of greasy smoke I would imagine. Thank God for that. Now, I beg you, the Portuguese are coming ashore and I promised them some gold for their pains."

"They shall have it. Come with me."

Kushoni turned away from the gaping pit, and calling to a couple of soldiers, led the way back to the keep. The Japons are usually most scrupulous in their business dealings. I followed, telling him in a strangely halting manner of my resolve to find a passage on the Portuguese vessel. Even though it was no more than a continuation of my earlier plans, I still felt a faint sense of guilt at leaving which communicated itself to my words.

"Good fortune and the speed of any God you believe in go with you." said Kushoni. We will always recall your exploits and not a Figo will live who will not remember your name."

I wondered quite what exploits he was referring to for there was a twinkle in his eye, but they were fine words, and happily spoken in the treasure chamber of the keep, where a profusion of gold and silver bars dazzled the eye. I wondered what Ieyasu's fortune looked like. Kushoni handed two gold bars to each of the soldiers and such was their size that it was as much as any man could carry. He then deliberated for a second.

"This commodity is somewhat prized in your country, is it not?" I assured him that it was.

"In that event perhaps you might find it useful to bear a bar with you."

I nodded and received another ingot into my arms which I hugged to me as covetously as any mother does her first born. With this and a little skilful dealing, my future was assured. But, despite my elation, I was discreet in my gratitude for I knew that, to a Samurai, money is ordure and the pursuit of riches beneath contempt.

We went back to the castle gates and there found a boat load of wary Portuguese, making much show of their muskets. Their eyes lit up when they saw the gold and they touched it as if not certain that it could be real. I interrupted their drooling to ask if they might take Somi and myself with them and after some deliberation and a few longing glances at my gold bar they said that their captain would probably agree to do so. It occurred to me that I would have to go careful to ensure that I did not wake up with my throat

cut. I bid them wait a few moments and went to fetch
Somi.

When I returned to the chamber she was not there,
but a glance from the window revealed her in the
niwa or ornamental gardens. I went down and can
recall how fine she looked; like a flower in its perfect setting. Perhaps it is my maudlin fantasy delud-
ing me in hindsight, but I believe that at that moment
I was as near to loving her as I have been to any human being—barring myself of course.

She was in a long robe of great simplicity, which
must have been based on drawings I had made of the
garb of English ladies of fashion—she had always been
much interested in such things—and which I took to
mean that she had finally decided to abandon the Japonian side of her nature. She was standing by a small
shrine, neatly fenced off, before which were implanted
some captured Satsuma lances with pennants attached
to them, no doubt some kind of offering for our deliverance.

"How have you fared?" said she eagerly.

"Well, I believe. I have secured our passage and
also some gold which will make our travels easier.
Have you gathered together your things?"

"Why? Are we off so soon?"

"Do not say that you have changed your mind
again."

"No, no," said she, "but I have waited so long that
now I cannot believe we are really going. I will miss
these gardens, their beauty has given me much cheer
in the past weeks."

Curse the woman, I breathed to myself. Was there
ever one who was not contrary in this kind of situation.

"They are indeed most handsome. Now, we must

be gone eer our Portuguese friends change their minds."

I knew there was no danger of it now that they had seen the gold but I was keen to bring an end to her heart-searching.

"I will come, but, I beg you, let me rest here a few moments more."

Foolishly, as it came about, I did so and stepped back with a shrug of the shoulders. Somi was plucking the camelia heads and meditatively casting them into one of the streams that meandered from pool to pool. I watched the fish darting above the whitesand and with half an eye followed the progress of one of the blossoms as it drifted under an ornamental bridge. I watched to see it emerge on the other side.

"Come, we must go."

The camelia had not come out. In its place the water billowed red. Was there some dye in the flower, or—

"Wait!"

Suddenly suspicious, I began to scramble down the bank. As I did so there was a turmoil in the water beneath the bridge and a scarlet flood streaked out into the open. Blood. I ducked down to peer under the arch at the moment that a man burst from its farthest side. One arm was almost severed and hung by a few sinews as if under dissection. The other grasped a sword.

I knew the man.

The scar tissue still bubbled across his face like hardened wax. The truncated nostrils still formed a doorway into his brain. Half drained of blood he remained a terrifying sight. Nomura. And I weaponless. I turned to snatch up one of the lances and at that moment he came for us. Somi was nearest to him but his eye was on me and she might have saved herself had she ran. But she did not. As I stood quaking like a cotquean she threw herself between us and screamed hate into his face as if the words might halt him. For a moment his motion faltered like a burst dam swelling up to overflow some obstacle in its path. Then his sword bit into her side and she was spilling her blood six feet away.

Her action saved me for it woke me from my trance, and in my fear and desperation liberated a spark of spirit to match her own. As the brute came for me I jerked up my lance and lunged forward so that by blessed fate the tip pierced him just below the throat. I pressed home the thrust and the bamboo lance buckled beneath the strain. Nomura loosed his grip on his sword to pluck at the shaft, and in that moment as it tumbled to the ground, I believed that I might take him. Now, there was a cold, beastly fury in my actions and I leaned onto the lance making it bend still further as Nomura sought to claw it from its resting place. If it snapped I might still be done for, and the fiend was thrusting forward, contributing to both this danger and his own downfall. Before the battle he might have snapped it like a twig but now, one-armed and drained of blood, I felt his sinews wilting as the minutes passed and knew that I need only bide my time. This I did with grim relish given a greater dimension by the sight of Somi stirring in a pool of her own blood. Step by step I drove Nomura backward until his foot stumbled on the brink of the stream and with a further thrust I could send him to measure his length in a handspan of water. He fought to struggle free but I leaned my whole weight upon the lance and forced his head down so that it bubbled and frothed below the water and the small fish flashed sil-

ver in the billowing clouds of crimson, as if spilling out
of his mouth. I held him thus until he had not moved
for several minutes and released the lance so that the
body lifted slightly like a drifting log.

As I looked up from my grisly labours it was to see
people streaming towards us. I ran to Somi and took
her hand but it was a useless gesture I could see she
was done for. Poor child, the wound in her side gaped
like a hound's jaws. I raised her up and she tried to
smile.

"I will not be coming with you," said she in a voice
so faint that it already seemed to be speaking from
death's door.

"But for your show of spirit I would be done for,"
said I. "You are a brave, brave girl."

She opened her mouth to speak again but as I bent
to catch her words her head dropped forward and she
was gone.

So by that cruel stroke of fate I was robbed of a
travelling companion, yet able to level my score with
the beast Nomura. I let Somi slip into the arms that
reached out to take her and, exhausted, stumbled
through the crowd that divided before me like the
Red Sea. Even now I flinched as I glanced into the
water but the bloated hulk still lay there, motionless
on its scarlet bier.

Kushoni appeared beside me and seemed most
agitated by the girl's death, saying that the gardens
should have been searched; but I told him, meaning
it, that no blame could be attached to any man. My
melancholy spirits of the previous evening had warned
me that tragedy of some kind was in the air.

"Say no more of it, good friend," said I. "The reason
is in the stars. Now farewell again."

These words were spoken in the presence of the

Portuguese who eyed my bloodstained body with some
suspicion which was not abated by me telling them
that I would now be travelling alone. It may seem
callous, and it probably was so, but my mind was
adjusting with great rapidity to Somi's death. I hugged
my gold bar and wondered if she was not some guardian angel who had been sent in error—it must have
been in error—to guard over me, and who now had
served her purpose. I hopped on to the boat and
singled out Kushoni for my farewell salutations. Looking into his grizzled features like those of some faithful pug, I knew I would not see his like again.

The thought played on my mind the more as I listened to the Portuguese now bending over their oars.

"What do you make of his clothes, Manuel?" asked
one.

"You mean their style or the blood on them? Of the
latter, I think he has spilled his breakfast."

"You think he eats human flesh?"

"Oh yes. What do you think became of the girl? If
he wears their clothes, he is likely to indulge all their
habits."

"Perhaps he is one of them. Look at his topknot."

"Yes, even his eyes are like two virgins' quims."

A fine fall, I thought, to find myself despised by
scabs like these. Was this what I was returning to after
being treated like a lord?

"Hey, slant eyes," called out one of them, "I do not
believe that you are English. Speak a few words to
prove it."

We were passing through the gap in the wall and already men were beginning to repair it. When this was
done the water would be pumped out and in time the
land would grow rice again. It suddenly occurred to
me to question why I was leaving. My worst enemies

were slain, one by my own hand, and I was close to the bosom of the most powerful men in the Kingdom. What was waiting for me in England? A rope's end if I ventured near Plymouth, and what was my guarantee of reaching Albion with these cut-throats? My gold bar would purchase only my own death. And, with so much gold and silver in the country, and myself held in such esteem, why settle for so little? I could become a man of affairs—a Samurai even. I had developed a taste for Sake and found the women pleasing enough. The cities knew no equal in Albion and the food was endurable. What more could I expect to gain. It was worth putting my wits to work and seeing what could be achieved—if nothing, then I could soon be on my way again.

"Take me back," I said.

"What does he say? Is that English, Manuel?"

I repeated the request in Portuguese.

"Are you a madman? Have you left something in the castle? What do you mean?"

"Take me back," I repeated.

"But the gold."

"You can keep it—your share of it."

The boat swung round with alacrity.

"He is mad, poor loon."

"Shh! Do not persuade him to change his mind."

They rowed carefully as if a sudden jolt might bring me to my senses. On the strand I could see a puzzled Kushoni coming to the water's edge. I would take a bath. Yes, that would provide an opportunity for contemplation and amusement. I felt better already. I clambered over the side and thrusting a water-logged corpse aside with my gold bar, began to wade towards the shore.

A Study of History   ARNOLD J. TOYNBEE

Abridged by D. C. Somervell

TWO HANDSOME PAPERBACK VOLUMES
IN A BEAUTIFULLY DESIGNED SLIP COVER

Now—Dell presents the long-awaited two-volume abridgment of Toynbee's monumental masterpiece, which *The New York Times* has called, ". . . unquestionably one of the great works of our times."

This remarkably concise abridgment is the work of D. C. Somervell who, with marvelous skill, has retained all of Toynbee's immense depth and breadth of thought. He has managed to preserve not only its texture and atmosphere, but—for the most part—the author's own words.

Two-volume boxed set $2.25

If you cannot obtain copies of these titles from your local bookseller, just send the price (plus 25c per copy for handling and postage) to Dell Books, Post Office Box 1000, Pinebrook, N. J. 07058.